BAIT FOR MEN
THE COMPLETE CASES OF THE
LADY FROM HELL, VOLUME 1

BAIT FOR MEN
THE COMPLETE CASES OF THE
LADY FROM HELL, VOLUME 1

EUGENE THOMAS

ILLUSTRATED BY
JOSEPH A. FARREN

COVER BY
LEJAREN HILLER

POPULAR PUBLICATIONS · 2022

PUBLISHING HISTORY

"The Lady from Hell" originally appeared in the January 19, 1935 issue of *Detective Fiction Weekly* magazine (Vol. 90, No. 5). Copyright © 1935 by The Frank A. Munsey Company. Copyright renewed © 1962 and assigned to Steeger Properties, LLC. All rights reserved. "Bait for Men" originally appeared in the January 26, 1935 issue of *Detective Fiction Weekly* magazine (Vol. 90, No. 6). Copyright © 1935 by The Frank A. Munsey Company. Copyright renewed © 1962 and assigned to Steeger Properties, LLC. All rights reserved. "The Episode of the Secret Service Blackmail" originally appeared in the February 9, 1935 issue of *Detective Fiction Weekly* magazine (Vol. 91, No. 2). Copyright © 1935 by The Frank A. Munsey Company. Copyright renewed © 1962 and assigned to Steeger Properties, LLC. All rights reserved. "The Episode of the Forty Murderers" originally appeared in the February 16, 1935 issue of *Detective Fiction Weekly* magazine (Vol. 91, No. 3). Copyright © 1935 by The Frank A. Munsey Company. Copyright renewed © 1962 and assigned to Steeger Properties, LLC. All rights reserved. "The Episode of the Grave Robbers" originally appeared in the March 2, 1935 issue of *Detective Fiction Weekly* magazine (Vol. 91, No. 5). Copyright © 1935 by The Frank A. Munsey Company. Copyright renewed © 1962 and assigned to Steeger Properties, LLC. All rights reserved. "The Episode of the Levantine Monster" originally appeared in the March 9, 1935 issue of *Detective Fiction Weekly* magazine (Vol. 91, No. 6). Copyright © 1935 by The Frank A. Munsey Company. Copyright renewed © 1962 and assigned to Steeger Properties, LLC. All rights reserved. "The Episode of the League of Death" originally appeared in the March 16, 1935 issue of *Detective Fiction Weekly* magazine (Vol. 92, No. 1). Copyright © 1935 by The Frank A. Munsey Company. Copyright renewed © 1962 and assigned to Steeger Properties, LLC. All rights reserved. "The Episode of the Orient Express Robbery" originally appeared in the April 20, 1935 issue of *Detective Fiction Weekly* magazine (Vol. 92, No. 6). Copyright © 1935 by The Frank A. Munsey Company. Copyright renewed © 1962 and assigned to Steeger Properties, LLC. All rights reserved. "The Episode of the House of Secrets" originally appeared in the May 4, 1935 issue of *Detective Fiction Weekly* magazine (Vol. 93, No. 2). Copyright © 1935 by The Frank A. Munsey Company. Copyright renewed © 1962 and assigned to Steeger Properties, LLC. All rights reserved. "The Episode of the Pounce of Death" originally appeared in the May 11, 1935 issue of *Detective Fiction Weekly* magazine (Vol. 93, No. 3). Copyright © 1935 by The Frank A. Munsey Company. Copyright renewed © 1962 and assigned to Steeger Properties, LLC. All rights reserved.

TABLE OF CONTENTS

THE LADY FROM HELL

That Red-Headed Siren, Vi Legrand,
Began Her Career of International
Blackmail by Pouring Sixty Drops of
Poison into Her Father's Glass

1

RED-HEADED VIVIAN LEGRAND was an exotic and breath-taking beauty. She fascinated men, and when they babbled their secrets she bled them of their wealth. The rich and influential of three continents were her victims.

She operated a school that trained blackmailers in the art of extortion. Her agents numbered hundreds, for she forced her victims to ferret out the secrets of their friends, and to pay her in information as well as money. Anybody in contact with the rich might be in Vi Legrand's pay, and the agents she recruited by blackmail included social leaders and public officials and royalty whom the world believed above suspicion!

This is the first of a series of stories about the exploits of this siren who came from Bubbling Well Road, Shanghai, and flamed across three continents.

DUKE DONELLAN DIDN'T have a friend in the world, and was proud of it. He was even proud of having few known enemies—because few dared to admit how much they hated him. The young man he was confronting now was deathly pale and very obviously afraid.

Donellan hailed from the coal and steel regions of Pennsylvania. Police in Pittsburgh and other cities had excellent reasons for remembering him. But at this time he was lording it over a bright and sordid corner of the Orient. The Duke, after violence, crime and murder, had found a lucra-

*Duke fell with a
sharp cry of agony*

tive haven as owner and operator of a notorious gambling
resort in the Bubbling Well Road, Shanghai.

The young man trembling before him wore the uniform
of the sanitary service of the port. He was smartly turned
out and rather good looking, though his eyes were a bit
too closely set.

Duke Donellan put a huge hand on the uniformed
shoulder. He began propelling the other toward a black
door at the end of the corridor.

Donellan was red-headed, florid, burly and brutal

looking, yet also commanding and shrewd. Some women considered him handsome—and not only the ones who worked for him as "European entertainers" here at the place deceptively named the Mansion.

The young health officer wasn't resisting. Duke Donellan stood a head taller, and sixty pounds heavier. He was muscular, light on his feet. His left hand swept the door open, his right thrust Alan Legrand into the room. He switched on the light, banged the door shut, and violently lodged his visitor in the depths of a large armchair.

"You skulking, double-dealing rat!" he stormed.

"But, Duke—"

Young Legrand, in panic, sought to interrupt.

"No more belly-aching excuses!" said Donellan grimly. "You went to McNab, Darcy and that Frenchman—d'Eschlein. All good customers of mine. Men you met out here.

And you asked each of 'em to lend you money to pay to me—"

"Only what I owe you, Duke," he managed to gasp.

"—to shake off the hold I got on you. That's what you told Mark Darcy." Donellan stood over him, and his fury, if exaggerated before, was now seething and dangerously genuine. "You even had the gall to drag Vivian into it. Selling 'em a sob-story about my own daughter! Wanting to save her from such evil associations, huh?"

Alan Legrand kept his eyes fixed on a circular stain marking the walnut desk. Suddenly he burst out:

"You know how I feel about Vi. I've asked her to marry me—"

"She's not of age. And she wouldn't wipe her feet on you."

Donellan's fierce derision made the other wince. He retorted hotly:

"You don't even know she's different from the rest you keep here."

LEGRAND STOPPED WITH a sobbing breath, startled by his own defiance. The proprietor of the shady Mansion broke into a roar of taunting laughter.

"Go ahead, tell me I'm too vile and dumb to appreciate Vi. Maybe I'm a gypsy and just stole her when she was a kid!" His bellowing laugh vibrated in the small private office. "Why, damn it, she's going to make me a millionaire before we're through. I'm just marking time here, sap—giving the girl a chance to grow up and learn what's good for her and who's boss of the outfit. Wouldn't she be happy, throwing herself away on a four-flushing crook like you!"

"You can't call me a crook because of those IOU's."

"The hell I can't! And the hell with your IOU's! It's something else that I only got wise to late today, after I'd heard by chance how Vi looked sideways at you. She's got the loveliest eyes this side of Singapore. Your trouble's been that you just couldn't keep away from her.

"She kind of liked you. You're polished and refined. And I sort of felt sorry for you, Legrand. You owed me nearly three thousand dollars, gambling. I let you give me three notes with regular and proper endorsements. Said if I was pushed I could discount 'em in any bank in Shanghai. Just like commercial paper!

"Well, I wasn't pushed. I kept your notes here. And here they've picked up a lot of value." With smirking, sinister relish he watched his victim and began drawing open a desk drawer. Legrand twisted his fingers uneasily, moistened dry lips, did not glance up. Duke peered into the drawer, grinning, but took no papers from it. "Imagine my pleasure," he chuckled, "to find all three endorsements are forgeries!"

"That's a lie!" Legrand exploded.

On a furious impulse he sprang to his feet, plucked at a hip pocket, drew a Browning revolver.

Duke's mighty paw swung up from the open desk drawer, struck the other's wrist sharply. The gun seemed to leap into his possession. He held it a moment, then he dropped the weapon casually into the drawer.

He turned belligerently on Legrand.

"If any pup had called me liar or pulled a rod on me yesterday, I'd have sent him to the hospital to get my heel marks ironed out of his mug. But today you look to me like something I can take to a bank. Seeing how you use a pen has made me awful impatient."

Alan Legrand struggled to free himself:

"Let me go, Duke. I'll pay you all I owe."

"You sure will. Plus my bonus on the artwork. Three thousand, plus another three thousand for the proofs of forgery—"

"That's blackmail!"

Donellan's grip tightened. "Be damned glad it is. If I went moral on you and took those notes to the consular court, you'd be convicted of first degree forgery and get sent away for a stretch of five years."

"God, Duke, you wouldn't do that!"

"Not while you've a family to appeal to. Your brothers here in the diplomatic service. Got you your job—"

"Stanley's only my half-brother."

"I know. Tough luck you had even at birth. I had your folks looked up when you first came shining around Vi. And they're not bush leaguers, as we'd say in the States. Your mother was English—Stanley's was an American, and what's more, a niece of Simon Ashebrook. That makes Stanley now one of the Ashebrook heirs. He'll get three or four millions when old Simon finally wears himself out.

"Stanley owns real prospects and can raise the ready cash. Ask him to help you and escape a public disgrace. Your names are the same. That 'only a half-brother' stuff wouldn't spare him much. And diplomats need to have families as pure and white as the spats they wear."

"But he's already lent me all he can afford—"

"Since you're a health officer, make him pay you to protect his health," said Donellan with a leer. "Until he marries, you're his next of kin. His death would make you an Ashebrook heir. Ever think of that?"

"You swine!"

Duke Donellan's repellent eyes grew small and ruby-bright. Young Legrand instantly repented his outburst.

"I mean, Duke," he almost whimpered, "it's horrible even to joke like that. If you'll only give me time—"

"I'll give you a week. After that, I'll turn you over to the consular court—for five years in the pen!"

2

GRAY-FACED AND STRICKEN, Alan Legrand dragged
his feet along the corridor and down the front staircase, a
ghost descending upon a scene of tawdry gaiety.

A stunning girl in a white evening gown noticed him
and saw that he was going to avoid her. She watched him
for a moment, then sent a Chinese "boy" to summon him.
With undisguised reluctance Legrand turned aside.

"Alan, what's the matter with you?"

"Maybe Duke will tell you, Vi."

"You tell me," she urged. "What's happened? You haven't
been down here gambling—you can't be cleaned out."

The flickering, malignant glitter in his eyes made her
pause. What had hit him so hard?

Vivian Donellan—known to her father's associates as
Vi—was not quite eighteen. Yet she already possessed a
mature and bewildering beauty. Tall, slender, self-pos-
sessed, she had an exquisite, graceful figure and red hair
that glowed like metal. Her eyes were large and low-lidded,
giving her face an exotic lure.

No one ever felt certain of the girl's attitude toward the
sordid affairs of the gambling resort. Even habitual rois-
terers treated her with marked consideration. No doubt
they remembered her formidable parent. Yet Duke Donellan brazenly used her enchantments to draw men to his

gaming rooms, the one part of the sprawling establish-
ment in which she regularly appeared. And had any of the
Donellan clients been able to read the future, they might
have thought less of Duke and been afraid of Vi herself.

"You had better go home, Alan," she was saying. "Get a
good night's Sleep. Tomorrow perhaps I'll drive over—"

"Vi!"

Duke's angry tone was a clap of thunder. The proprietor
had come to the head of the stairs. It enraged him to find
Legrand still hanging around the possession he valued at
a million or more.

His voice made the Chinese servants jump. Patrons
within range of it looked up. The girl looked up.

Then she glanced anxiously at Alan Legrand. He was
perceptibly shivering. A man, a real man, could have taken
her away from the abominable Mansion then and there.
But Legrand was in the grip of a terrible fear. He was just
another puppet manipulated by her father.

Yet she still liked him. His appearance and manifest
gentility attracted her, even though she saw in him now a
rather ineffectual, unstable, self-indulgent weakling. He
was no hero and not well-to-do; but he was really a gentleman, had come of good stock, and knew what it meant to
grow up in cultivated surroundings.

Vi, who would eventually become the most audacious,
bewitching, resourceful blackmailer known to the police
of three continents, was to be, as her father had elegantly
phrased it, "a sucker for refinement" all through her bewildering, colorful career. Breeding and culture fascinated
her. Shabby upbringing or companions, lawless pursuits
couldn't curb her aspirations. She meant to get on in the

world, mingle with superior people, and feel wholly at ease among them.

"See you tomorrow, then," Legrand whispered, and turned to slink away.

"Come up here!" Duke was barking.

Head erect, she started to ascend the staircase. Poise and grace personified, she was hiding the nervous tremor that always swept over her in the presence of her father.

It was nearly two years since Duke had struck her, beaten her—cruelly and deliberately hurting her and yet, as he bragged at the time, "leaving no expensive, disfiguring scars." She had neither forgotten nor forgiven him that chastisement.

ON HER GORGEOUS hair a momentary gleam of light shone as if it flashed from a burnished helmet. Was she marching to battle? She feared so, and was icy cold. Below a tipsy young tourist and a Mongolian servant stood near together, each observing her till she disappeared, eyes blinking, jaws slack, in utterly enthralled admiration.

Duke Donellan gestured, and she followed him to his private office.

"What was Legrand telling you?" he demanded.

She watched him narrowly as he shut the door. He did not lock it, a hopeful sign.

"Not a thing," she denied daringly.

"Don't lie!" her father threatened.

"I never lie. He looked sick—I asked him what was wrong. He scarcely spoke. What did you do to him?" She put her question as indifferently as she could.

"Me—I just told him plenty," Duke growled. "Say, you ain't still sweet on that—"

"Still? When was I ever?"

"Oh, come now—don't play too innocent. I don't mind you stringing some of these guys along."

"In fact, you insist upon it."

Duke grinned. He sprawled before his desk. A bottle, a glass, three photostatic copies of Alan Legrand's promis-

Vivian Legrand

sory notes lay before him. He looked huge, self-satisfied, callous.

"Legrand's just a cheap crook—that's what he is."

"Then," she said, edging toward the door, "I suppose we won't see him around here any more—"

"You don't care?"

"Why should I? If he's broke as well as crooked—"

"That's the girl!" Duke held out a huge hand in what he meant for a gesture of parental esteem. She was now very close to the door. "Hold a minute—they won't miss you below yet," he exclaimed. "Feast your pretty eyes on these. All three endorsements forged by God!"

She had to step closer, yet hardly glanced at the evidence.

"Poor fool!" she murmured. Her contempt seemed to cover all the men she knew. She suddenly felt possessed by a queer inner feeling of warmth and bravado. Was she getting bold enough to face Duke Donellan? His own daughter at last!

"What," she asked, "are these mistakes going to cost his family?"

"Looking for your cut? A new dress or a ring, maybe. It was you that made him toss away his dough."

She shrugged. "Could I buy those notes?" she suggested.

"What for?"

"Oh, just to save a nasty scandal. Maybe I'm sentimental about ruining my first sucker."

Duke wasn't deceived by the bantering conclusion.

"He can't raise enough, but you think you can. How?"

"Call it some of what you owe me. For instance, about how much extra have I been drawing to those crooked games of yours?"

He had started to take a gulp of liquor. Now he held his glass suspended at the level of his chin, his expression black and incredulous.

"No more'n you cost me," he grunted.

"A thousand a month, counting with one eye shut, the way you always count cuts. That's what I've been drawing. And how much do I cost you? Three thousand a year, hotel rates! Allowing I cost as much as three, I deserve a fifty-fifty split of twelve thousand at least. So you owe me three thousand."

Duke profanely set down his glass, heaved himself out of his chair. If this was his night for animal taming—

Vi did not flinch. For a long moment father and daughter glared at each other. His evil, bloodshot eyes were first to waver.

"One of that Legrand's financial ideas," he jeered.

"I don't need him or any man to give me ideas, and I never will. Fair's fair, Duke. You know what I'm worth here."

"You ain't worth a dime," he rasped out, "if you forget who's boss and don't do as you're told. It's been some time since you gave me any of your lip, Vi."

He stepped toward her with that astonishing, catlike quickness of his. His right hand took a firm hold upon her lustrous hair. As he jerked it her head snapped back sharply. With a half-choked moan she sank to her knees.

Duke Donellan was all savage now. Even a million dollars' worth of merchantable loveliness was not enough to subdue his desire to inflict pain and conquer her.

She permitted herself no second outcry. Her arms upraised, she fiercely clawed at his hand and forearm. Her polished nails gashed him painfully.

He merely grinned. "Not many would still look handsome as you do," he remarked, "when they were being hurt and scared so—"

"I'm *not* scared!"

"No? That's great. We must drink to your new independence."

3

HE HELD HER in the cruel vise of his hand and knee. With the other hand he reached over and swept the whisky bottle from his desk, took a long, gurgling pull at it, then vindictively started lowering it, closer and closer to her parted lips.

When she struggled again, he applied more pressure, hurting her severely. She had to cease resisting, and slowly, with careful aim, he began trickling the liquor into her mouth.

She sputtered—managed to twist her head a little. But he forced it back to the position he desired.

She was choking, strangling on the fiery liquor. Yet only when the bottle ran dry did Duke stop.

Face purple from the torture, gown limp and drenched, the girl collapsed at his feet. Duke seated himself, dabbing at his lacerated wrist with his tongue. Vi's gradual recovery he noted with the unconcern of one who has seen consciousness come flickering back in many another victim.

At length she was able to raise herself up and look around. The first thing she saw clearly through the mists of her receding torment was a face—her father's red, derisive, hateful face. Her first clear thought was a resolve and a plan to kill him.

SHE WAS PHYSICALLY unable to drive to the International Settlement next day, or even the day after. But she managed to smuggle out a note to Alan Legrand. He shared an apartment in the French Concession with two young colleagues of the local sanitary service. And on the third day Vi went there in secret, her plan now matured.

Legrand's own desperate concerns were swarming darkly around him. Stanley, his half-brother, had been sent off unexpectedly on a mission to Nanking. Alan would either have to wait to make an appeal to him, his one resource, or else obtain leave and go after him. He was uncertain what to do; helpless, vacillating, and brooding darkly. Meanwhile, his week's grace was slipping away hour by hour. Worried though he was, he soon perceived the change in Duke's incredibly alluring daughter.

"You've quarreled with him?" he exclaimed.

She described just what had occurred.

"The beast—the filthy beast—"

"Never mind that now. What do you propose to do about those notes?"

"I don't know. I felt sure I'd be able to redeem them long before."

"Suppose I recover them for you?"

"But, good Lord, how?"

She told him. He was startled at first, but desperation had put a stout curb on his conscience.

"You must know just what drug to use, and how to get me some," she urged.

"It'll be too dangerous. Might prove fatal—"

"It's self-defense, Alan. What he did to me the other

night might have been fatal. And even what he now threatens to do to you—"

Legrand sprang up uneasily, growing pale. "Who—who could my trouble be fatal to? Vi, your father didn't say anything to you about—about Stanley?"

"Why, no. Your brother will survive your disgrace, I guess. I meant you might not survive a prison sentence. You'd feel driven to—"

"Make way with myself! Lord, how I have thought of that!"

"Stop thinking of it," she commanded. "I've found a way out for both of us, haven't I? Get me just the right drug. Knockout drops. Something to make him sick, lay him up a while, give me a running start. Tell me just the right dose to give, Alan, and I'll be very careful, I promise."

HERE WAS THE first of scores of such promises that Vi would make to smitten men of all ages and nationalities. The melting green eyes were already wonderful weapons with which to disarm any skeptic.

"You'll get me back my notes—money for yourself," he was rehearsing. "Money that's certainly due you, my dear. But then—then you'll have to run away and hide where Duke can't trace you. Till you're of age. Where will you go, Vi? What about us?"

"I can't go far. Manila or Honolulu, maybe. I'm an American born. I feel Uncle Sam can protect me, even from Duke. We will keep in close touch, Alan. I'll miss Shanghai and probably want to come back here," she lied. "As soon as I'm forgotten and my disappearance has ceased to matter, even to Duke."

He tried to take her into his arms, exclaiming:

"You will never be forgotten, or cease to matter!"

"Later," she admonished, avoiding his embrace. "Now, let's get on about this drug."

Legrand paced the floor. "Yes," he said at length. "I know the very thing."

He went out, and returned almost immediately with a tiny dark bottle. It didn't strike Vi as strange that he should have in his home "the very thing." Knockout drops were always at hand in the gambling house, but she dared not touch those—for reasons of her own.

Perhaps Alan Legrand had been toying with the notion of poisoning his half-brother, becoming an heir to Simon Ashebrook's fortune, which would put him in the preferred class with money lenders the world over.

Duke Donellan had maliciously planted the seed of a greater crime to cover his first unlawful act. But Vi knew nothing of Stanley.

"What is it?" she asked, taking the bottle from him.

"Hyoscine. Opium derivative, probably. I'm not sure. However, I am sure of its exact potency." He hesitated, looking out of the window.

"How many drops?" she asked. "Just for a knockout?"

They were deceiving each other flagrantly.

Alan Legrand was of that tribe of egotists in whom self-ishness or self-indulgence are magnified to the strength and driving force of a religious conviction. He wanted most ardently to be free of the blackmailing threats of Duke Donellan. Yet he wanted to win Duke's daughter just as ardently.

He saw no reason now for not trying to have his own way in both directions. Fifteen drops of the drug he vaguely identified would have done what Vi alleged she wished to do.

Legrand looked straight into her eyes. "Give him no more than thirty drops, mind," he said. "Thirty is your limit."

She nodded almost absently. For she also was an egotist, formed in a sterner mold. She had suffered her last torment from Duke Donellan, the cruel parent who enjoyed inflicting pain. She decided to double the dose.

And Alan, watching her closely to see if she suspected his ruse, wondered if thirty would be fatal to such a brute as Donellan. He wished now he had said thirty-five. Of course, an overdose of poison often induced a nausea that prevented a lethal effect.

He felt sure that if Duke died suddenly that Vi would not leave Shanghai. She would be too smart to risk throwing suspicion upon herself and her "mistake." He studied her intently. What a lovely picture she made, holding the small brown bottle on high to let the afternoon light shine through!

It was worth killing any man to keep her here in China.

4

FORTY-EIGHT HOURS VI waited, and then her perfect chance came. She had contrived to keep watch upon her father's small office. Whenever the door stood ajar she managed to be near at hand.

It was late. Duke was not in the gaming rooms. She made an excuse to come upstairs. Light shone from his door.

A Chinese boy passed her, taking some message. She heard her father's bellowing voice, cursing.

She found a curtained alcove and hid as she had done more than once in that upper corridor since returning with the bottle of poison.

Duke went stamping along the hall and down the staircase, the China boy pattering after him warily. Duke's temper was up. But when in Heaven's name wasn't it up?

Vi drifted like greenish white smoke into the private room. He had left the door open, lights blazing—and, yes, a bottle on the stained desk.

This was too good to be true. A glass half full of liquor stood beside the bottle. He would be angrier than ever when he returned. She could see him, had so often seen him, toss off his forgotten drink at one gulp.

Out came the poison bottle.

She began her fatal count.

"—Twenty-nine—thirty." Thirty drops into the half glass of whisky. Legrand hadn't said what influence spirits might have if the hyoscine was administered in an alcoholic drink. Yet he must have known she would have better access to Donellan's liquor than to his food.

She went on. At forty drops her hand shook ever so slightly. She was not losing her nerve. It was an inner warning that Duke would soon return.

She counted to fifty drops, fifty-five, then sixty.

She raised the glass and sniffed. The tiny dark bottle had an odor. But that odor did not cling to Duke's glass. Rotating it slowly, she made certain of a mixture.

There was only a very little of the poison left. Perhaps five drops more. On impulse she dumped it into the lethal glass.

What was that? Yes—now she did hear it—Duke was stamping majestically back to his lair.

In a second she looked around, saw she had disarranged nothing, then fled from the lighted room. Shadows in the corridor helped to hide her.

Duke passed within a yard of her. He was rubbing his hands, she could hear. Which meant he had struck one of the native servants, most likely the one having the least to do with whatever it had been that disturbed him.

She stole on now to her own bedroom, around the turn. But she left the door ajar, and waited with a throbbing in her throat, listening.

The small brown bottle had somehow slipped from her grasp. Where had she dropped it? Had it borne any marking whatsoever which might later on be found to incriminate her or Alan Legrand?

This worry surged upon her swiftly, and for perhaps the first time she became aware of the gravity of her offense. Possibly that worry pointed her to her ultimate career of blackmailing and magnificent swindling. Certainly it warned her forever away from a life of violence and revenge.

"God—"

She heard very distinctly Duke's strangling outcry. He seemed to be choking, just as the liquor he had trickled down her throat had made her choke.

She remembered having heard that poison often caused suffocation. And now she heard him staggering out into the corridor. Since she would have a part to play, she nerved herself to go through with it.

She must not hurry or seem to know immediately what was wrong with him. She did not.

FATHER AND DAUGHTER came face to face in the upper hall, near the head of the stairs. He was groping his way blindly, his eyes glazed, his evil countenance altered curiously by awful pain.

"Duke?" she cried. "What is it? What's the matter?"

It was the first offer of aid he had encountered, and he received it characteristically.

"None of your business!" he gasped.

Vi recoiled. But he was staggering drunkenly. She must appear to help him somehow.

"Please, Duke—" she implored.

"Keep away, do you hear, you—"

Below they were staring up. Servants and patrons could only assume the master of the Mansion was wholly himself.

He tottered an instant at the top of the staircase.

Vi reached out to save a stricken man from a precipitate and crushing fall.

Duke's eyes were clear for a momentary glimpse of her. Rage burned in them, and dark insanity. He struck at her. She parried the blow with the hands outstretched to balance him.

His own vicious momentum carried him over and down. He fell with a sharp cry of agony, landed on his back and shoulders very awkwardly, and lay still in a broken and contorted heap.

Vi hurried down to him, found him slack and insensible. She issued crisp, immediate orders.

She was playing the shocked and anxious daughter, but not overplaying.

Chinese boys carried Duke to a bedroom. Patrons were encouraged to depart. The doctor arrived rather slowly.

Meanwhile, Vi had found an interval in which to go again into the private office. The glass lay on its side next to the bottle. She could not find the poison phial. She used whisky to rinse the glass, dribbled more whisky over the damp stain where some of the poisoned liquor had spilled.

What else could she do?

It was much too soon to look for Alan's damning forgeries or the roll of money she would require to care for immediate needs. Just as Legrand had surmised, she was not planning to hurry away from Shanghai or even the odious Mansion. If her father died in this mystifying way, she must solemnly bury him, settle his complex estate, and take her departure with proper and unhurried dignity.

Surely he would prove to have funds enough to enable

her to climb to a decent position in some other quarter of the world?

A Chinese boy came to say the doctor was now through with his examination and ready to speak to her.

Vi went at once to hear the news of her crime.

"A strange case, my dear," said the Mansion's regularly retained physician. "Something seems to have hit him hard. It's too soon for a thorough diagnosis, and with your consent I'd like to call some colleague into consultation. Say, Dubois from the French Concession?"

"Why, of course," she agreed, experiencing a twinge of alarm.

"It isn't possible to decide what caused your father to fall as he did. Some internal disorder of very perplexing and acute characteristics! But I am sorry to say, my dear girl, the results of his fall are only too apparent. Not but what such a condition can improve—"

"Please tell me, Doctor."

"He has suffered a severe spinal injury.

"There is grave likelihood that, if he survives—and I believe he will—he will be paralyzed below the waist for the rest of his days."

5

VI LAUGHED HYSTERICALLY. She had meant to get rid of a monstrous tyrant. Instead, she had elected herself, for years perhaps, to endure the tyranny of a harsh, exacting parent's invalidism.

The morning's medical consultation resulted as the physician had predicted. Duke Donellan's remarkable constitution had withstood a twice doubled dose of poison. He was terribly ill. But the unidentified drug had counteracted itself.

Duke's spine, however, was fractured. Months hence an operation might restore him to partial mobility. But all surgical science would never make him the blustering, striding, violent Duke again. In all likelihood he was condemned to an invalid's chair so long as he should live.

Vi furtively visited Alan Legrand.

"I wanted to kill him," she confessed.

He gulped. "I wanted you to kill him. We have bungled the whole business horribly." And he explained his exaggeration of the hyoscine dose, which in turn she had more than doubled.

"Anyhow, here are your notes," she exclaimed.

He clutched at them eagerly, and then he groaned.

"Facsimile copies," he said. "You found no others?"

"There were other papers; I glanced over them hastily. I didn't see your name anywhere, Alan."

He urged her to return and search even more diligently, as circumstances might permit. She hesitated long before describing her loss; of the poison bottle.

Legrand, when he heard that, nearly fainted.

"I got it from the laboratory," he cried. "Microscopic examination by the police would probably turn up an identification. Most manufacturers can trace their own bottles—"

"But Duke is going to live. There won't be any police investigation!"

That cheered him a very little. But soon he was complaining:

"If you don't find the notes, it means that he has kept them somewhere else—a safe-deposit box probably. And my ruin is certain."

Vi hastened homeward. She had the right to search now. Her father lay helpless and stricken. Where was his money? She found less than three thousand dollars. The moment he had landed at the foot of the stairs greedy hands must have begun dividing up the gambling house funds. Duke, if ever himself again, would know who had robbed him, and how to force a restitution.

But Vi, kept unfamiliar with her parent's finances, simply had to accept the inevitable.

Other photostats which turned up in Duke's possession astonished her. Obviously he had gone in extensively for blackmail.

It seemed to her almost too subtle and adroit a game for any one of her father's bullying, violent propensities. She didn't stop to realize that most blackmailers are merely cheap bullies of Duke Donellan's stamp. The kind of blackmailer Vi had visualized didn't as yet exist in the upper reaches of the international underworld. For that was the astounding sort of blackmailer which Vi herself became.

She found Alan Legrand's revolver. She didn't know it was his—he hadn't remembered to ask her about it—and so she ignored it. That oversight had serious consequences.

She tried in vain to find even a fragment of the brown poison bottle. She found nothing. If she had dropped it, fleeing from the office, shouldn't it have smashed?

THE FACT WAS, a Chinese servant had found the phial, and was holding it against the time when Duke might be well enough to treat with him privately. This shrewd Oriental had no suspicion of anybody as the would-be murderer of his master. But he felt that he had been deprived of certain ante-mortem pickings when the staff of the Mansion first began to look out for themselves. And he wisely assumed that of all people concerned about the attempt on Duke Donellan's life, the crippled Duke himself would pay the most for the bit of evidence.

When Vi reported again to Alan Legrand, his worst fears seemed to have been realized. Duke was not going to die.

His actual forgeries were now securely hidden away. Vi hadn't even uncovered funds enough to lend him the sum of money that Duke Donellan—even stricken as he was— would try to extort from him as soon as he got around to remembering the unredeemed forgeries.

Duke, as a matter of fact, was already remembering. He lay abed in helpless torment. And it seemed clear as day to him that the craven Legrand had hired a native spy to poison him. Occidental crooks and weaklings were often influenced like that by the guile and cunning of the Orient. Alan Legrand was really his murderer, then. Duke at this moment deemed himself a good deal worse than dead.

But how to get even? How to punish Alan so craftily that only harm would come to him and only profit to his enemy?

The wily servant had shown Duke the brown bottle. He had straightway been promised rich rewards, and sent off to thread his way through the intricate maze of alleys and byways in Shanghai's native quarter. Duke was flat on his back, but swinging into action.

He had innumerable Oriental connections, had dipped a slimy claw into every form of evil traffic besetting the China coast. Duke meant to have the small bottle traced. It would, he felt sure, lead ultimately to the sanitary service of the port and Alan Legrand.

Meanwhile, there was solace of a sort to be found in revolving schemes of revenge. Duke hoped to strike secretly and savagely at the young health officer, who was now—though the invalid didn't know it—his son-in-law.

6

EVER SINCE DUKE DONELLAN regained consciousness, Alan's fears about the forgeries and the missing poison phial had pinned him upon a red hot griddle of panic. He thought of flight, of confessing everything to Stanley, just returned from his mission to Nanking, of this and that refuge or subterfuge. But all to no purpose.

Finally, with his implacable selfishness, he had found the lone solution to his dilemma in an event he desired more than all celestial glories. Vi must marry him.

"We are deep in this together—the only witnesses against each other," he argued, adding the lie, "I've heard mighty disturbing rumors, Vi. White men despised Duke, but he seems to have had a lot of powerful Chink friends. They keep pestering the police—"

A whole lot of this gradually wore down her belief that "attempted homicide" was not a serious or impending charge in China.

Naturally, Alan Legrand did not press his suit in terms of pure expediency. Didn't she knew he was crazy about her? Hadn't he really got himself into this desperate plight because he couldn't keep away from the Mansion and miss meeting her?

And so she falsified her age, and they were secretly married. Husband and wife cannot be made to testify against each other. So far as ever *proving* the attempted crime, the fear that the attempted crime would ever be proven was thrust well back in Alan's consciousness.

But he had many surviving cares. Vi had to stay on at the Mansion.

"The servants have never stopped wondering about Duke's 'accident,'" said she. "If we announced our marriage, or I even left the place, it would be a dead give-away. I've little money for any independent move. And I still hope to get the real notes he holds against you."

In short, it was no joyous honeymoon. And then the last blow fell. Duke communicated with Alan, reminding him of the notes, demanding that he and his half-brother come to the Mansion and arrange an agreement "clearing up" the debts and other payments "somewhat overdue."

The brown phial had been traced. It came to rest so close to Legrand's door that Duke needed no further confirmation. He sent for a certain elderly, wrinkled Chinaman, and they conversed in private.

Duke was being very mean and mysterious about his funds. Even as he lay helpless, he could hold fast to the purse strings. He even imagined that Vi visited him daily because of this new hold he had upon her.

He arranged to pay the old Chinese a large sum in gold. Two new, shifty-eyed young servants arrived at the gambling resort next day.

Duke had to send other threats to Alan, who spoke to Vi about them. He thought the time had come to admit the marriage.

The girl laughed bitterly.

"Are you mad?" she asked. "He has never credited me

with courage enough to try to harm him. But I am sure now he knows the whisky was poisoned. You had reason to fear him. You are surely among his suspects. Announce our secret marriage and he will know in a second who supplied the drug—and who had the really best chance to slip it into his drink, I suppose he hasn't so far suspected me, because he doesn't know how I could have obtained a poison."

After much palpitation, Alan saw there was no way out but a strong way. He went and told Stanley about the forgeries. And that capable diplomat at once agreed to the meeting with Donellan.

Stanley and his crestfallen half-brother were due at the gambling resort at five o'clock in the afternoon. Vi was unaware of their coming.

DUKE HAD EVERYTHING planned as carefully and thoroughly as one would expect in a monstrous mind shackled to a broken body. He talked with the new Chinese servants, giving one of them Alan Legrand's revolver. Both these shifty-eyed young toughs were hired assassins.

Means of escape were already provided. They would be deep in some wild interior province before any formal police search was started.

The Legrands were as unlike as possible. Perhaps Stanley's good fortune in finding himself an Ashebrook heir had given him that added tone of manliness and cool assurance. He said a word or two of tactful sympathy to Duke, and then came straight to the point:

Alan had behaved like a silly young ass—and had done a criminal thing besides. He owed Donellan legitimately a substantial sum, as well as the IOU's for gambling debts. Donellan was clearly entitled to his money.

As for selling back the proofs of forgery, why pile one offense upon another said Stanley, with his winning diplomatic smile. Such a bargain would be extortion—would be common blackmail. Blackmail, in truth, was common enough. But it was rather hard to engineer any crime from a sick bed.

"Oh, you think so?" Duke said.

"I do."

"Well, we shall see."

In his throat Duke made a strange, low, chirping sound.

A curtain parted. A swarthy Chinese visage came through, then a hand and arm. There was a Browning revolver in the hand.

"God, Stan! Look out!" Alan yelled.

In that moment he was a heroic and devoted brother. He flung himself forward. But the assassin was an expert shot. He fired over Alan's shoulder and brought Stanley down. Fired a second shot, to make sure of a fatal result.

The assassin's partner leaped in, as prearranged, and spilled Alan beside Duke's bed with a wrestling trick. The assassin bent and thrust the gun into Alan's fumbling hand.

Both gunmen then vanished utterly from the Mansion.

Duke Donellan, though he regretted his victim, lay on his broken back and chuckled with croaking triumph.

"Get up, Alan," he urged. "You're entirely safe with me. I'll even help you hide your gun, lad."

Legrand rose, staggered a little; then crossed over and knelt sadly beside his relative.

"You've gone and made yourself an Ashebrook heir. You can borrow large amounts, here, there, anywhere," said Duke. "And I'm the only witness in the world who knows how you plotted to get rid of Stanley. I'll protect your secret and your life, Alan, as if they were my very own.

"It's going to be long and tough for me. Only the greatest specialists may set me on my rotten feet again. But, man alive, when old Simon Ashebrook dies, will you and I divide your fortune?"

The two shots had brought servants and Vi herself to her father's room. She stood bewildered and aghast in the doorway. Duke was chortling and croaking like a fiend.

Alan suddenly snapped out of his trance. He saw the gun in his hand—his own Browning.

He snapped up the Browning. Vi screamed and rushed toward him. He fired. Duke's stricken massive frame gave an odd kind of half-convulsive leap on the bed. A ghastly red stain spread over the white sheets.

7

"A FOOL TO the very end," Duke Donellan murmured. Vi and the servants had disarmed Alan, were now seeking the wound to check the bubbling flow of blood. His voice receded and grew husky as he spoke.

"You'll hang for this, Legrand," he said, "when you might have been rich and safe. Vi'll stick to me. She'll prosecute you, you slinking rat. I'll be gone, but she'll see you hang—"

But Vi—Vi Legrand now, the name she would make internationally notorious—had suffered enough with these two men. She went from the room.

She must have money. She gathered up the blackmail evidence she had discovered.

She was leaving the Mansion unobtrusively when the blue-uniformed Russian police auxiliaries of the Shanghai Municipal Council drove up.

She was a material witness of great importance, and knew they would soon start searching for her. But before they had time to start she visited certain persons in Shanghai. She was starting as blackmailer, and she went through that cosmopolitan metropolis like a blend of cash register and typhoon.

She soon got wind that the authorities were now doubly eager to apprehend her, and got away to Macao in an Oriental disguise. There she changed to a school-girlish

American costume—she was just passing eighteen—and so proceeded blandly to Manila.

Alan Legrand drew a long prison term. Duke's safe-deposit box was found, and in it the notes with forged endorsements, giving a clear motive for Alan's shooting of the gambling house proprietor.

Vi knew nothing at the time of the Ashebrook estate or Alan's potential inheritance. In due course she quietly divorced him, as he was a convict. And still later she came to regret it. But that belongs to the history of the Legrand ring of international crooks.

BAIT FOR MEN

*The Sinister Allure and the Treacherous
Smile of Vivian Legrand Cost a Malay
Prince a Ruby and a Rajah's Throne*

1

THE PLAZA GOITI in Manila belies its name. It is an alley that slinks in the shadow of unpretentious houses. At the far end the house of the sinister Mandarin Hoang Fi Tu in 1904 presented a blank front flush with the street... a house that seemed to have secrets and guarded them all.

Curious eyes followed the woman who one evening walked up to the door of this house, for every man in the Chinese Section of Manila, in those days, knew that the blank front of that house concealed things that were best not discussed if a man valued his life. The woman jerked the strap that hung through the door; the sound of a silver bell came to her as she stood there in the green mists of dusk.

With a last furtive look at the street behind her the woman—girl, rather, for she was just nineteen—opened her hand bag and gave a last reassuring look into a little mirror on the flap, smoothed back the black wig that hid her red hair and scrutinized her flawless face, which was cleverly made up to resemble a half-caste's. She was a voluptuous, full-blown orchid.

A panel in the door was drawn back. A yellow mask peered through and a voice in the shrill dialect of Hanoi demanded to know who was wanted and why.

"Tell his excellency that I wish to see him on a matter

of business," the woman returned, arrogantly in the same dialect.

The panel closed quickly. After a moment the door opened and the girl stepped inside.

The door closed behind her. It was sheathed with heavy steel on the inside. She was in a hall where a *dong* swinging from brass chains kindled an orange flame against the semi-darkness. A stale, sweetish scent clung to the gloom… the unmistakable odor of opium.

An ordinary woman would have shrunk from entering that house in Manila, the headquarters of one of the most feared criminals of the Orient. Many had gone into this house, to vanish utterly from sight. But this girl was not an ordinary woman. She had beauty that possessed the subtle and almost terrifying fascination of a cobra. Her body had the smooth sleekness of a panther. She was utterly arrogant and utterly unafraid.

She followed the houseboy who had admitted her through a series of doors to a corridor where a sliding door was pushed back. She stepped through it into a dimly illuminated area.

A lamp with a yellow shade hung by invisible means from an invisible ceiling, casting a pyramid of ochre light upon a figure that squatted on silken cushions beneath it… a figure arrayed in a loose yellow garment and the embroidered boots of a mandarin's undress. He was grossly obese, with drooping gray mustaches and oblique, beady eyes. This was the Mandarin Haong Fi Tu.

HE ROSE WITH visible effort, smiled blandly and shook his own hands within his brocaded sleeves.

"You will do me the honor to be seated?" he inquired,

*Captain Swanstrom
flung himself at
the Malay prince*

gesturing toward a pile of cushions opposite him. "My house is flattered that one of such beauty should lighten it with her presence."

A slightly contemptuous smile, the mask with which she faced the world, deepened in the girl's eyes and in the corners of her brilliantly rouged mouth. She studied the mandarin a moment.

"I desire your help," she stated bluntly.

"Desire is the essence of life," murmured the Chinese.

"I want a passport made out in another name and a passage on the first steamer to San Francisco."

"And what makes you think that I would... if I could... gratify these desires?" queried the Oriental criminal.

Fire flashed instantly into the girl's eyes.

"The fact that I know every detail of many of your schemes... know who plotted the murder of Iang Wan Kee in Shanghai... know who substituted Japanese-made imitations of the treasures of the Imperial City, kept in the

Pekin Museum, and sold the originals to collectors in New York... know—"

The mandarin's voice broke in with the soft rasping sound of a sword drawn slowly from a metal sheath.

"In my turn, I know who tried to poison her father in Shanghai... know who stole certain papers from his safe and blackmailed certain people... know who is wanted, badly, by the Shanghai police... Do you play chess, Mrs. Legrand? If you did, you would recognize the meaning of the phrase 'stalemate.'"

Vivian Legrand's thoughts were lightning swift, and the gleam in her narrowed eyes was dangerous. So he knew her! Knew her in spite of the dark wig, in spite of her altered appearance. He was clever, and dangerous. She smiled a trifle. Her delicately arched eyebrows raised. She reached for her bag, took out her vanity case, powdered her nose carefully, and dabbled her mouth with a scarlet lip stick. Then she stood up.

"Very well. Then we each play our own game." She leaned forward, both hands on a little table, so that she faced the mandarin. "But let's get this thing straight. I know you. I know your reputation. Don't make the mistake of thinking that I can be made to vanish as others have. Oh, no. When I play a man's game, I play it a man's way. Unless I am out of this house within an hour every shred of information about you that I have will be in the hands of the Manila police half an hour later."

The mandarin raised a hand. "I did not say I would not help," he said smoothly. "I will help. But there are conditions."

"How much?" the girl shot at him.

"It is not a question of money, but of service. There is a scheme on hand that requires the services of a beautiful woman. If you are willing to perform that service… a passport, sufficient cash and passage to the States. If you are not willing… we will each take such action as each deems best."

The girl was silent a moment.

"A service that requires a woman," she said slowly. "A woman to be bait for some man, I suppose? Well, I have no love for men. Men are fools to be made greater fools by a woman."

His excellency nodded.

"The situation is this: there is a certain Malay prince who owns a ruby mine. This prince has a brother who has consulted us as our—client. He desires us to help him regain his share of the family property which the ruling prince withholds from him.

"There is no redress at law. The prince is the law, and he, like all the Malay princes, acknowledges the rule of the British Raj. And, like the other Malay princes, he is absolute ruler of his own people. So our client must resort to guile and strategy. He has promised us a handsome share of whatever we help him recover. And that is where you come in."

He looked at her inquiringly.

"It's a bargain," the girl agreed. "And then you will give me what I need—the passport, the money to get to the States?"

"Yes," the mandarin said.

2

BACK IN SHANGHAI, Vivian Legrand was wanted as the most important witness in the murder of her father, the brutal, notorious Duke Donellan. But she had no intention of giving testimony for or against Alan Legrand, her father's murderer, whose secret bride she was. Legrand had killed her father because he was tangled in Duke's blackmailing toils. Vivian herself had attempted to poison her father, had failed, and had married Legrand to cover up her attempted crime. But there was no love lost between them, and it was without regret that she had left Legrand to face the situation alone.

In order to escape in a hurry from Shanghai, she had extracted substantial sums from half a dozen persons, using such information as her evil father had been keeping in his safe for extortion purposes of his own. That had been her debut as a blackmailer; a debut that was to cause her to blossom into the most glamorous blackmailer and swindler that the world has ever known. When she had collected what she could she had fled in disguise.

Among the papers in her father's safe had been several relating to the activities of the Mandarin Hoang Fi Tu in Manila, a man whose hand was behind most of the major crimes of the Orient. In them she had seen her opportunity... an opportunity that an ordinary woman would not have dared tackle. An opportunity to achieve safety by blackmailing the Oriental criminal. It was a daring and a dangerous thing to attempt. But possessed of a supreme self-confidence, she had never considered the risks of a venture, only the outcome.

She was exotic. She had a mysterious, semi-hypnotic power over men… and was ruthless with them.

WITHIN HALF AN hour after her conference with the mandarin, Vivian Legrand had met his companion in crime, Adrian Wylie. And that was an historic meeting in the annals of worldwide crime. "Doc" Wylie, in the years to come, would be chief of staff of the Legrand king of blackmailers and swindlers.

Wylie was, at this time, an opium addict, a brilliant mind sinking into decay. Contact with the subtle, venturesome daughter of Duke Donellan was to change the whole course of his career. He remained a crook, a consummate schemer and swindler, but he was to stop using the drug and spend his leisure and illicit gains upon distinguished, intelligent hobbies.

But even at the outset, Vivian Legrand found both Wylie and the mandarin a vast improvement over the companions thrust upon her at her father's gambling resort. They seemed to conduct their lawless affairs so that the police never laid hands upon them. They used their wits—blending American and Asian—with results often spectacular. And what an odd assortment of accomplishments each possessed!

It was early in the evening of the second day when the brother of the Malayan prince turned up at the mandarin's house. He had good reason to arrive by stealth, and to steer widely around both police and port authorities.

He was known as Tuan Lepar, and was a feared outcast from a wealthy and powerful Penang family. Savage crimes and indescribable cruelties were charged against him. He had even trafficked with *Klah* desperadoes, most vicious criminal outlaws in the Federated Malay States. There was as yet no price upon his head. The power of his family had protected him. But there was more than one person who would have been glad to bury a knife in his body.

He came to the mandarin's under cover of darkness. He wore the native garb of a low caste Malay, was heavily armed and jumpy because of the risks he was taking. Manila was not a British possession, and police there would not be lenient with him because his brother was a ruling prince.

"We must leave within forty-eight hours," he told Wylie and the mandarin on arrival. His English was remarkably good. Like his brother, he had been educated in England. "Are you ready?"

"We are," Wylie assured him. "Our plan is a shrewd one. Wait until you see our new partner."

The Malay's eyes suddenly blazed.

"Do you so soon forget our bargain? It was to be just the three of us."

"But wait until you see her," put in Wylie.

"A woman? But there you are mistaken. A native would not catch the eye of my brother. He was educated in Europe."

"Not a native girl, Tuan. An American."

The man's eyes widened.

"You have kidnaped her?"

"No. She joins us of her own free will. An equal partner—and a prize, I assure you."

"But the risk?" Lepar asked uneasily.

"There is no risk," Wylie assured him. "She needs us
even more than we need her. She is wanted in Shanghai
for murder."

Tuan Lepar's eyes narrowed. "Still," he said thoughtfully,
"I don't like it."

The mandarin clapped his hands twice. At the signal
Vivian Legrand came slowly down the stairs.

The cloth of silver gown she was wearing fitted her
body like the closed petals of a flower. Her neck and face
rose from the silver sheath like the stamen of some exotic
jungle orchid. There was no need to wear her disguise in
the sanctuary of the mandarin's house, and her red hair
gleamed like a flickering flame above her enigmatic face.
Her slightly contemptuous smile, the symbol of her arrogance, added to her allure. It gave her an air of detachment,
of remoteness, that was as fuel to the fire of men's desire.

Tuan Lepar's pulse ran high at sight of her. Unholy spec-
ulation lighted his fierce, dark eyes. He bowed low in mock
humility, and then wet his lips like a hungry tiger. But his
voice faltered a little when he spoke, and his accent became
more pronounced.

"She is enchanting," he agreed.

Brother of a ruling prince, he owned a ruthless and
unruly will. His thoughts now would have worried his
confederates.

3

"**YOUR BROTHER STANDS** high with the British authorities," Wylie was saying. "With a Western education and point of view he is considered by them modern, loyal and utterly reliable. But that same Western education has undermined, to some extent, the confidence of the people in their ruler. Now, our plan is this: we will land at your brother's chief port. Mrs. Legrand will drive about the streets, visit the palace—be seen as much as possible—make sure that there are numerous people who will remember her.

"Then she will be smuggled back to the ship, where she will be hidden. Posing as her uncle and guardian, I will hurry to the British authorities with a story that the prince has kidnaped her. It will be your part to see that the news of the 'kidnaping' is spread among the people. Then I will manage to 'rescue' her in such a way that the whole town will believe that a white girl—an American—has been rescued from the palace of the prince."

"I do not see the value of that," said Lepar, puzzled.

"The result will be that the prince will fall into complete disfavor with the British. In one of lower rank, any such treatment of a British or American woman would be a hanging offense. In addition, his people will believe that he is infatuated with one not of the true faith. That, coupled with the fact that his people have resented his being educated in Europe, will cost him the loyalty of his humblest subject. Can't you hear the rumors growing from village to village?"

Tuan Lepar's eyes flamed. "I congratulate you!" he cried. "To discredit my brother with the British and at the same time stir up his people against him—that is genius! And if we spread the news every mullah in every village will denounce my brother. Then, at the right moment, I can appear at the head of my men and force his abdication and become rajah myself."

"At a price," put in the mandarin softly.

"At a price," agreed Lepar.

"Half the ruby mine," suggested the mandarin.

"It is agreed," said the other with grandiose gesture.

It was easy to make promises. But the mandarin was eying Lepar with marked suspicion. An Oriental himself, he distrusted any agreement where there was no bargaining as to the price.

"You agreed to raise the money for the expedition," he reminded Lepar.

"I have done more. Found the ship we may use in safety. And as for raising funds—"

His eyes flashed a moment toward Vivian Legrand. Then from the folds of his robe he brought forth a small red leather pouch. With a swift, dramatic gesture he rolled out two rubies upon the table.

"A gift from my devoted brother," Lepar said. "What an amusing thing—to use them to insure his downfall."

He reached over and picked up one of the gems,

extended it to Vivian Legrand. Something flickered in the brown depths of the Malay's eyes.

"For you," he said. "The other is for our expenses."

There was no hesitation in Vivian Legrand's movements. She took the gem and cupped it in her palm, letting the light play through its crimson depths.

"It is lovely," she said.

She looked at him, green eyes smiling and calculating through long, dark curling lashes. Their eyes met for an instant. Again Vivian Legrand noted that almost imperceptible flicker behind his smooth, brown lips. Noted it, and read its meaning correctly.

"You are lovelier," Lepar said.

He watched her turn and go up the stairs. Vivian Legrand, knowing that he would watch until she was out of sight, turned at the head of the narrow stairs and smiled enticingly down upon him.

That smile of hers would have held less invitation could she have read the Malay's thoughts. And it would have been wiser had he been followed on leaving the house, for the conference he held half an hour later would have proved illuminating to the three conspirators. But he was not followed, and they were unaware of the plot that he was hatching.

4

FOR DAYS THE Bessie S. steamed down the lonely China Sea. Another woman might have been uneasy at the unsightly tramp steamer, or the sullen Lascar crew, or Captain Swanstrom, whose thoughts were reflected quite plainly in his eyes whenever he looked at Vivian Legrand. But she was used to seeing that look in men's eyes, and she had a supreme confidence in her ability to handle whatever situation might arise. Lepar, too, had changed; and as the ship steamed nearer and nearer to his jungle shores he seemed to become less and less the man she had met in Manila and more and more the savage.

It was long after sunset of the fifth day when the Bessie S. dropped anchor in a little sheltered cove a few miles to the north of Penang. There Lepar was scheduled to leave them, to carry out his part of the conspiracy in the interior, while the plotters themselves proceeded on to the prince's chief port.

The girl stood at the rail for a few minutes after they dropped anchor. The glow of the moon, as yet invisible behind the tall trees, was an evil copper-green, like the reflection from some witch's cauldron. A white cockatoo or two, ghostly in the darkness, flitted in front of the trees. Vivian Legrand remained on deck for several hours. It was after ten when she went below.

Hours later she awoke with a start. What it was caused her to awake she did not know. Perhaps it was the sixth sense that never seemed to desert her. She restrained an impulse to sit up in her berth. She lay still and stared about her little cabin. The tropical moonlight, floating through a porthole, crusted the floor with a band of pearl. A shadow flitted across it. She realized suddenly, and not without a shock, that the shadow was not a shadow, but a human form.

There was someone in the room.

Vivian Legrand lay still, listening for the slightest sound. A faint scraping noise... What was it? A footfall? An oblong of light suddenly grew on the further side of the room. She knew that her cabin door was being opened.

Then the lights flashed on.

In the doorway stood Tuan Lepar, and beside him the lithe form of the Malay boy who had wriggled through the porthole and opened her door from the inside.

Vivian Legrand sat up, anger flashing in her eyes.

"What do you want here?" she demanded.

"You," answered Lepar succinctly.

For a moment they eyed each other.

Vivian Legrand's smile, maddening in its arrogance, flitted across her face.

"I am honored," she said evenly. "I had not realized..."

She allowed the sentence to die away, leaving the implication hanging in the air between them. The remark disarmed Lepar. He stepped forward, almost apologetically.

"I did not know you would take it so," he said awkwardly.

"No one ever knows how I will take a thing," she

replied. "I do not know myself until the moment arrives. That is one of the things that makes me interesting."

"I am glad that I have found favor in your eyes." The Malay took another step forward.

Vivian Legrand eyed him coldly. "Well, now that you

Doc Wylie

know, don't you think that you could find a more opportune time than this? I wish to sleep. There are many days—and nights—to come."

"*This* is the opportune time," Lepar insisted. "Your friends and the crew are locked below decks. My men possess the ship. I will give you five minutes in which to dress and accompany me ashore."

This was a new turn of affairs. Vivian Legrand's mind flew fast, while her eyes scanned the cabin for a possible weapon.

"But why are you doing this?" she demanded. "Don't you realize that this will wreck our plans? Prevent you from taking your brother's place on the throne?"

Lepar laughed.

"That was their plan. Mine is better. You do not know my brother as I do. He holds the honor of his house even above his own personal honor. And he will pay well to prevent any breath of scandal falling upon it. When he knows that his brother—that I—have kidnaped a white girl, he will pay well for her release.

"And while my messengers are negotiating for the ransom, you and I will be enjoying the sweetness of love in my headquarters in the interior." His tone changed. "Now hurry. In five minutes I will come in again and expect to find you dressed."

It was a few minutes less than the allotted five when Vivian Legrand threw open the door of her cabin and confronted Lepar, seated in a chair in the dining salon.

"I AM READY," she said curtly. Her alert brain was working, seeking a loophole. Mentally she damned herself for not being sufficiently foresighted to have a revolver within arm's reach in her cabin. It would have been so easy to have shot Lepar down as he stood there waiting for her. In that moment was born the resolution never to be without a gun again. And she never was.

Lepar took her by the arm. "This way," he urged, hurrying her up the companion stairs and along the silent, deserted deck.

Then came a sudden diversion. As they crossed the deck the door of the charthouse on the bridge was flung open. Lepar had forgotten that there was a bunk in the charthouse and that Captain Swanstrom sometimes slept there. With a roar the captain rushed down the bridge ladder and flung himself at the Malay.

Lepar ducked the blow and swung up with a knife. A blow from Swanstrom parried the slash, but not entirely. Blood welled from a gash on the captain's shoulder. He roared again, the roar of a maddened bull, but before he could close in on Lepar the latter had flung himself forward with the speed of a striking cobra, and with an effect as deadly. The knife sank into Swanstrom's breast. The captain sank slowly to his knees, then pitched forward flat on the deck, sobbing out his last breath.

The thing had been so quick, so sudden, that Vivian Legrand had no time to take action. But now, as Swanstrom fell, she suddenly whirled and ran toward the door leading toward the crew's quarters. If only she might open that, and free them!

She flung it open—and was dragged back from the threshold as Lepar's hand clutched her shoulder.

The Malay lost no time. Snatching her in his arms he stumbled toward the rail, where a group of sampans waited at the foot of the lowered accommodation ladder. As he began to descend the crew began to pour out of the opened door.

Vivian Legrand fought desperately, but she might have saved herself the trouble. She was dumped in the bottom of one of the sampans. A long cloak flung over her as they shoved off.

A rifle cracked from the deck of the steamer, followed by an irregular volley. Lepar cursed suddenly. Vivian Legrand threw off the cloak, and, in the moonlight, saw blood welling from his upper arm, where a bullet had struck him.

But that was the only shot that went home. In a few minutes more the overhanging shadows of the mangrove trees closed over them, and the sampans swerved into a narrow tidal creek that ran back into the jungle.

It was as the sampans swerved into this creek that Vivian made a final effort to save herself. The velvet darkness under the low arching branches hid her movement, and it passed unnoticed.

5

DURING THAT FLIGHT through the night Vivian Legrand seemed to have entered a new world, a world inhabited only by Lepar, and by shadows that took on human shape.

Hours later there came a squelch as the sampans furrowed mud. Lepar made no move to help her from the boat. She climbed over the side, sinking ankle deep in mud.

Hardly more than a hundred feet from the water's edge was a stockade, inside which were bamboo houses, log-raised, huddled in close packed groups. Some distance from the gate, perhaps a hundred yards, was a monster building, a jumbled pile of grass roofs and wattled walls flung upon poles. At close range she perceived that instead of one great building it was a series of houses joined by narrow verandas.

At the entrance several women stood. Intuitively she knew them to be Lepar's wives. Was she destined to become one of them?

She was conducted through a labyrinth of rooms with sagging floors and across frail verandas to an apartment in the very heart of the place, where Lepar played at being ruler. It was empty except for two chests and a bed. The bed, a truly Malay affair, was curtained. It had gold-embroidered valances and seven stiff, brocaded pillows.

A few minutes later one of the women returned with

food. Vivian Legrand waved it away. It was dawn before she slept.

Despite her fatigue she woke before noon. She had scarcely finished dressing when Lepar entered. He was in a bad temper. His wounded arm was throbbing. The wound had begun to fester.

"We will now write a note to my esteemed brother— may Allah curse him!" he began abruptly. "Tell him you are being held prisoner by Tuan Lepar, and that your release will come about upon the payment of five thousand English pounds in gold to be delivered to me here. Failure to make the payment will result in your being delivered—a finger, a toe, an eye, an ear at a time—to the British Governor at Singapore."

A shudder went through Vivian Legrand's body. She caught her breath sharply. He had touched upon the one thing that had power to frighten her. A threat to her beauty—the beauty that she prized more than life itself— was the one thing that struck home to this unusual woman. She could smile in the face of a gun.

Across the room she could see her face in a long, cheap French mirror. Her mouth was a scarlet slash in a field of snow. Lepar smiled at her—the smile of a tiger who knows that his prey cannot escape.

"Of course," he said, "I would not disfigure you that way—if you are reasonable. And you will be reasonable, I am sure."

"Naturally," Vivian Legrand said quietly, and picked up the pen.

He read the note through carefully when she had finished it.

"Very good," he said. "Now, to make sure that my brother does not think that I am trying a game with him—"

His keen-edged *kris* snipped off a lock of her red hair which he folded carefully into the note.

"Convincing proof," he said. "Malay women do not have hair like that."

He clapped his hands sharply and gave swift, staccato instructions in Malay to the man who entered.

"By tonight," he said, "my brother should have received your appeal. In the meanwhile, shall we not become better acquainted?"

Vivian Legrand's eyes narrowed in the way that was characteristic of her in moments of stress. Then she raised her head, and the smile she gave him was friendly and disarming. She chattered in a friendly way as she moved by his side through the rambling rooms of the old structure.

It was only the intense pain in Lepar's wounded arm that permitted her to return to her room alone that night. As she prepared for bed she realized that ransom or no ransom, unless she wished to spend the rest of her life as a member of Lepar's harem she must use her wits as she had never used them before.

IT WAS LATE that night when she heard the faintest of rustling sounds at the *attap* of woven palm leaves that shielded the window. It might have been a lizard—but somehow she did not think it was. Instantly she was on her feet, tiptoeing across the yielding floor of split bamboo; peering out into the night.

Then a figure stepped into her line of vision. Doc Wylie!

"Vivian!" he breathed.

"Doc!" she exclaimed. "You followed me!"

"Couldn't have, if you hadn't hung that white scarf of yours on the limb at the creek entrance. When we saw that we knew he'd taken you up the creek. Otherwise we'd never have known whether he took you somewhere by sea, through the jungle, or what. I've got to get you out of here, quick. The rajah is outside with his men, but he doesn't dare attack while you are here. At the sound of the first shot Lepar would kill you. Are you dressed?"

"I will be in a moment," she said hastily. In a few minutes she crawled through the window. Doc caught her as she jumped.

"Once we're outside the stockade the rajah will attack the village," Wylie whispered as they crept along in the shadow of the building. "His men have cut a hole in the bamboo stockade. The rajah is determined to put an end to his brother. They're only waiting for you."

"How did the rajah get here so quickly?" Vivian asked.

"I sent a launch around to the port," Wylie answered. "He and his men joined us at the ship before daylight. We came up the creek. Had the launch tow a long string of Sampans filled with his soldiers, until we reached a point where we were afraid Lepar might hear the engine. Rest of the way on foot through the jungle."

They had reached the corner of the building now. Ahead lay the somber shadow of the stockade—and safety. But between them lay a tract of ground brilliantly illuminated by the tropical moon. To attempt to approach the stockade across that illuminated area would be madness. And further along, where Wylie had crept to her rescue in the shadow of the buildings, the attempt would now be equally dangerous. For there they could hear the rumble of voices.

The only chance was to make a dash for the hole in the stockade. It was a very slim chance, but one that must be taken.

Wylie pressed a slim-bladed knife into her hand.

"See that tall tree outside the stockade?" he asked. At the answering pressure of her hand he went on: "Just under it, hidden by a clump of hibiscus bushes on the inside, is the opening. Make a dash for that spot. If Lepar catches you and finds that his brother's forces are outside—it's taps."

Wylie's hand found the girl's and received an answering pressure. There was a revolver in his pocket, but he dared not shoot, except as a last desperate expedient. The sound would bring the whole town about his ears in half a minute.

Suddenly, without warning, a dark form burst through the shadows—was upon them. On the instant Wylie's body shot forward, hurtling at his assailant. His left arm went about the man's neck and shoulders, tightening over his mouth, preventing any outcry.

"Run," he said hoarsely.

A throaty sound, animal and inarticulate, came from the throat of the man. Then the butt of Doc's revolver fell— again and again. Vivian Legrand saw the man fall as she took to her heels, heading for the opening in the stockade.

But she had waited too long. Before she had taken a dozen steps lithe forms were upon her. A hand caught her throat. Her last sight, before a sarong was thrown over her head, was of Doc going down, fighting beneath a mass of men. She felt herself being carried. Then she was placed on her feet. The sarong was whipped off, and the interior of the room on whose threshold she was standing jumped at her with a brutal massing of colors and sounds.

6

FLARING TORCHES OF palm fiber soaked in coconut oil flamed red in the blackness of the long room, lit up the place. The face of Tuan Lepar had the aspect of a devil standing in the glare of hell-fire. She knew from the look on his face that death lay in store for her.

Lepar was the first to speak.

"So my little white flower would run away," he jeered.

Vivian Legrand could feel the black thrill of Lepar's anger rising and hanging in the air like a tangible thing. A cruel smile animated his face. She wondered if by look or gesture on her part, or through intuition the Malay had guessed the plan that had been born in her brain.

"What have you done with Wylie, Tuan Lepar?" she asked.

Lepar smiled.

"He is where he will be safe until I have finished with you."

"I want to make a bargain with you."

It was the bait—displayed for the fish to see.

"I have no time for bargains—or need of them," Lepar said.

"Not even if I know where the mandarin and Wylie keep money enough to last the two of us all our lives?"

Lepar stared at her without speaking. Distrust flickered in his eyes like the shimmer of a naked blade.

"You want money, don't you, Tuan Lepar?"

"I shall have it," he declared grimly.

"I can give you more."

"Where?"

A new look had come into the Malay's face. The fish had seen the bait.

"Do you want me to tell you before all your men?" she asked.

An inscrutable expression flitted across Lepar's eyes. He did not reply immediately.

But Vivian Legrand knew what lay behind that silence. The smile on the man's face bit into her consciousness like acid. She knew why Lepar had leaned forward; read it in the licking tongue that moistened his dry lips, in the smile like that of an animal crouching for the kill.

"Where is the money?" demanded Lepar.

She watched him calculatingly.

"First the bargain," she said.

He lifted a hand threateningly—as only an Oriental can threaten with a gesture. It was more than a mere waving of hand and arm.

But Vivian Legrand did not recoil, as the Malay had expected. Instead she took a step forward. She must get nearer to Lepar before her plan could succeed.

"What is your bargain?"

Exultation swept through Vivian Legrand. The fish was ready to be hooked.

"If you'll agree not to hurt Wylie, and to give me half

of the money, I'll tell you where the gold and the jewels of the mandarin are hidden."

The stretch of flooring between herself and Lepar seemed vast.

"Your brother is outside with his troops. I can tell him that I was not kidnaped. That I came to you of my own free will. Then we can go to Manila—and the money."

A cunning grin twisted Lepar's face.

"It is a bargain—if you go with it."

"It is a bargain," she said, and walked toward him, smiling.

SHE KNEW THAT the moment had come. Her hand crept beneath her gown, withdrew the knife Doc had given her. Swiftly, with all the strength at her command, she slashed downward, striking for the little hollow at the base of Lepar's throat.

But the blow was futile.

The knife was wrenched from her hand. One of Lepar's yellow hands dragged her head back. The other pressed the sharp edge of the knife against her throat.

Lepar's hand straightened. He held her at arm's length. The knife slid slowly, caressingly across her throat.

A whispering silence was in the room, like the rustle of forest leaves.

And then, suddenly, there came a tiny sound. It was like a puff of breath, quickly released. A sound that under normal conditions would have gone unheard.

Lepar loosened his grip. He sprang to his feet, clawing frantically at the side of his face, where a tiny sliver of bamboo, tipped with the down of the silk-cotton tree, had penetrated the skin.

Even then Vivian Legrand would not have realized, would not have known what saved her life if she had not seen the form of the Malay soldier at the window: a tall man who still held the ten-foot *sumpitan* from which he had blown the poisoned dart.

So swift was the action of the poison that before the men at the far end of the room could move, before anything could be done, it was over.

Lepar screamed; a horrible, bubbling scream of agony. Screamed again and again, until the room rang with his cries, his hands clawing at his throat. The perspiration of a man in terrible agony poured down his face. His eyes strained, stared, seemed about to jump from their sockets. The veins in his forehead strained to the breaking point— and he fell. He writhed in agony on the floor for a moment; then lay stiff and quiet, his face set in a mask of death.

Soldiers appeared at the windows, *sumpitans* and muskets trained on the little knot of Lepar's followers. The big door was flung open and a tall, slender man in a silken sarong stood in the opening. By the side of the prince stood Doc Wylie, and behind him a group of soldiers, armed with modern repeating rifles.

In an instant Vivian Legrand was in Wylie's arms. He comforted her—and as he did so he managed to whisper:

"You're a movie actress… I'm director. We're making a jungle picture. Came here for animal shots. Lepar kidnaped you. Don't forget."

She nodded as the rajah turned from the body of his brother toward her.

"Miss Legrand," he said in English that was almost flaw-less, "my profound apologies. Please try to forget how you have suffered at the hands of this rebel. He was once my brother, and, as the head of my house, I shall try to make amends. Won't you and your director be my guests, for the time being at least?"

Vivian Legrand nodded. An ironic flicker came into her eyes. She was just remembering that the rajah was the owner of the ruby mine.

THE EPISODE OF THE SECRET SERVICE BLACKMAIL

From the Fortress of the Bald Doctor with
the Yellow Eyes Vivian Legrand Snatches
a Letter Worth Three Thousand Pounds

1

COL. SIR MARK CAYWOOD, Chief of the British Secret Service in the Far East, was an exceedingly worried man on two counts this June night.

The first worry rose from a cablegram in code received that morning from the Viceroy of India giving him to understand, in no uncertain terms, that the Viceroy expected results in the matter that was just then occupying the undivided attention of the secret service as well as causing new wrinkles and gray hair among the higher members of British India officialdom.

The second worry rose from a note received an hour or so before, signed Mrs. Legrand, and stating that the writer would call at his office at eight that night for an interview of importance. No answer had been requested, and, apparently, none had been expected, the writer taking it for granted that the interview would be granted her.

In his files were several reports on Vivian Legrand, who was wanted in Shanghai in connection with the murder of her father, the notorious Duke Donellan. Under ordinary conditions, Sir Mark would have simply ordered the lady held for the Shanghai police. The matter was not so simple, however. As a matter of fact, Sir Mark did not dare arrest her, for she was present in Rangoon as the guest of a native potentate, the ruling Rajah of Salingar. To arrest

The steel door behind the painting swung open

his guest would be an offense to the rajah that Sir Mark did not care to commit.

So, as the clock approached eight, he sat alone in his study beneath a madly whirring fan and sweltered and swore. Not once did Sir Mark suspect that there might be a most important connection between that note and the cablegram.

A houseboy appeared like a white wraith. Sir Mark looked up.

"A lady who says that you desire an appointment with her, O Presence."

The colonel stared. The effrontery of the woman, making it appear that the appointment was of his seeking! He did not realize—nor did many another of her victims in later years realize—that Vivian Legrand almost invariably and at once placed the other person on the defensive. It gave her the advantage. The colonel bit his lip, then said slowly, "Show the lady in."

He watched the doorway and presently a figure materialized. He rose—and came out of the shell. His official reports on Vivian Legrand had not prepared him for what he saw. No man could question her beauty. Her red hair caught the shaded light on the colonel's study table and became a quivering flame above the exquisitely modeled, exotic face. The clinging black gown she wore seemed molded to her shapely form.

"You are Mrs. Legrand?"

"I am Mrs. Legrand," Vi responded in the husky contralto that was one of her charms. The smile she bestowed upon him was completely disarming.

"Since I received your note," the colonel told her, settling behind the desk, "I have, if you will pardon me, been more than a little puzzled. I cannot imagine anything that cannot be taken up with my secretary."

"I told you that I wanted to see you regarding a matter of importance."

SHE PAUSED AND smiled. Had Sir Mark known what was in her mind at the moment the smile might not have pleased him as much as it did. Vivian Legrand lay back in silence in the long rattan chair, quite at ease, her hands clasped in her lap, chin tilted, eyes looking upon him as a cat's eyes look upon the mouse it is about to play with.

"What happened on the night of June 14th?" she flung at him.

He glared at her, consternation written on his features.

"You don't mean—"

"But I do," she assured him.

He drummed upon the desk.

"You have not answered me," she reminded him after a moment. "Shall I tell *you* what happened that night, and what the consequences are likely to be?"

He raised a hand swiftly. "Please. These things are best not discussed."

She went on relentlessly. "On the night of June 14th a paper was stolen from your safe… a letter that had been written to you by a man named Ivan Stavinsky, a prisoner who had been sentenced for life to the penal colony on the Andaman Islands. If that letter falls into the hands of a certain power to the north of India, it might precipitate a war."

The colonel leaned forward tensely. "You know the contents of that letter?"

"What I know is locked away safely until the time is ripe to bring it forth. Meanwhile, I will say this much. That letter has not left Rangoon."

For a moment Sir Mark sat motionless and expressionless. Then he said briefly:

"Unless you are willing to answer my question truthfully, there is no need to continue the interview further."

She dismissed the implication with a shrug. "Frankly, I do not know the contents," she said. "But I do know where it is."

Instantly he was on his feet. "You do?"

She nodded. "How much is it worth to you if I recover that document, Sir Mark?"

He stared at her in amazement.

"You—recover it? But that is impossible!" He stopped, struck by a sudden thought, and she laughed.

"Wrong, Sir Mark. I am not the person who stole that letter. But I repeat that I know who did—know where it is—and if it is worth—shall we say three thousand pounds to you—you may have it back again."

It was with difficulty that Sir Mark suppressed an impulse to smile. He said soberly:

"I'll confess that I do not know how you learned of this matter. But since you do, won't you be more explicit? To—ah—propose to blackmail the British Secret Service seems rather incredible."

In her turn, Vivian Legrand suppressed an impulse to smile. She wondered what Sir Mark would say were she to tell him that the secret service of the Mandarin Hoang Fi Tu, underworld leader of Manila, was fully as good as that of the British; and when it came to gathering information among the underworld occupants of the Far East, much better than the British.

She said swiftly, stabbing each word at him as if it were a weapon.

"I mean, quite simply, Sir Mark, that I can and will do—for the sum of three thousand pounds—what your entire police and secret service have failed to do."

He chewed his lip. "Really, won't you throw a little more light on the subject?"

"No," she replied curtly. "Either you accept my offer, or you don't."

Sir Mark's forehead wrinkled in an official frown.

"This is most extraordinary. Is that a—er—threat?"

It seemed impossible that a girl as superbly beautiful as this one should be sitting across the desk from him calmly blackmailing him, and through him, the British Empire!

Vivian Legrand laughed, that laugh that rippled low in her throat.

"Dare one threaten the British Secret Service?" she purred.

Sir Mark drummed upon the surface of the desk again. His thoughts at that moment were none too pleasant.

"Well, what are your terms?" came at length from him.

She was aware that she was mistress of the situation and she enjoyed the position.

"I wish, first of all, an invitation for myself and Mr. Adrian Wylie to the Official Ball to be held next Wednesday. I want you to have at that ball three thousand pounds in bank notes, and be prepared to pay them to me that night upon delivery of the letter. And lastly, I wish you to arrange with the municipal police of Shanghai that any charges against me in connection with the death of my father be dropped."

Sir Mark stared at her in amazement.

"You ask the impossible."

She made an impatient gesture.

"You are not dealing with a fool or a child, Sir Mark. I know that the municipal police in Shanghai, upon your request, will wipe out all record of any charge against me."

Their eyes met and there followed a quick duel. The man's smile was a signal of defeat.

"You are a very resourceful woman," he said.

"I have to be," she said. "You accept?"

"I accept," he said. "The charge will be quashed. You shall have your invitations tomorrow. And I shall be prepared to carry out my part of the bargain on the night of the ball. The cash will be ready."

She smiled her approval, gave him her hand and moved to the door; melted into the dusky hallway, leaving Sir Mark seated at his desk with a feeling of bafflement.

2

FOR SIX WEEKS Vivian Legrand and her companion in crime had been the guests of the Rajah of Salinger, following her rescue by the rajah from his own brother in the depths of the Malayan jungle. Vivian Legrand and Adrian Wylie had plotted with the Mandarin Hoang Fi Tu to topple the rajah from his throne. Yet when their plot failed Vivian and Wylie had made the rajah believe that they were motion picture people, making pictures in the jungle, Wylie being the director and Vivian Legrand the actress.

The rajah had offered the two of them his hospitality as recompense, in some part, for the injuries she had suffered at the hands of his brother, and Vivian Legrand, still thinking of a ruby mine which the rajah owned, had accepted.

When she returned from her meeting with Colonel Sir Mark Caywood she found Wylie waiting for her on the after deck of the rajah's yacht. She dropped down into a chair beside him.

"Well," she said briefly, "we are to deliver the letter to him next Wednesday night in return for the payment of three thousand pounds—cash on the nail."

"Very nice," Wylie reflected, a touch of sarcasm in his manner. "Now all we have to do is the thing that the whole British Secret Service in the Far East has failed to do—

discover who has the letter, get it away from them, and deliver it. Of course we'll find that quite simple."

Doc Wylie had not yet discovered what would be quite plain to him in later years of their partnership in crime— namely, that Vivian Legrand never took a step in one of their schemes without the next step being clear before her.

"I know who has it, and know how to get it," she assured him.

Wylie sat up, astonishment written on his face.

"You do?" he said incredulously. "I received the manda- rin's cablegram only this morning. In less than twelve hours, in a strange port, you've discovered what the Brit- ish Secret Service failed completely to find a trace of?"

Vivian Legrand bent closer and lowered her voice.

"I reasoned," she said, "that because Russia was involved the secret service would be looking for a Russian angle. And I reasoned that the man clever enough to steal that letter would also be clever enough to make sure that there was no visible thread connecting him with Russia—that it would be someone on whom the breath of suspicion would never fall.

"And I reasoned also that a document containing as much political dynamite as that letter would never be entrusted to a subordinate. It would be delivered by the principal himself to the Russian authorities—to make sure of getting the credit.

"The first thing I did was to check the steamship sail- ings. There has been no boat sailing from here for a Russian port, or a port where connections could be made for Russia, since June 14th. The first boat is next Saturday. I discovered that three persons had booked passage through to Harbin, where connections can be made on the Chinese Eastern Railroad for Siberia and St. Petersburg. Two of them were obviously impossible suspects. The third seemed impossible, and yet if my line of reasoning was correct, it had to be he. I went down into the Chinese quarter, managed to get hold of a discharged Chinese servant—and I was right."

"Who is it?" Wylie asked.

"Dr. Basil Orbison," Vivian Legrand responded.

Wylie thought a moment. "Never heard of him."

"HE IS A doctor, half Greek, half English who is making an exhaustive study of tropical diseases," she told him. "He lives some seven miles out from the town. He is an exceedingly peculiar individual, yet well liked by the English. A friend of the Governor's, who is often called in by the hospitals here when something beyond their medical experience comes up. Not the slightest breath of suspicion that he might be connected with Russia, and yet his house is surrounded by a high wall and guarded like a fortress. And unless I'm a fool the letter we want is in that house."

Wylie looked at her seriously. "Where it's likely to stay if that house is as well guarded as you say."

"That's why I asked for—and got—invitations to the Official Ball on Wednesday night."

Then she made a swift gesture to Wylie as the tall form of the Rajah of Salingar loomed in the shadows of the deck. The rajah was their anchor to windward, their safeguard. As guests on his yacht they could go almost anywhere, move in circles that otherwise they could not enter. He must not be permitted to suspect, even for a moment, that they were not motion picture people. And then, too, there was the matter of the ruby mine that was a part of the royal properties of Salingar.

Educated at Oxford, the rajah's English was practically flawless, as he stopped beside them in the shadows and greeted his guests warmly. Vivian Legrand leaned back a trifle, so that the glow from a lantern at the companion-way made highlights in the red of her hair and etched her exotic face in soft relief. Then she patted a cushion beside her and the rajah sank down upon it.

Wylie watched the absorbed face of the Malay ruler for a moment as the man talked with Vivian, and then with a grim smile of satisfaction got to his feet and went below to his cabin.

3

THE ORCHESTRA WAS playing a slow waltz when Vivian Legrand came up the steps of Government House on the arm of the Prince of Salingar, with Doc Wylie following discreetly behind.

A cap of cloth of silver hid her flaming hair, and a flame-like spray of egrets swayed above her head. Gown and hands and throat were shimmering with jewels—some of them given her by the rajah, others that he had loaned her. Pendants dangled beside cheeks that were pale as if all the blood had been drained out of them, but her lips were blood red.

The Governor and his wife greeted them courteously, and if their eyes widened a trifle at the sight of a white woman attending the Official Ball on the arm of a native rajah, it was not noticeable.

Vivian Legrand's greenish eyes, shadowed with lids as purple as grapes, flitted here and there about the long room. She was searching for someone, and presently she caught sight of the man she sought—Basil Orbison.

He was talking to a woman, and for the first time Vivian had a good look at him. His gaunt face was as pale as anything that lives in darkness. A bony, fleshless sort of face, plastered over with lifeless skin; ugly and interesting.

The eyes glittered in bony sockets. Dark hair flowed back from a high forehead.

The woman with him claimed Vivian Legrand's close attention, for she was the key to her plan. Without her, Vivian was helpless. By a coincidence that was no coincidence on Vivian's part the two women wore the same type of headdress—silver cap fitting over the hair, from which rose the flame-like spray of egrets. It had cost Vivian Legrand fifty dollars to find what kind of head dress the woman would wear, and to have the Chinese dressmaker make a duplicate of it for her.

Wylie, walking down the room beside her, was the only one who caught the whisper that came from her lips.

"That's the woman—talking to Orbison—you know what you've got to do—be ready when I get Orbison out on the veranda."

The next moment Vivian Legrand was smiling up into the eyes of the Rajah of Salingar.

With the rajah at her side she moved slowly about the room. Several times she stood close enough to the woman with Orbison, who was addressed as Madame Carpenter, to hear her voice. It was a low-pitched, well-modulated voice, and Vivian Legrand fixed its tones firmly in her mind.

Within an hour she had contrived to meet Dr. Basil Orbison and had steered him deftly to a corner of the veranda. His back was to the clustered shrubbery which bordered the veranda, and even if he had heard a faint rustling in the shrubbery he would have put it down to the passage of a night bird.

They stood there talking for a few minutes. There was

not the slightest change in Vivian Legrand's manner or voice to indicate that she saw the stealthy shape that loomed up in the shrubbery behind the doctor. So cleverly did she hold his attention that he never knew what hit him.

His limp form slumped to the floor, and almost instantly Wylie had vaulted over the railing, still holding the black-jack.

"Get him over the railing, quick," Vivian Legrand said tensely.

Together they raised him and lowered him. While Vivian Legrand stood on the balcony above, Wylie swiftly went through the man's pockets and found the thing for which he was looking—a key ring.

"How long will he be out?" Vivian Legrand asked as he passed the keys up to her.

"Fifteen minutes—maybe twenty," Wylie said.

"It will have to do," she said tersely. She moved swiftly down the veranda and descended the steps to the garden. Wylie met her where the sanded path passed beneath the overhanging branches of a ylang-ylang tree. She took a silken wrap that he carried and flung it over her dress. She turned up the collar, hiding her face from view.

Side by side they passed through the garden gate and approached the spot where Orbison's powerful car was parked. As they came opposite the spot where the chauf-feur sat, Wylie paused and extended his hand.

"So sorry you're not feeling well, Madame Carpenter," he said with just the right touch of concern in his voice. "You're sure you don't want me to go with you?"

"Quite sure," Vivian Legrand answered, making her tones as like that of the woman who was Orbison's companion as she could. It was not the last time that her gift for mimicry would stand her in good stead. "I shall be quite all right. I am so sorry to leave so early, but Dr. Orbison understands. Good night."

Then, before the chauffeur could get out of the car, she opened the door and slipped into the rear.

"Home," she said quietly. Then, as the big car slid smoothly from the curb she leaned back with a sigh of relief. So far her scheme had worked without a hitch. If only she had a little more luck she would win.

FROM GOVERNMENT HOUSE to Orbison's fortress-like home was seven miles, but the car did it in fifteen minutes. The chauffeur let his passenger out of the Rolls and inquired:

"Shall I wait for *madame?*"

Vivian Legrand gestured a negative, crossed the porch and rang the bell.

The butler opened the door, saw what he deemed to be the woman who had left the house with the doctor standing on the threshold, and flung the door open.

Quite unsuspiciously he closed the door behind him, shot the bolt—found a revolver jammed into his ribs.

"Don't move. And don't speak," Vivian Legrand whispered.

The butler stood with his fingers jammed against the wall, utterly unable to comprehend the turn of events. His face went pale, not so much from fear of the gun as fear of what his master might do when he found that entry had been effected so easily into a house that was guarded like a fortress.

"Now," whispered Vivian Legrand, "where are the other servants?"

"In their quarters," came the surly answer.

"Where does your master keep his safe?" she demanded.

"I don't know," he spat back at her.

"At three I shoot," Vivian Legrand said curtly. "One—two—"

"Upstairs in his study," the man cut in hurriedly. "Take that gun further away. I don't like it so damn close."

"Lead me to the study. And don't try any funny stuff. I'll shoot first and ask questions afterwards. And don't figure that because I'm a woman I won't shoot. I will."

The man started forward, then stopped abruptly. From the rear of the house the sound of voices and the blare of a phonograph had come suddenly as a door was opened. The servants were making merry in their master's absence. Then the door was closed again and the noise cut off as abruptly as it had begun. There were tiny beads of perspiration on the butler's forehead.

"That was lucky for you," Vivian Legrand said grimly. "You'll be the first to get hurt. Go ahead."

Surrendering to the menace behind him, the butler moved forward across the red-tiled floor and slowly ascended the carpeted stairs. At the head of the stairs he indicated a door at the right of the hallway.

"That's the study," he said sullenly. "You won't be able to get in. He keeps it locked all the time."

Vivian Legrand's answer was to take the bunch of keys from her hand bag.

"Unlock the door," she said curtly to the butler. Under

the muzzle of the menacing revolver the man tried the keys. The second fitted. The door swung open.

"Inside," she told him curtly. Once the man was inside she touched the light switch on the wall, and then closed the door with her foot. The butler turned and peered at her, again endeavoring to see her face. She checked him.

"No tricks, unless you want to commit suicide," she warned him curtly. "Here!" She touched a big chair with her foot. "Sit here."

Whipping a scarf from the table in the center of the room she effectively blindfolded the man. No sense in leaving a trail that could be followed, she felt—and that was to become one of the cardinal principles of the Legrand ring of blackmailers in later years, one of the things that baffled the police of three continents. There was rarely a trail that led to one of the gang.

Slowly her eyes went from object to object in the room, measuring, identifying. It was unlikely that Dr. Orbison would have a letter as important as was this one lying around loose. It was undoubtedly well hidden. She discarded the big writing desk with one cursory glance. That would be the first place that a searcher would look, and the doctor would realize that.

There was no safe in sight, but a large painting on the far side of the room caught her eye. It was out of harmony with the rest of the room. No reason for it to be there. And no reason either for it to be set into the wall, instead of hanging as a painting normally would.

A quick search and she found a spot on the wall beside it where the wall paper was smudged, as though fingers had been often pressed there. She pressed with her thumb. A click and the painting swung outward, disclosing the steel door of a safe behind it.

Again the key ring that she had taken from Orbison's pocket went into play and the steel door swung open.

There was nothing in it, however, except a small box with a few bills, a package of letters, and a thin rod of steel with a cross piece at one end. A hasty inspection showed that the letter she sought was not among the bundle lying in the safe.

Glancing at the butler, who was sitting taut in his chair, listening to every movement, Vivian Legrand picked up the T-shaped rod of steel and inserted it in a round opening in the back of the safe. There was a faint click and the door of a hidden compartment swung outward. Lying in the compartment was a long envelope. She opened it swiftly. It held the letter for which she was in search.

4

VIVIAN LEGRAND KNEW enough of the political background of the Far East to grasp at the first reading the tremendous import of that document. She knew the importance to England of the Khyber Pass, the only practicable route from the north into India, the route through which every invader of India from the time of Alexander the Great has come, the pass through the mountains that has been so heavily fortified by England that it would be impossible for an invading army to force it.

And here was a letter to the British Secret Service from a Russian agent offering to barter to the English knowledge of a hitherto unknown pass through the mountains for his freedom.

The writer went on to say that he had discovered this pass, and had been mixed up with a riot in the Calcutta bazaars, arrested and sentenced to life in the Andaman Islands before he could report his discovery to his superiors in St. Petersburg.

Vivian Legrand's greenish eyes narrowed thoughtfully as the full import of the thing flashed over her. No wonder Sir Mark Caywood had been willing to pay three thousand pounds for the return of this letter. Knowledge of this unguarded pass into India from the north, in the hands of Russia, was a constant threat to the security of the British rule in India. And Russia? What would the knowledge be worth to her? Not a single implication of the potential possibilities that the situation held was escaping Vivian Legrand's mind.

So engrossed was she in the contents of the letter that she did not notice the butler's right hand groping for the cord of a bell pull that hung quite near. When she looked up from the letter the man's arms were again resting on the arms of the chair.

She was in the act of folding the letter when the room door flung open, and four of Orbison's men hurled themselves in. For a split second they stared in amazement at finding a woman in jewels and plumes in that place. Vivian Legrand's arm reached the alabaster globe above her head. She turned the lights out.

She was through the group like an eel as they sprang for her. She was down the stairs, across the hall, with the front door open, inserting the key in the outside, before the first of her pursuers reached the bottom of the staircase. And then she stopped short in consternation. Just walking up to the front door was Dr. Basil Orbison.

He looked at Vivian Legrand, and his thin mouth moved in a slow smile. He bowed in exaggerated courtesy.

"So, it is the lovely lady of the Official Ball who honors me with a visit—in my absence. So fortunate that I returned in time! I would have regretted missing you."

His eyes flickered from Vivian Legrand to the armed men who stood in the hallway behind her. Then he took her arm and urged her gently back into the house and into a room on the right. The butler followed them, a gun poised in readiness.

Vivian Legrand halted just inside the door. She stood beside one of a pair of tall vases of blue pottery, wide of neck and bellying out as they curved toward rounded bases. The vases stood on each side of the doorway.

Dr. Orbison dropped into a chair and peered up at her like an expectant vulture.

"I congratulate the British Secret Service. I really did not credit them with sufficient intelligence to trace this little affair to me."

Vivian Legrand did not move.

"She was looking for a paper of some sort," the butler burst out. "And she got it!"

"Your handbag," demanded Orbison.

Vivian Legrand extended the bag. He went through it rapidly, dropping the small revolver it contained on the table. Then he returned it to her and shot a string of sibilant words that Vivian Legrand took to be Russian to the butler. The latter went to the door and a moment later a Chinese woman appeared at the doorway.

"Chu-Chi will search you," Orbison announced. "I have called her, not from motives of delicacy, but because a woman is more likely to find a woman's hiding place than a man."

He watched in silence as the Chinese woman searched Vivian Legrand swiftly and expertly, overlooking no possible place where a letter could be hidden. She reported in Chinese that there was nothing hidden upon the redheaded woman.

ORBISON'S THIN MOUTH curled up; the vulture's hairless head bobbed up and down as he waved the Chinese woman impatiently out of the room. His long fingers curved slightly, as if, filled with desire, they tensed to leap at Vivian Legrand's throat. There was strength in those fingers, she knew—enormous strength. Meeting the cold eyes she knew that this man would murder her without a qualm. But she did not flinch from his gaze. Instead she smiled quite calmly. The letter was safe. He did not suspect where it was—would probably never find it unless she revealed its hiding place. And she knew that she held the trump card.

"Where is the letter you took from my safe," he demanded.

"I took no letter," Vivian Legrand answered steadily. "Your butler summoned help before I could find it."

Orbison laughed, a sudden little laugh. Vivian Legrand realized where she had heard the counterpart of that laugh before—the same little laugh over sudden silence that may be heard just before the Chinese executioner raises his sword for the stroke that will sever his victim's head from his shoulders.

"I know that you lie," Orbison said. He stroked the curve of his mouth with his tongue's tip, very much as if tasting blood and liking it. "It would be wise to tell me now where it is. You will eventually."

"I didn't find it," Vivian told him. She put the right trace of impatience into her manner. "Can't you see that for yourself? Your men came while I was searching. I had to run for it. You caught me just as I was about to leave the house. Common sense should tell you that I am not lying."

As she talked a great satisfaction came into her heart. Orbison had made one fatal error. All she needed now was time and luck to win clear.

"I think we can refresh her memory," Orbison went on, speaking to the butler. He made Vivian Legrand a little bow. "You will excuse me a moment, I am sure."

Opening a door on the further side of the room he disappeared. Vivian Legrand could see that it was a room of gleaming white enamel, with strange instruments and tubes on white tables. Taking her eyes from the door she glided sidewise, crabwise, toward the table in the center of the room. Her movements were almost imperceptible. Her eyes flickered for a second over the safety catch of the butler's gun. It was still locked. Did the man know it? Upon the answer to that question hung life or death.

Then Orbison entered the room again, carrying in one hand a small test tube and in the other a hypodermic syringe.

"You really are an utter fool," Vivian Legrand told the doctor.

"So?" he murmured softly. He filled the hypodermic. "And what leads you to that conclusion?"

"Because," Vivian Legrand said with superb indifference. "You haven't the ability to distinguish the truth from a lie. I came here to get that letter—yes. But I had no connection with the British Secret Service. My scheme was to steal the letter to show you that I was a better woman to have as an ally than an enemy—and once I had blackmailed you into obtaining me a post in the Russian Secret Service, to return the letter to you."

The doctor laid the hypodermic down carefully; took out a cigarette. His case fell to the floor. Vivian Legrand took a step, picked it up and returned it. Orbison was clever. But even he saw nothing in the movement that brought her a step closer to the table.

"A man of real cleverness would be able to see the advantage of having me as an ally," she went on. "Also, he would realize that I wouldn't come here without certain—er—precautions. There will be inquiries if I do not return."

"There will be no inquiries," the doctor returned indifferently.

Again Vivian Legrand took a sidewise step. Again her eyes flickered to the safety catch. It was still down.

The doctor picked up the hypodermic. "Now we will make the injection," he murmured. "It would really be useless to resist."

Vivian Legrand did not reply. She was within reaching distance of the library table now—and on the table lay her own gun, dropped there by Orbison when he searched her bag.

She made a careless step toward the table—and whirled, gun in hand, facing the two men. The butler pulled the trigger of his gun. There was no explosion.

"Hands up!" snapped Vivian. Orbison's head turned like that of a startled vulture at the crisp command. "Drop that gun, you!"

5

THE TWO MEN stood as if frozen. Then the butler's gun dropped to the floor, and his hands followed Orbison's above his head. Now it was that Vivian Legrand's greenish eyes bit into the vulture features of Orbison. She moved backwards toward the door to the hall. So engrossed was she by the men's upraised hands, and the gun on the floor, that she failed to see the sudden grimness that darkened the face of the doctor.

She felt the high heels of her evening slippers touch the door sill. Her free hand reached out and down into one of the blue vases, where she had dropped the letter. Then, with the precious document in her hand, she reached for the door knob.

Without warning the doctor's upraised hands darted for a weapon.

Vivian Legrand whipped about with the swiftness of a striking serpent. With a half turn of her body, she shot. Orbison dropped, face down.

Through narrow green eyes she glared at the butler. He glanced once at his dead master. Then his hands reached higher, trembling.

Vivian Legrand opened the front door. A moment later the roar of an automobile told that she was escaping in safety.

TWO HOURS LATER Vivian entered the salon of the rajah's yacht and dropped a package of Bank of England notes in front of Wylie.

"Three thousand pounds," she said curtly. "It was worth five."

"You delivered the letter?" Wylie asked.

"I delivered the letter," she said. "But I read it first. And we must sail in an hour."

Wylie sat up alertly. "What's up? Danger?"

She shook her head.

"No. Money. There is a prisoner on the Andaman Islands worth a fortune to whoever reaches him first. And if we can outsail and outwit the Russian and the British secret services, we'll have something they'll pawn their souls to ransom."

"But the ruby mine," Wylie protested.

"That can wait," Vivian Legrand said firmly. "When we have no further use for the rajah as a blind—then will come the time for securing his ruby mine."

THE EPISODE OF THE FORTY MURDERERS

*Behind a Half-Opened Door Vivian
Legrand Sways in a Siren's Dance and Tricks
Forty Pirates Out of Liberty and Life*

1

VIVIAN LEGRAND WAS fully aware of the sinister reputation of the man whose shop she was entering. He had the reputation of having in stock many things difficult to purchase anywhere else. Such things as a knife and a hand to wield it on a dark street.

She knew that he would have at his finger tips a most intimate knowledge of life in Port Blair, capital of India's Penal Colony in the Andaman Islands. And what he did not know, he would find out for you.

The latter was Vivian's reason for seeking out Wing Li, the Chinese bird-seller on Port Blair's principal street. She was in Port Blair to kidnap one Ivan Stavinsky from under the noses of his British jailers. Stavinsky, a Russian secret service agent, had been sentenced to a life term in the Andamans for a civil crime committed in Calcutta.

A Chinese sitting cross-legged on a cushion in the rear of the shop rose at her entrance and came forward.

"You wanchee buy?" he inquired in pidgin, the common tongue of the Islands.

Vivian Legrand shook her head and answered in fluent Cantonese.

"I desire to buy," she said, "but I am afraid that you have not the object I wish to purchase."

She seated herself on a stool beside the counter and

looked up at him quietly. Her eyes, heavy lidded, and of a greenish color, were baffling. Flaming red hair clouded her face.

"I have many things," the Chinese told her.

"I am seeking a bird. But only one kind will do. And I can pay only one price. Three pounds, sixpence."

Their eyes met and they exchanged one long, calculating glance.

"Is it a native bird?" inquired the Chinese.

"It is a Chinese bird," Vivian Legrand responded. "But now it roosts in Manila."

A swift smile broke the impassive yellow mask. "I am he whom you seek," he said. "What are the instructions of the Mandarin Hoang Fi Tu?"

THE CHINESE SHOPKEEPER was one of the agents of the sinister mandarin, whose long-nailed fingers reached through the underworld of the whole Far East. The formula Vivian Legrand had used, simple as it was, had identified her as an agent of the mandarin.

"Do you know a prisoner whose name is Ivan Stavinsky?" she asked.

The Chinese reflected a moment, then nodded.

"Can you get a message to him?"

"It will not be difficult. Just now he is a gardener on the grounds of the Chief Commissioner's house."

"I want you," Vivian Legrand said, "to get word to him that he is to be rescued and placed aboard the yacht, Southern Cross, in the harbor. You will know the best hour and the best place for the rescue to be made, and you will have a boat waiting for me somewhere on the water front. It will be impossible for me to use the yacht's launch."

"*I'll kill the first man!*"

The Chinese raised protesting hands.

"It cannot be done," he expostulated. "There would be no way of getting him aboard the yacht during the day without being seen. And because he is not a ticket-of-leave man, at night he is locked up.

"But even if he were free at night, it could not be done. The water front is well patrolled, and the Indian police are constantly on the alert about the harbor. Besides, this Stavinsky is a dangerous man. He has the instinct of the killer... the instinct of the tiger. He would have no gratitude toward you for rescuing him. He would not hesitate to kill you if it would serve his purpose."

Vivian Legrand looked at him with the unreadable, faintly-slant-eyed gaze that, had he known her better, would have told him that trouble was brewing. Her voice was suddenly harsh.

"That is my business. It will be yours to give me the information I want and to carry out my orders."

The Chinese quailed.

"I but meant to be helpful," he murmured.

"I want information, not advice," she said curtly. "When is the best time to free this prisoner?"

The man hesitated. "He is always guarded."

"Police or soldier?" Vivian Legrand queried.

"Neither," the man responded. "A ticket-of-leave man. And him you could not bribe. He knows that for Stavinsky to escape while in his charge would mean life imprisonment without privileges for him."

"A blow on the head?" Vivian Legrand suggested.

The Chinese shook his head. Stavinsky could not pass through the streets, and even if he were to reach the water front he could never leave the dock. No, he must be smuggled aboard. And the Chinese didn't know how.

"I do," Vivian Legrand said suddenly. "I think I see a way to make the prison authorities place him aboard the yacht themselves."

She talked rapidly for a few minutes. The Chinese listened, while a look of admiration spread over his face. And in the end he agreed that, if luck was with her, she might be able to work it. Then he said humbly:

"Is it permitted that this unworthy one advise you that the boats in the harbor, even the yacht of the Rajah of Salingar on which you are a guest, will be searched at once?

And if you leave before the search is made, they will send a boat with soldiers after you to search the ship."

"They can search to their heart's content," Vivian Legrand told him. "They will never find him, where he will be hidden. You may tell him that; also that I have already received permission from the High Commissioner to visit a village of the Andamese, the one called Karawas, which is about twenty miles down the coast.

"Immediately after the escape of the prisoner is discovered and the ship searched, we will sail for Karawas, remain there one night as a blind, return to Port Blair to pay our respects to the High Commissioner, and then sail again."

Vivian Legrand left the shop of the bird-seller.

Meanwhile, from Calcutta a British gunboat was steaming for Port Blair, her fires roaring under forced draft. There was occasion for hurry. Her commander had been placed under the orders of Colonel Sir Mark Caywood, Chief of the British secret service in the Far East, and Sir Mark had informed him curtly that neither coal nor men were to be spared in reaching the Penal Colony. The sailor was not informed that a certain prisoner there had discovered a hidden pass through the mountains that guard the northern frontier of India. The secret was of immense value to Great Britain—and to Russia.

From Penang a Dutch cargo boat... Dutch at least in registry... was lumbering southward. She was Russian in crew. Her captain was a commander in the Imperial Russian Navy, although few persons outside of the secret service headquarters in St. Petersburg were aware of that fact. Haste was a part of her program also.

The cablegram in code that her captain had received in

Saigon, ostensibly relating to a cargo of jute to be picked up in Bombay, had in reality been orders for him to proceed to the Andaman Islands with all possible speed.

The object of the gunboat, the cargo boat and Vivian Legrand, was the same.

2

THE OFFICE OF the doctor who administers to the convicts of Port Blair stands on a slight hill from which can be seen the dusty streets of the little town, the blue water of the bay, and the boats at anchor there.

It was just after the siesta hour that Vivian Legrand rang the doctor's door bell.

The man who admitted her was an orderly. He conducted her into an empty hall and disappeared. In a moment or two he returned, and opening a door on the right, ushered her into a reception room.

The man who rose from behind the desk in the center of the room was tall and broad enough to give the impression of being unusually powerful. There was about him a terrible vitality that battered against the will of the observer. This impression may have been due, in some measure, to the eyes. They were dark, with a peculiar reddish glow like very dark garnets.

Vivian Legrand looked into them as she approached, and saw that their owner had the power to turn off almost at will their curious red gleam, almost as though a camera shutter had clicked shut over them.

"Please be seated, Miss"—he glanced at the card he still held in his hand—"Mrs. Legrand. I am Doctor Ferguson."

"I want to consult you professionally," Vivian Legrand explained.

"I see." The doctor was noncommittal. "You realize, of course, that I am the prison doctor, and that my practice is confined, ordinarily, to convicts?"

"Quite," Vivian Legrand said pleasantly. "But unfortunately we have no doctor on the Rajah of Salingar's yacht, on which I am a guest, and from what I have heard of the half-caste doctor who administers to the civilians in Port Blair, I do not think that I care to place the case in his hands. And on the other hand I would have no hesitation in leaving it in yours."

"You are most kind." The red flared again, and then the eyes played their camera-shutter trick. "Perhaps you did not realize that I am not supposed to handle outside cases."

"Without special permission," Vivian Legrand amended with her most charming smile. "I have here a note of introduction from the High Commissioner." She extended it. "I realize that you are a busy man. I merely wish a diagnosis and an outline of treatment."

"I see. Just what is your trouble, Mrs. Legrand?"

"Oh, it isn't for myself." Vivian Legrand laughed as if the idea of her needing treatment from a doctor were quite amusing. "But for someone for whom I am in a measure responsible."

"And his trouble?"

"A belief that he is being robbed… a temporary belief, of course… but one that is becoming increasingly frequent. To explain, he has had this trouble for some time, and I brought him along with us on the yachting trip in the belief that the voyage might aid the condition. But of late it has seemed to increase. A day or two ago he insisted that I had deprived him of a favorite pair of shoes. He would become angry when I insisted that I knew nothing of them. Then, in a day or so, the matter would be completely forgotten."

"Quite a common paranoia, Mrs. Legrand. There is nothing so unusual in that."

"Perhaps not," Vivian Legrand agreed. "But these attacks or whatever they may be are becoming increasingly frequent. Only last night he insisted that I had robbed him of a large sum of money. When, as a matter of fact, he has no money, and is completely dependent upon me. I was only able to quiet him by telling him that the money would be restored today. On that condition he agreed to meet me here."

"Here?" the thin tone had a note of disapproval.

"Yes. You see, I was quite anxious to have you examine him during one of these attacks."

"There was really no occasion to bring him here," the doctor said. "It would have been quite all right for me to visit him upon the yacht."

"But he wouldn't have seen you, if he had known you were a doctor. It was necessary to trick him into coming here. All that I ask is that you examine him, give me your opinion on whether this condition is likely to increase, and what treatment is best."

"Very well," the doctor said. "When do you expect him?"

"At any moment now," Vivian Legrand answered, glancing at her watch. "I imagine that you are a busy man. If you have work to do, just leave me here in your reception room, and when your patient arrives, the orderly can call you."

She held her breath. On the doctor's reaction to this

suggestion hung the success or failure of her plan. If he reacted as she figured that he would, and luck was with her, she would have in her hands the man who held the key to the secret for which two nations would be willing to pay—and pay well.

The doctor nodded. "I am quite busy," he said. "You will find magazines and books there on the table."

WAITING UNTIL THE door to the ward had closed behind him, Vivian Legrand made a swift examination of the room. There were two doors, one leading to the hall, the other to the hospital proper. Windows were on only one side, facing the roadway. A large settee was in one corner, a heavy, clumsy article of furniture. She opened the door to the hall a trifle and peered out. No one there.

Picking up a three months' old magazine she crossed to one of the windows, drew aside the curtains a trifle, and leaned against the casement. To a casual observer she would have seemed merely engaged in turning the pages of a magazine in a rather bored manner.

She did not have long to wait. Scarcely ten minutes later she saw two men on foot turn in at the gate beside the road. From the description she knew that one of them was Stavinsky. The other man must be his guard. Instantly she was alert. Crossing swiftly to the door leading to the hospital, she listened. There was no sound there. Then she ran soundlessly into the hall.

Before Stavinsky's guard had time to ring, the door was opened and Vivian Legrand stood on the threshold. Her hat and handbag lay behind a row of books on the table. There was no indication that she was not an occupant of the doctor's quarters.

"The doctor is expecting you," she said quietly. "He is performing an important operation just now, and left word that the two of you were to wait in here."

She indicated the open door of the reception room. The two preceded her into the room. She entered after them and carefully closed the door behind her.

The guard dropped on to the settee, his rifle held between his knees. Stavinsky dropped into a chair near the table. For a few seconds there was silence.

Stavinsky was wide-shouldered, and the chest at his open shirt front was a mat of curly hair. His head was cropped, and his face was one to remember—big-nosed, square-jawed, with piercing black eyes. Just at the moment there was a look in those eyes of a caged animal who sees the door of his cage slowly opening, and wonders if he can make the dash to liberty before it closes again.

Vivian Legrand picked up her handbag and strolled casually toward the door. She turned, just as she reached the settee, opened her bag, took out a little mirror and inspected her face. The guard glanced at her indifferently, and then his gaze shifted.

He never knew what hit him. The blackjack that Vivian Legrand had in her handbag struck him savagely across the head. He went out like a light.

With a leap like an agile cat Stavinsky caught the rifle before it clattered to the floor.

"Put him behind the settee," Vivian Legrand ordered tensely. If the orderly or the doctor came in just then they were lost. "Put his rifle back there, too."

Together they dropped the unconscious man behind the clumsy article of furniture so that he was completely hidden from sight. Then from beneath her dress Vivian Legrand whipped a white shirt and a pair of flannel trousers.

"Get these on in a hurry," she ordered tensely. "Throw your prison clothes behind there with the guard. You know what you've got to do?"

"Wing Li told me," the other responded in a swift whisper. Already he was ripping off his clothes. "I pretended to be sick... a touch of the sun... so the guard got permission to bring me up to the hospital."

"Keep your feet out of sight," she ordered. "You're still wearing prison shoes, remember. I couldn't bring you shoes. Didn't know your size, even if it had been possible."

She crossed the room and tapped upon the door leading to the hospital. A moment later the doctor appeared.

"He's here," she said in a low voice. "And worse than ever. I can't do anything with him."

"I'll talk to him," the doctor said and walked into the room.

STAVINSKY WAS STANDING at the far side of the table, leaning on it. He glared at the doctor as he approached and said in a loud voice:

"I want my money."

"Of course, of course," Dr. Ferguson said soothingly. "I'll see that you get your money. But first I want to talk to you."

"I don't want to talk," Stavinsky said furiously. "I want my money. I want my money, and if I don't get it I'll break your neck." He turned toward Vivian Legrand. "You told me if I'd come up here I'd get my money, and I want it."

He picked up a heavy book-end on the table and poised it, as if to throw.

"I want my money."

Attracted by the loud tones an orderly appeared in the doorway behind them. The doctor said something to him rapidly and then turned toward Vivian Legrand.

"Impossible to do anything with him in this condition."

"But I can't leave him like this," Vivian Legrand said hopelessly. "Can't you do something to quiet him?"

"I'm going to give him a hypodermic," the doctor said.

The assistant appeared in the door behind him, and handed the doctor a filled hypodermic, then slowly moved to a position behind Stavinsky, who still stood behind the table demanding his money.

With a swift gesture the orderly threw his arms about Stavinsky's shoulders and tightened them so that the man gasped for breath. The doctor rolled up the shirt sleeve and pressed the hypodermic home.

"There," he said, stepping back, "he'll be all right now." Then he said to the orderly, "Just hold him for a few minutes."

"I'm so sorry," Vivian Legrand said. "I wouldn't have subjected you to this annoyance for the world. The poor fellow has been getting worse for days, but I had no idea when he left me this morning, that he would be like this."

"It frequently happens," the doctor remarked.

Even as he spoke Stavinsky's struggles became less violent.

"It's a sad case," Vivian Legrand said. "I'm very much afraid that he will have to be sent to an asylum." Then she hesitated. "I hate to ask you, but is there any way you can assist me in getting him back to the ship?"

"Of course," the doctor said. "We'll send him down in the hospital ambulance."

He turned to the orderly.

"Have this man placed in the ambulance and taken aboard Mrs. Legrand's yacht," he said.

And fifteen minutes later, with Vivian Legrand in attendance, Stavinsky was placed aboard the yacht by men whose duty it was to prevent his escape.

3

FIVE HOURS LATER the last soldier had departed over the side of the trim White yacht. Every possible hiding place on the ship had been searched. The coal bunkers had been probed with iron bars, the water tanks opened and examined. But of the missing Stavinsky they had found no trace. He was safely hidden in the opening between the cabin wall and the hull of the ship that Wylie had had made beneath his bunk.

It was a cramped space for a large man, to be sure, and gave him room to only lie fiat, like a man in a coffin. But it represented safety and Stavinsky had not demurred.

Within a few minutes after the soldiers had left, the anchor came clanking aboard and the ship's nose was turned toward the point of land around which lay the native village, off which they were to spend the night.

Vivian Legrand breathed a sigh of relief as the roofs of Port Blair fell astern. The one thing that she had feared had been questions concerning the man who had been brought aboard from the hospital. But there had been no visitors from ashore to ask embarrassing questions, and as the rajah had been ashore himself he knew nothing of it. The following afternoon they would return to Port Blair, pay a formal visit of farewell to the High Commissioner—

and then Rangoon and the sale of Stavinsky's secret to the highest bidder.

Vivian Legrand always slept like a cat. The normal sounds of her surroundings did not penetrate her slumber, but let any alien sound intrude itself and she was awake. That night she slept even more lightly than usual.

She did not know what had awakened her, later that night, while the yacht lay off the native village, but she suddenly found herself sitting up in her berth listening intently. She reached out for the revolver which she never failed to place beside her bed. With a little tingling shock her fingers encountered only emptiness where the revolver had been.

Hastily throwing a robe over her nightdress, she flung open the door and stepped into the dining saloon into which her room opened. There she stumbled over a pair of shoes. A slight sound caused her to look up. She saw a pair of stockinged feet disappearing up the stairs that led to the deck.

She gazed after the disappearing feet in perplexity. If they belonged to Adrian Wylie, what did he intend to do? She wanted to call to him. She did call in a low voice. But there was no answer.

She stood there a moment undecided, listening, watching. Then a hoarse shout broke the silence. Wylie's voice. There was a note of surprise in it, and it was followed by another that was unmistakably one of warning. Other shouts came, and sounds of heavy feet.

She was no longer uncertain as to what was happening. Curses, shouting, running feet. Clubs striking steel plates—they could only mean a battle, and instinctively she knew that Wylie was attacked.

On the wall at the far end of the dining saloon hung a collection of native weapons—knives, blowguns, bows and arrows. Hastily snatching a slim-bladed *kris* from the collection she ran up the stairs to the deck.

She was just in time to see a dark figure leap over the rail and run toward the forward deck whence came the sound of battle. She ran to the rail. Below her, down there under the ship's rail, was a rowboat. The faces of half a dozen of them were looking upward in the starlight. Scarcely a dozen feet away another boat, laden with men, was approaching the ship.

Her first thought had been that her plot had been discovered, that soldiers from ashore were boarding the vessel. But a glance told her that these men were not soldiers. And then she knew the truth. These men were escaped convicts seeking to capture the yacht.

At her feet lay a heavy piece of iron. She stooped over and lifted it. With the down roll of the ship, Vivian again peered over the rail. Below was the black shape of the rowboat. She hurled the iron straight down. It went through the shell of the little boat with a rending smash of planking. A swift slash of her knife and the knotted rope up which the man had climbed, dropped into the water. Then she turned and raced toward the forward deck. Harsh voices leaped out to meet her, mingled with the screams and wild cries of the men in the sunken boat.

Forward the rajah, the captain and officers of the ship were already lined up against the further rail. Adrian Wylie was retreating slowly down the center of the deck before the clubs of three men.

Wylie was hard pressed, and as he backed against the open portion of the deck, one man slipped past for a rear attack.

VIVIAN LEGRAND SCREAMED, but too late. The club crashed across Wylie's head and he went down. The three men turned their attention to her. She backed against the rail.

"I'll kill the first man to touch me," she said in a low voice.

But the three men armed with clubs, deploying from the prone figure on the deck, were moving swiftly to the left and right and center. But this remarkable woman was not afraid, even though there seemed no chance for escape. In another moment a club might come crashing across her skull, as it had crashed across Wylie's—but that thought never entered her head.

In later years, when peril loomed in one of the schemes in which Wylie and Vivian Legrand were engaged, the former often wondered whether she were the bravest woman in the world, or merely a fool who did not know the meaning of danger. He says he never found out.

She seemed to explode in flaming movement.

The slimmer of the three men, whose name was Morgan, fell back before the sweep of her knife. She whirled in mid-air and launched herself at Stavinsky. He was caught unawares, too slow in his movements. The blade ripped down the length of his right forearm.

The others retreated hastily before that whirlwind of fury, but almost beside her a dripping figure arose—one of the men from the sunken boat. His arm shot out and wrenched hers viciously. The knife clattered to the floor.

"The little hellcat!" Stavinsky snarled. "Tap her on the head. Lock her up. Anything, so that you can take care of this arm."

Blood was spurting from the wound. He was trying to stop it with the other hand.

"I wish it had been your heart," Vivian Legrand said with deliberate venom.

The convicts were undisputed masters of the ship. Even in the short space of time since she had been disarmed the rope had again been fastened to the railing and men were swarming up. The deck was alive with them. Having the ship, what were they going to do with it? And, more specifically, what were they going to do with the passengers, with her, with Wylie, lying there on the deck, with the rajah? In addition to escaping prison, they had committed piracy. Facing death for that, they were not likely to stop at anything further. The punishment for additional crime could be no worse.

As if to place a period to her thoughts, Vivian Legrand heard Stavinsky speak, as he lifted the arm of a lascar sailor, the man who had been on watch, and let it drop to the deck with a sodden thump.

"Getting stiff already," he grunted. "Throw him overboard. He's no good to anybody any more."

Three men sprang to obey his orders. Without expression on their faces they lifted the body and carried it to the rail.

4

GRAY DAWN HAD already crept into the sky as Vivian Legrand watched the body slide over the side. Her mind was working desperately. Even in times of greatest peril, she never lost an opportunity to take a trick—never passed up an opportunity, however small, to turn a seemingly hopeless situation to her own advantage. But she could see no loophole here.

Then, as the body disappeared beneath the water, Stavinsky turned to the little group of prisoners.

"We're masters of the ship," he began abruptly. "Unfortunately, none of us know how to navigate." He thrust his face out toward the captain. "That's where you come in. Navigate the ship to the point I indicate, and you won't be harmed. Try any tricks and you'll feed the fishes."

The captain, a lean-faced, bronzed Scotchman, swore deeply.

"I'll see you in hell first," he said roundly.

Stavinsky moved so swiftly that the deed was done almost before the words were out of the captain's mouth. The knife went into the captain's throat as though the flesh were soft butter. A dark knife handle jutted out from the captain's throat. The blade was buried deeply in the flesh.

For a split second the captain stood as though carved from stone. He raised groping hands to his throat. Gurgled chokingly, and slumped to the deck, a bright stream of crimson trickling from beneath his chin.

All that had happened in a brace of seconds. There had been no other sound. Almost before Vivian Legrand realized what had happened, Stavinsky had whirled and was facing the mate of the yacht.

"Are *you* willing to navigate us wherever I say?" he asked silkily, his hands slipping slowly toward the belt where a second knife rested.

The man raised eyes that were sick pools of horror and stared at Stavinsky. Words refused to come from his choken throat, but he nodded assent.

"You are a wise man," Stavinsky said evenly. "Don't make the mistake of thinking we are not serious. We are." He glanced around at the little knot of engineers and deck officers. "Any objections to getting the ship under way?"

There was no answer. Stavinsky spoke again.

"Very well. Get steam up and get the ship out to sea as fast as you can. When we're out of sight of land I'll give you our destination. Now get this: the crew will not be permitted on deck, except such men as are needed for the running of the ship, and then only under guard. The officers will be locked in their cabins except when they are actually on duty. Engineers will remain below decks at all times. All right, boys, take 'em below."

"What will we do with this one?" queried one of the men, indicating Wylie.

"Throw him in his cabin and lock the door. If he lives, all right. If he doesn't, that's just his hard luck."

Vivian Legrand watched without a word as the escaped convicts herded the rajah and the officers below, two of them bearing Wylie. Meanwhile, Morgan walked across to Stavinsky.

In the early sunlight she had her first good look at Morgan and she studied him with calculating eyes. He was smaller than Stavinsky, wiry of build, with a lean face under a soft, silky beard, thin nostrils, and thin lips.

His speech was quick, jerky; his movement nervous. And it was evident from his manner, from his speech, that while Stavinsky might be the guiding spirit in this affair, that here was a man who would not be content to accept orders placidly.

"That was useless, Ivan," he said curtly, indicating the body of the slain captain. "No sense in killing unless you have to."

"I'm the best judge of that," Stavinsky said angrily. "I engineered your escape, as well as that of the others, and I'm handling this affair."

Morgan flushed resentfully.

"The captain could have been shown that it was better to navigate the ship, rather than die," he said. "He would have given in. You gave him no chance."

Stavinsky glared at him.

"I told you," he said between tight lips, "that I'm running this affair. You're forgetting that, aren't you? And I'll run it the way that seems best to me. If you're getting chicken-hearted at the sight of a little blood, then you'd better jump overboard and swim back to prison."

Morgan did not answer, but Vivian Legrand could see the effort he was making to keep his temper. Stavinsky went on.

"All right, if you've come to your senses, we'll straighten

things out. One of us must be on guard on the bridge all the time. We should have steam up and be ready to sail by eight o'clock. I'll stand guard on the bridge for six hours, and then you can relieve me."

Then for the first time Stavinsky noticed that Vivian Legrand was still on deck.

"What are you doing here, you hellcat?" he demanded. "I thought you went below with the others."

"Why, you don't intend to lock me in my cabin, do you?" she queried innocently. "You're not afraid of me, are you?"

STAVINSKY EXPLODED IN a bellow of laughter. "I ought to wring your neck for what you did to me," he said, indicating the blood stained strip from his shirt about the arm. "But I won't. It's too pretty. I won't lock you in your cabin after we get out of sight of land. But until then you'll be locked in. And just to make sure, I'll lock you in myself."

Taking her arm he led her below.

"If you're wise you'll stay out of sight as much as possible," he told her. "There are forty men on this ship—escaped prisoners—murderers—all sentenced to the Andaman Islands for life. This is their chance at a getaway and if you think they'll let a little thing like a woman stand in their way, you don't know them."

They halted at the door of her cabin.

"We'll be neighbors," he said with a grin. "The captain won't need his cabin any more, so I'll just move in there, since I'm the captain now."

Vivian Legrand's eyes flickered the merest trifle. The captain's cabin was two doors past hers down the corridor. To get to the deck, Stavinsky would have to pass her cabin. In that moment was born a plan, desperate, harebrained, and presenting the only opportunity of escape she had seen.

All that day she deliberately kept away from Stavinsky. Now and then she permitted him a brief glimpse of her, cool and distant in her white clothes, as she sat in a chair on the after deck. When Stavinsky was off duty, she was locked in her cabin. Until night. Then she waited in her chair until he was beside her, then rose.

"Oh, I didn't see you," she lied.

"I suppose if you had, you'd be gone," he said grimly. "You needn't be afraid. I won't eat you."

She hesitated prettily, consummate actress that she was, before speaking.

"I wasn't sure how you'd feel about that," she said, and indicated his bandaged arm.

Stavinsky exploded in a bellow of laughter—and over her shoulder Vivian Legrand saw Morgan peering down at them from the bridge.

"That pin-prick," he said. "That's nothing."

"I'm glad," Vivian Legrand said softly, "that it wasn't worse. But you couldn't expect me to do anything... then."

The next morning she was up early. A trip to the cook furnished her with several bottles of ammonia, which she was going to need. Then she found the frightened Malay cabin boy. To him she gave a folded slip of paper, with instructions that it be delivered at once.

Then she waited until she heard one of the convicts call Stavinsky to go on watch on the bridge. Waited until she heard the sound of his door opening.

Then Vivian Legrand, a Delilah with flaming red hair, began spinning her web.

She stood before the long glass in her cabin. In it she could see the entire length of her body, in her long, straight cobweb-thin gown; a tube of sheerest black. The weblike embroidery over her breasts rose and fell with her breathing.

A queer, cold expression had settled upon her face. Only her eyes were warm. She smiled, a rather terrible smile, as she stood there, every nerve keyed.

There was a sound of a footstep outside. She had purposely left the door ajar—a crack of only an inch or two, but one that it would be almost impossible for a person passing in the corridor to miss seeing.

The footstep halted. Vivian Legrand began to hum a slow, lazy waltz, in her deep contralto. There was a faint creak and she saw the crack in the door open a trifle.

She lifted her bare arms above her head as high as she could, stretching. She locked her pointed fingers. With a slow, stroking movement she slid her hands down, tightening the silk about her body until her hands pressed taut above her hips. As the hands moved downward she breathed slowly, lifting and arching her bosom. She stared at herself—and at the effect the scene was having on the man at the crack in the doorway—peering intently into the mirror, her eyes watching the rise of her high, pointed breasts.

Then she whirled, her arms crossed protectively across her body, her eyes fixed in cleverly simulated fright on the door.

"Who is there?" she called, and no man living could have told that the note of fear in her voice was not genuine.

Years later a famous French theatrical producer who

knew Vivian Legrand, to his own sorrow, said that if she had not taken up blackmail as a profession, she could have been the greatest actress the world had ever known.

5

THE DOOR OPENED a little more. Framed in the aperture was the stark and sinister figure of Ivan Stavinsky.

"I thought I heard you call," he said by way of explanation. His eyes fluttered greedily over her silk-clad body.

"No, I didn't call." Her embarrassment was a work of art. Yet she was playing the most terrific gamble in her career. She was banking, betting, coldly and unruffledly on an unpredictable factor—a man's emotions.

Moving to her berth, she threw a mandarin coat over her sheer gown. She shot a glance at the clock. It was nearly eight. "But I am glad you… you thought you heard me call. I *am* afraid."

He came further into the room. "You need not be afraid. No one will hurt you."

"Perhaps *you* won't." She dropped her long lashes over her greenish eyes, and then looked up at him again. This man was no fool. He knew the value of the secret of which he was the possessor, and her instinct had already warned her that he was not the type of man from whom a woman could worm a secret easily. "But you aren't the only one on board. There are forty and if *you* were gone—"

She stopped, letting the sentence die away, leaving the unspoken implication hanging in the air between them.

He crossed the room with swift strides, his easily aroused suspicions flaming; grasped her hands.

"What do you mean—if I were gone?" he demanded.

"Nothing," she protested in distress. "Nothing. I shouldn't have said it. I wouldn't have—but I was so afraid—and you were the only one I thought I could trust to protect me—and when I heard—"

Again she stopped. Again that break, that unspoken implication.

She was playing the most dangerous game in the world, and she was playing it not merely against a criminal, but against a man who held human life as the cheapest thing at his command. Her life would go out like a snuffed candle if her opponent suspected for a single instant the game she was playing.

"Heard what?" Stavinsky demanded.

"Oh, don't make me tell," she moaned.

"What did you hear?" he demanded. "Tell me, or I'll break every bone in your damned body."

Instead of answering, she countered with a question.

"Are you the leader of those men or is someone else?"

"I am, by God," he answered harshly. "What did you hear?"

"I heard someone talking," she said with reluctance, as if the words were being dragged from her against her will. "I couldn't see who it was. They were on deck and I was at the foot of the stairs. It was during the night. I had gone out to get a drink of water... and I heard something about taking the leadership away from you—about killing you—"

"Who was it?" he shot at her.

"I don't know," she protested. "I couldn't see them. It was dark. The voice sounded like an Englishman's."

"Morgan! The English swine!" He swore in Russian. "Was that all you heard?"

"Almost. They passed on down the deck and I didn't follow them."

"What else was there?"

"Something about some of the men being loyal to you because you arranged their escape—and something else about trying to win them over. And then someone said something about tonight—about killing you tonight. And that's all."

She came closer to him, looked up at him with eyes wide and trusting. "You won't let them hurt me?"

There was silence in the room for a moment. Vivian Legrand's brain was working coolly, methodically, judicially, but in her eyes was something more remorseless and deadly than any sudden flare of impetuous and unbridled anger. The cold unwinking stare of the snake about to strike.

Stavinsky slipped an arm over her shoulder. Her softness, the sight of her rounded shoulders showing beneath the thin covering, excited him.

"Don't worry, I won't let them harm you," he swore.

"I knew I could trust you," she said, and her body relaxed in the curve of his arm.

He bent over and kissed her. She strained away from him, and then, as she saw the door of her cabin begin to open, struggled furiously. She got one arm free and slapped him with all her force. He recoiled—and then over her shoulder caught sight of Morgan standing on the threshold, scowling. Stavinsky loosened his hold and whirled on the other.

"What are you doing here?" the Russian demanded savagely.

"**HOW ABOUT YOU?**" demanded Morgan curtly. He still held in one hand a slip of paper that Vivian Legrand knew must be the note she had sent him. "I thought we'd agreed that for the sake of peace on board, the woman was to be left alone? You know damn well that if the others find you're not playing straight with them about this girl, there'll be hell to pay."

Stavinsky thrust his head forward in a gorilla-like gesture.

"How about yourself?" he asked.

"Don't worry about me. I can handle my own affairs," the Englishman said evenly. "Now, you'd better get out, Ivan."

"Get out!" Stavinsky exploded. His mood was ugly, and for a moment it seemed that the two would come to blows there in her cabin. And that, Vivian Legrand knew, would spoil whatever chances her plan had of being successful. She moved between them.

"Yes, please go," she said to Stavinsky. And then, in the softest of whispers, added for his ears alone:

"You must not make him suspicious."

For a moment anger and craft warred in Stavinsky. The latter won. Without a word he turned on his heel and strode from the cabin. But his eyes as they swept across Morgan, in passing, were venomous.

A little thrill went through Vivian Legrand. She knew the seed she had planted would sprout and blossom. She waited until Stavinsky's footsteps clumped up the companionway stairs, outside. Then she swayed and reached out blindly for support.

"I think... I'm... going to faint," she murmured.

The Englishman crossed the room swiftly; caught her in his arms. She lay there supine for a moment, her eyes looking up into his, the flame of her hair cascading down across his arms. Then she pushed him away resolutely.

"You mustn't," she whispered tensely. "Oh, you don't know—you don't know—he's going to kill you."

"Not he," the Englishman scoffed. "He values his damned hide too much to try it."

"But he is, I tell you." There was a choken sob in her voice. She caught his hand, held it fiercely. The eyes she raised to his pleaded mutely for belief. "Tonight—he was telling me about it before you came in—I don't know all the details... but I know he plans to kill you and some of your men. He said some of the men were loyal to you, and those he couldn't win over to his side, he'd kill—along with you—tonight."

"Why, the damned crook," the Englishman marveled.

Vivian Legrand's brain was working swiftly, yet carefully.

"I didn't know when I wrote you that note. But I was afraid of him, and I wanted to ask you to protect me... and I was waiting here for you when the door opened and he came in... and then he told me... that he was going to kill you... and take the ship—" she paused dramatically—"and me.

"Oh, you won't let him, will you? If he kills you and becomes the undisputed leader, there is no one to protect me. Oh, you won't let him, will you? He can't win—you're the better man."

"Don't worry," the Englishman said grimly, "he won't win."

Vivian Legrand took his hand and moved him gently toward the door. There was a shadow of a smile in her eyes, but he did not see it.

"You must go now. You mustn't stay here. He might become suspicious. Might kill you without warning. If you wait until tonight—when he starts something—then you can be ready for him."

"I'll wait," Morgan said, and his lips were tight. "And I'll be ready."

She closed the door behind him and began hastily to dress. Her plan was under way. But there were many things to do.

6

SHE WAS PLAYING a desperate game, one of the most desperate games of her long and varied career. Any little trifle might betray to Stavinsky and Morgan the game she was playing. As the day went on, she knew that storm clouds were gathering about the two men. The forty murderers aboard seemed to be more and more, as hour after hour passed, gathering into two camps. There were glowering looks, muttered words.

Once a squabble between two men turned into a fight. She held her breath lest the moment for which she was planning came too soon. But the two leaders quelled the fight with a stern hand.

The rajah she had not seen since the night the forty murderers had boarded them. In common with all officers of the ship, he was locked in his cabin, the keys in possession of one of the escaped prisoners who had been appointed jailer. The engine room crew were kept below decks, working under the menace of guns in the hands of their captors, who stood guard upon the engine room grating.

She managed a furtive meeting with Wylie, and outlined her plan to him and the part that he was to play. Unknown to their captors, she had a key to Wylie's cabin. Shortly before eight that night she would unlock his door. They would sneak to the deck and play their respective parts in the drama that was to follow—the drama that would result in freedom for themselves, or, if their plans failed, death at the hands of the infuriated criminals.

Vivian Legrand was reasonably familiar with a ship, as familiar as the average passenger, and she felt certain that she would carry out the plan she had set herself. It was shortly after seven when she softly slipped the key into the lock of Wylie's cabin and opened the door. Beneath her arm she carried a bulky package. Her white clothes had been changed for something dark that merged with the shadows of the night.

Wylie was waiting, tensely alert. She pressed a revolver into his hand, a revolver that she had stolen from one of the escaped convicts that afternoon.

"Everything set?" Wylie asked. She nodded.

"I'll wait," she said, "until I hear the first shot. Then I'll start."

Together they stole quietly to the deck. The ship was running through a moonless night, and a strange silence hung over her. Protective shadows clung thickly about the deck, cloaking the two masses of men huddling at opposite ends of the ship. Clustered about the bridge, where Vivian Legrand knew that Stavinsky was standing guard over the helmsman and officer on duty, were vague shapes she knew to be the Russian's adherents. Aft, beneath the awning, was the huddled group of Morgan's followers.

Wylie melted noiselessly into a shadow along the railing, vanished into the lee of a cluster of ventilators. Satisfied, Vivian Legrand turned, ran down the stairs, along a passage and turned into a little passage that ended in an open door.

Hot, moist air struck her in the face. She was on a narrow steel grating. Steel steps went down steeply. Below was the top of the engine and the tangle of piping and pumps that filled the cramped confines of the engine room. There was another platform just below the top of the engine. On it lounged the forms of the two convict guards. It was those two men on the platform with whom she was concerned.

Now she made her bid for freedom. Swiftly and noiselessly she undid the package under her arm, waited tensely there in the doorway, out of sight of the men below, for the signal.

It came. The sound of a shot from the deck above, clear above the pounding of the engine, and then a yell:

"Kill Stavinsky!"

Wylie was doing his part. He had fired that shot, just as he had planned, and then yelled that phrase. She knew that it would be confirmation of the tale that she had told Stavinsky. That he would immediately retaliate in kind on Morgan's faction, believing that the shot had come from them.

Instantly she tossed one of the bottles she held onto the platform where the two guards lounged. It shattered with a crash. She threw another and another. The floor of the platform was covered with a fuming liquid. The two figures that had been standing erect were wabbling now. Hands were pawing at blinded eyes, and they were gasping as the fumes of the powerful ammonia choked them.

ABOVE, ON THE deck were shouts, yells, shots. Vivian

Legrand leaned over the edge of the grating and called down to the men in the engine room.

"Come up!" she called. "The guards are blinded, and the men who captured the ship are fighting among themselves. This is our chance to get the ship back again. Hurry and free the rest of the crew!"

Then she raced for the deck. She still had something to do. It was no part of her plan that Stavinsky should be killed. He was too valuable to be wasted.

On the deck turmoil raged. Her plan had worked to perfection. The two rival factions, headed by Stavinsky and Morgan, were at one another's throats. Stavinsky's voice lifted above the turmoil of shouting men. She recognized it at once, among all the others. That voice held a tigerish, inhuman quality, like no other she had ever heard. A man came running past the entrance where she stood, then crashed to the deck and squeaked as he went down from a shot from the bridge.

Knives were flashing in the starlight, shots spat from shadows. The entrance to the companionway stairs was in the line of fire. Even as she reached it a bullet struck the steel lintel and whined off at a tangent.

Dropping to the deck she crawled along in the lee of the railing, whose canvas windbreak made a ribbon of impenetrable shadow along the lightness of the deck. Up on the bridge was Stavinsky, and she must reach that bridge.

A man lay sprawled on the deck near the railing, the gun he had been clutching when death overtook him lying within a few inches of his hand. She reached out and appropriated it.

She was almost at the foot of the bridge ladder when the

first of the crew burst out from below. Shovels, crowbars, slice bars from the engine room formed their weapons. From the hand of one of them a revolver spat venomously toward the yelling, fighting knot of men on the deck, proving that the weapons on the two guards below had not been overlooked.

Their presence gave her the opportunity she was looking for. Stavinsky did not see her figure swing lightly up the ladder. The chief mate did. All during the fight he had been held motionless under the gun of the man on the bridge with Stavinsky. Now he redeemed himself.

He drove his right foot up from the floor with all the strength he could muster. The hard toe of the shoe slammed powerfully against the wrist of the guard's arm. The gun he held sailed down to the deck below.

Almost at the same instant Vivian Legrand's gun spoke. Stavinsky's companion gave a grunt and sank to the floor, even as the chief mate's fist slammed into Stavinsky's chin, again, and again until the man wilted and went down.

Vivian Legrand turned. Wylie was by her side. Their pistols spat flame and lead at the prisoners on the deck below. The first officer ran down to join in the fracas.

And even as he did so, a pencil of light streaked out—a searchlight stabbing across the water. Unnoticed by Vivian Legrand or the others, a ship had been steadily approaching them. Now she saw that it was a naval vessel.

Swiftly she dropped her gun, and with Wylie's assistance got the unconscious Stavinsky down to the latter's cabin. Then the two ran back to the deck.

The fight was over now. The escaped prisoners, those that were left, were a sorry sight. Bruised, battered and cut they stood disarmed in a ring of glowering men as a boatload of sailors from the British gunboat pulled alongside.

The Rajah of Salingar, released from his cabin by one of the officers, came on deck, exceedingly worried.

The officer who released him had told him of Vivian's courage in routing the forty murderers. The Rajah sought her out, deep gratitude on his lips.

"It was the least I could do," she said softly. "I got you into this mess. All that I ask is that you forgive me, and that you do the suggesting from now on."

The rajah was flattered.

"There is nothing to forgive," he said. "But if I may suggest, I would suggest the Riviera. I am sure you would enjoy it."

"Yes," Vivian said absently, for her startled eyes had seen Sir Mark Caywood, Chief of the British secret service in the Far East, coming over the rail with sailors from the gunboat. "I'm sure I would." Was this to be the end, after all her trouble?

Then she smiled her most serene smile; she knew that, search as Sir Mark might, he would never find Stavinsky. And she was right. They did not find him.

In the excitement of transferring the escaped convicts to be returned to Port Blair none of them noticed the lights of a Dutch cargo boat, bound to Port Blair on an errand that would never be accomplished.

7

TWO WEEKS LATER, in Rangoon, she faced Sir Mark Caywood again. Their interview was almost at an end. In Vivian Legrand's handbag was a bundle of Bank of England notes that totaled up more money than she ever knew existed. Two hours after the rajah's yacht sailed from Rangoon, Sir Mark would receive a letter telling him where Stavinsky was being held, safely doped, in the Chinese section of the city.

Sir Mark rose from his desk as she turned to go.

"If ever you are in trouble out here, Mrs. Legrand," he said earnestly, "just manage to get word to me. I might be able to help you."

"Thank you," said Vivian Legrand demurely, "but I am sailing tomorrow for the Riviera. I am negotiating for an interest in a ruby mine—and I expect to acquire it there."

THE EPISODE OF THE
GRAVE ROBBERS

From the Confession of a Tortured Apache
Vivian Legrand Frames a Devilish Scheme
to Blackmail the Monte Carlo Banker:
The Episode of the Grave Robbers

1

"**BRING HIM IN!**" Vivian Legrand herself had opened the door of the little villa on the outskirts of Monte Carlo. Her greenish eyes narrowed and a grim smile of triumph flickered across her beautiful face as she saw that one of the three men who stood on the doorstep was a prisoner, with a gun shoved into his ribs.

Night and day, for more than a week, this prisoner had been dogging the footsteps of an old woman whom Vivian Legrand had selected as a likely victim to enrich the Legrand gang. And night and day her confederates had dogged the footsteps of both the man and the old woman, seeking some whispered hint of the information that Vivian Legrand sought. Now the long and patient shadowing was bearing fruit.

She stepped back to permit the two men to shove their prisoner through the door, then closed and locked it.

"Was there any trouble?" she inquired of Adrian Wylie, her chief assistant.

"No trouble," Wylie said. He looked as grim as the gun he was thrusting back into the concealed holster. "He came like a lamb to the slaughter."

The captive winced at the implication.

"Just wait until Raoul Valente hears of this," he said defiantly.

"Oh, so Raoul Valente is interested in the Signora Toma-sino?" Vivian Legrand said softly, switching to French as flawless as that of a Parisienne. She looked at her prisoner with the unreadable, faintly slant-eyed gaze that, had he known her better, would have told him meant trouble. "I wondered... but I did not think of him. I was right, then. The affair is worthwhile."

Raoul Valente, at this time, shortly before the World War, was one of the leading figures of the Monte Carlo underworld. Clever, audacious, he had been suspected by the police of many things, but they had been unable to pin anything on him.

Vivian Legrand followed as the prisoner was hustled into a small room opening off the hall. She drew the heavy hangings across the windows.

"I do not think that I shall worry about Valente," she said. "He had best be careful himself, lest he find himself in the same trap that closed about his spy." She turned to Wylie. "Tie him up."

The man yelped shrilly and tried to dodge as the two men seized him, but his resistance was futile against the strength of the two. The other man held him down while Wylie tied each arm to the chair, lashed the feet together and fastened a running noose around his neck, the other end of the rope being tied to the rung of the chair.

Vivian Legrand watched with a lazy smile twitching at her lips. She had picked up a fluffy Persian cat that lay dozing on a chair and held its head close to her cheek.

"Dear Cleo," she cooed to the animal, her eyes watching the man in the chair. "So lazy, so useless—but so beautiful."

The resemblance between the eyes of the cat and her

*They watched
Sammard bury
the stolen money*

own was remarkable. In them both was the same greenish glint, and in their depths lay the same hint of latent cruelty that might spring to life at any moment. As she stroked the animal her bracelet caught in its thick fur and pulled. A feline paw came out and raked Vivian's white arm.

A BLAZE OF ferocity shown in the eyes of the woman. With a swift gesture she hurled the beautiful animal across the room. It struck the stone fireplace with a thud, dropped to the floor and lay there motionless, mewing a little, with eyes fixed piteously on the woman who had been stroking it a moment before.

But Vivian Legrand did not accord the stricken animal a second glance. She leaned forward, her hands on the edge of the table, her smile cruel as she watched the shrinking figure in the chair. Her voice, when she spoke, was as soft as the purr of the cat she had held.

"You have just one chance of leaving this room alive,

Vincente Delgado," she advised him. "Tell me what I want to know, and you can go."

The shadow of the callous cruelty he had just witnessed had not left the man's face. He was tall and slender; a Greek or an Italian, dressed in spotless white flannels and sport shoes. The clear olive of his face was set off by a small waxen mustache under a slender aquiline nose. The hands were long and supple and slender; almost the hands of a woman—or a professional killer.

"What do you want to know?" he muttered in French.

"Where does the Signora Tomasino get the money that she loses at the gambling tables?"

"I don't know what you mean," the man said. "I do not know the Signora Tomasino. You have come to the wrong man for information."

"Don't lie!" Vivian Legrand spat at him. "I know that you watch her every night at the Casino. You follow her from table to table. Yet you are careful to keep out of her sight—careful that she does not know that you watch her. She is not wealthy. She lives in one room in a house that a pig would turn up its nose at. Yet she has a card for the Casino, and she loses thousands of francs nightly at roulette and *chemin de fer*. I know these things. But I wish to know where the money comes from. If you desire to live, tell me. If not—"

She shrugged. No need to finish the sentence to make her meaning clear.

Delgado's voice cracked as he said:

"I don't know. God help me, I don't know."

"That is too bad." Vivian Legrand said calmly. "Perhaps you will know more after a little—er—treatment."

"Treatment?" the man said uneasily.

"Yes," she said. Reaching over to the table, she picked up a little leather case. It contained a hypodermic needle and two tiny phials, one filled with a colored liquid and the other with a clear substance. "Even in the most obstinate cases of do-not-knowness, this has been known to work wonders."

Picking out the colored phial she held it before Delgado's eyes, so that he might see the label: *Poison.*

The man stared and stared.

Two drops of sweat splashed from his forehead. His eyes, venomous with hatred and fear, watched Vivian Legrand.

"You see, poison," she said sweetly. She drew the cork and carefully filled the barrel of the needle. "In the event that you are not familiar with the stuff, you might like to know that it kills—oh, quite painlessly—in about fifteen minutes after it is injected. That is, unless an antidote is injected before it is too late. This"—she held up the other phial—"is the antidote."

"But—you wouldn't poison me!" gasped Delgado, staring at the phial as though it were his death warrant.

"I shall inject the poison," Vivian Legrand went on evenly. "But if you are willing to talk, I shall inject the antidote. If not, when the fifteen minutes are up, the two men who brought you here will simply toss your body over the cliffs into the sea."

Wylie's companion looked closely at Vivian. Hardened Apache though he was, he was unable to credit her with the serious intention of putting the thing she threatened into practice. Several years later, when the exploits of the Legrand gang of blackmailers were the talk of the underworld, the Apache, boasting of his early connection with the gang, told his comrades that at first it seemed incredible to him that any woman could have the iron strength of will, the ruthlessness, to put such a thing through. But one look at Vivian Legrand's blazing eyes made him realize that this was not an empty threat.

SHE ROLLED UP the prisoner's sleeve. He shrank back, struggling to escape the needle she held poised. But it was useless. The tight ropes, allowed him no leeway. She pinched up the flesh of his upper arm and despite his frenzied protests, injected the contents of the syringe.

The man's face was drawn in terror as she stepped back.

"The first symptom," her relentless voice went on, "will be a slight pain in the arm, followed by a numbness, gradually spreading through the arm and from there to the shoulder. There will be no further pain. As the poison spreads through the system, the numbness will follow until it reaches the heart.

"After that," she added significantly, "it won't matter. So you had better talk before then."

"But I can't tell you anything!" Delgado wailed. He was straining forward against his bonds, gasping, greenish of face. His body shook. "I don't know anything! I swear I don't. I don't know the woman you are talking about. I tell you I don't!"

Vivian Legrand glanced at her watch. "The antidote must be injected at least three minutes before the fifteenth minute is up. You have now just eleven more minutes in which to talk."

Fear clung to the man like an aura, hung in the still room like a tangible thing. But still he insisted that he did not know the information she wanted. Minute after minute passed, and from time to time, Vivian Legrand spoke, her words falling in the silence like fateful things.

"Ten minutes more."

She paused and showed him the label on the phial.

Delgado's voice cracked and he gave a hollow groan.

"I don't know... I don't know!"

"Five minutes."

She washed out the syringe at the hand basin and filled it with the clear liquid from the other phial.

"Four minutes."

Clearly, ever so clearly, her words dropped into the stillness, flogging the man with the lash of fear. From the look in the man's eyes she knew that she had won.

"Valente... he would kill me... he is a devil, that one," the man moaned.

"Better possible death later than certain death now," Vivian Legrand pressed on relentlessly. "He need never know. He will not know."

She held the syringe over the wash basin, her thumb on the plunger.

"When the time is up I shall empty the syringe into the basin."

"The antidote, the antidote," the man pleaded. "Give me the antidote! I'll talk." His face was shrunken and drawn with fear, his breath coming in little panting gasps. "Give me the antidote, for God's sake."

"Talk," Vivian Legrand said relentlessly.

In a tumble of words, their flight winged by the death that hovered over him, the story was poured out. The Signora Tomasino formerly kept a small shop in Marseille, a fence for thieves. Then one day her daughter, Camilla, caught the eye of Paul Sammard, a private banker. He was pouring out money on Camilla like water.

And, true to her type, the old woman was bleeding her daughter, in order to have funds with which to gamble at the tables. Raoul Valente had been watching the old woman, hoping to stumble onto something that would give him a chance to share in the funds that the old woman wasted so liberally. That was why he, Delgado, had been watching her night after night.

Vivian Legrand nodded. She had learned the link in the chain that she wanted to know.

"Quick, the antidote. For God's sake!" gasped the man. Beads of sweat were on his face.

Vivian Legrand's answer was to cross to the basin and empty the syringe into it.

The man's eyes followed her, and as he grasped the significance of the movement, a bubbling scream of horror and despair rose to his lips.

"You fool," Vivian Legrand said scornfully to the huddled figure on the chair, "did you think that I would let you live to tell Raoul Valente that we are on the trail of the same fox? There was no antidote. That was only water in that other phial."

She turned to Wylie.

"It will only take about five minutes more," she said calmly. "I told him fifteen, but it actually takes twenty minutes. There are chains in the cellar. When it is over, fasten the chains to him and throw him over the cliff. The water is deep there."

Turning on her heel she walked out of the room as

another despairing, bubbling scream rose from the foam-
flecked lips of the dying man.

2

VIVIAN LEGRAND AND Wylie had come to Monte Carlo
as the guests of the reigning Rajah of Salingar. Making his
acquaintance in the Far East in a scheme in which she had
been the lure, they had become friends with him, and had
used the Rajah's official standing and his yacht as a front
to defy the English Secret Service.

Vivian Legrand herself had blackmailed Sir Mark
Caywood, chief of the Secret Service in the Far East, of
three thousands pounds for the return of an important
document that had been stolen. Following that, she had
kidnaped a political prisoner who held the key to a political secret and sold him to Sir Mark for a staggering sum.
The Rajah, altogether unsuspecting of the real character of
his lovely guest and her companion, had turned the yacht's
nose toward Monte Carlo.

Some ten days before he had been called to Paris on
business, and Vivian, ever alert for an opportunity to line
her pockets, had become more and more interested in
the old woman, Signora Tomasino, whom she saw in the
Casino nearly every night. It had not been long before she
was aware that others, too, were interested in the *signora*.
Wylie had shadowed her to the squalid house where she
lived several times, and each time he had noticed that the

same man who had been watching her in the Casino had followed her home also.

It had not taken them long to find that there was no wealthy Tomasino family with an elderly member addicted to gambling. Checking up on her through casual conversation with Casino attendants, Vivian Legrand found that the old woman had been losing large sums of money for several months. But try as they might, they could not determine the source of her wealth.

Then she had hit upon the expedient of extorting the information from the man who had been shadowing her. And now she had the thread in her hands. She knew, of course, who Sammard was—the junior partner of the private banking house of Courtois, Sammard et Cie., one of the most prominent on the Riviera.

But Sammard himself had never been considered a particularly wealthy man, and it would take a wealthy man to furnish the funds that the old woman squandered at the Casino. He was a partner in the business because of the fact that his late wife had been the daughter of Courtois, founder of the banking firm. Vivian Legrand was still turning the puzzle over in her mind when Adrian Wylie came into the room.

Wylie's brain was stuffed with every kind of ancient, medieval and modern lore. He never stopped reading and he never forgot anything. A scholar by inclination, he was only a professional crook and swindler in order to obtain money. And he could not have continued to be a successful crook had it not been for his association with the girl who sat before him.

"Well, we've got the trail of the fox at last," Wylie said with satisfaction, "and dead men tell no tales."

Vivian Legrand nodded, her thoughts still fixed upon the puzzle that confronted her. The man's fate troubled her no more than the fate of the cat she had hurled so callously against the stone fireplace. That was like her. Through the whole course of her career as the world's most successful blackmailer, she permitted nothing in the way of scruples to stand in her way. She swept a man's life as ruthlessly, as surely, as she would his career, or his reputation.

"This thing is bigger than I thought," she said slowly. "My first thought was that the old woman was blackmailing someone. But that's out. Now, how does Camilla get the money she gives her mother, plus the greater sums she squanders on herself? From Sammard, undoubtedly. And where does Sammard get it? He has not a great fortune. Most of his money came to him from his wife."

In the back of her eyes a light flamed and went out again. Wylie saw it, recognized it. He said once that it was the warning signal that came into her eyes when her mind was clicking. It was a little flicker of triumph that she could not control.

"There is only one place that Sammard can get that money," she told Wylie. "He is robbing the bank of which he is a partner, or he is robbing Courtois, or else he is robbing those who trust the banking house with their deposits. Doc, it's a perfect setup for us.

"Suppose he is?" Wylie asked. "We've no proof that we could hold over his head. If he is clever enough to rob his bank without being suspected, he is clever enough to cover it up deeply enough so that we could never discover it."

"Courtois, the partner of Sammard, is a man of the old school," Vivian said thoughtfully. "He would do anything to keep the name of Courtois from being smirched by scandal. Yes, Doc, the setup is quite perfect for us."

"You can't blackmail old Courtois because of his partner's thievery," Wylie expostulated. "He would simply make good the losses and kick Sammard out."

"Exactly," Vivian Legrand said triumphantly. "So we'll have to work through the girl, Camilla. She's no fool. She knows something is up." She turned toward the door. "Now listen!" And into Wylie's ears she poured a plan that made him gasp with admiration.

3

VIVIAN LEGRAND STOPPED her car a few doors from the
house she intended to break into, dismissed it and walked.
Though her scheme was wild enough, she could think of
no other way to put her plan into effect.

The building she sought had five stories and contained
ten apartments, two on each floor, with a big entrance
lobby always open. Rather than be seen using the elevator she mounted the stairs to the third floor. The hall was
deserted.

She rang the bell of one of the apartments, although she
was certain that the apartment was empty. There was no
reply. She tried the door. It was secured by a lock which she
could not break open without making a noise.

She moved down the hall to the back door, which gave
inward like the front. This door had a different lock. An
old-fashioned one. Taking out the slender rod of thin steel
which Wylie had given her, she forced it slowly back of the
weather strip on a level with the lock. The rod scraped on
metal. She worked it up and down, slowly pressing inward.
Bit by bit the sloping tongue of the lock was forced back
into its sheath, until the blade slipped through. A twist of
the door handle and she was looking into a large kitchen.

A moment later she was inside the apartment with the
door closed and locked as she had found it.

On quick, light feet she searched the place. The drawing room had windows on the street. Off this led an inner room, a bedroom.

Tense and alert she searched the drawers of the dresser, trained fingers leaving everything as they found it. The desk held nothing of interest. She cast about to look elsewhere.

Suddenly the front door slammed.

She stood motionless a moment, as sounds came from the drawing room that told that the newcomer was moving about. Then they ceased. Silently she tiptoed to the portiere that masked the door to the drawing room and peered through.

The room was empty.

Her eyes were still searching the room when there came a slight sound behind her. She whirled.

In the kitchen doorway stood Camilla, a revolver in her hand covering Vivian Legrand, the light from the window revealing her coils of glistening black hair, eyes like dark pools, white teeth and olive tinted skin. Standing there with her gun trained on Vivian, Camilla had all of the strained nonchalance of a woman who has unexpectedly walked into a cage of tigers.

"Put your hands up," she said in crisp French. "Do not move, or I shall shoot."

"Don't be a fool," Vivian Legrand answered arrogantly. She went on harshly.

"If you start anything I shall be compelled to arrest you—and I prefer not to."

A slight movement of the summer muff she carried disclosed the fact that her own gun, hidden in its depths, was covering the girl.

The whole thing was, plainly, not what the girl had expected. As for Vivian Legrand, her exquisite face betrayed no more than a slight smile: no sign of astonishment, no flutter of panic.

"Arrest me?" faltered the girl.

"Yes," Vivian Legrand told her quietly. "I am of the police. But I am not here officially. If I were, I would be compelled to arrest you. I am betraying my duty because of your mother."

"My mother?" the girl queried.

"Yes, the Signora Tomasino. Once, many years ago she did me a service. A very great service. And I have come to return that service by aiding her daughter."

The girl sat down slowly. She was still trembling, and for a moment the two women eyed one another after the manner of strange cats. But, despite the girl's evident fear, Vivian Legrand was conscious of her appraising look, a look that swept Vivian from the casque of flaming red hair to the hem of the sports dress she wore.

"How can you aid me?" the girl asked finally. "I have done nothing that the police could be interested in."

"Except receive stolen goods," Vivian Legrand snapped. "That is why I am here—to warn you. If you are wise, you will leave Monte Carlo. If you stay you will be arrested, tried and sent to prison with your lover."

"You mean—" faltered the girl completely unnerved by the fact that this woman seemed to know everything.

"Exactly," Vivian Legrand told her. "Paul Sammard, junior partner of the banking firm of Courtois, Sammard et Cie. The police know that he is your lover. They know that for months he has been robbing his bank of huge sums of money to squander on you. What they do not know, because I have been faithless to my duty and have not reported it, is that a large part of this money you have passed on to your mother. It was when I learned that she was your mother that I determined to try and save you, if I could."

For a moment the girl was silent, dubious. Then she said in a tremulous voice:

"But what shall I do?"

"Leave Monte Carlo," Vivian told her instantly. "Not today, or tonight, but before Monday morning. Because then the police will swoop down upon the bank. Sammard and his thievery will be discovered. If you are still here you will be arrested, also."

She moved toward the door.

"Just one thing more. On no condition tell Sammard of the warning that I have given you. There is still a great deal of money in the vaults of the bank that he has not stolen. If he knew he was suspected he would take all of the money and flee. So you must not warn him."

Without another word she slipped out of the door and closed it behind her.

There was a satisfied smile on Vivian Legrand's face as she rang for the elevator. The jaws of the trap were closing.

4

FOR TWO DAYS, scarcely a move of Sammard's had been missed by Vivian Legrand's agents. They had been close on his heels when he entered his bank the morning before. They had shadowed him when he left the bank for lunch. They knew that Camilla had repeated Vivian Legrand's conversation to him, as she had intended. They surmised, if they did not know, the contents of the bulging dispatch case that had accompanied him when he left the bank that evening.

Wylie himself had been at Sammard's elbow when he had purchased a compartment for Italy for Saturday night, and tonight's move was entirely expected.

Vivian Legrand and Wylie had been waiting in a car drawn up on the further side of the street when Sammard emerged from the girl's apartment, still carrying the brief-case, and got into a waiting car.

All her life Vivian Legrand was guided by what Wylie maintains was a rare sense of intuition. Something made her perfectly confident of Sammard. He had committed himself too deeply, she told her companion, to remain in Monte Carlo. He had known that the time would eventually come when he would have to flee, and he would never take a chance on the police finding any of his stolen loot in his possession by a surprise raid. He would hide it somewhere. But where? That was what she intended to find out that night, for upon that hung the success or failure of her scheme.

Sammard's car moved off down the street. She followed. As the two cars reached less congested streets on the outskirts of the city, Wylie, who was driving, had to fall further back to keep from being noticed, but managed to always keep the taillight in sight.

Then Sammard's car made a sudden left turn. For an instant its headlights shone along a side road. Then they vanished.

The end of the chase was at hand. Sammard's car had turned into a large cemetery that lay on the slopes between the mountains and the sea.

Stopping their car, Vivian and Wylie crept through the unguarded gates of the cemetery on foot and stole down the roadway until they could see Sammard.

They watched cautiously as he removed a wreath of flowers that lay beside a headstone, burrowed in the heaped up earth that covered the grave, and deposited in the hollow of a number of packages from the dispatch case he carried.

He was burying the money he had stolen from his banking firm in his wife's grave.

Silently the two watched until Sammard straightened up and glanced about furtively. They stole down the road toward their car.

There was only one road that Sammard could use to get back to town. Down this road Wylie drove their car. Just past an intersection he stopped, turned the car so that the headlights illuminated the road. They waited until they saw the lights of a car approaching. Vivian Legrand stepped into the glare of the headlights from their own car, and waved a handkerchief.

The car came to a halt a few feet from them. Sammard stepped out.

To him Vivian told her story. She was an American heiress, traveling with her guardian. Their car had broken down. Would he be kind enough to give her a lift into town, so that she could send back assistance to her guardian, who would in the meanwhile remain with their broken-down car?

Sammard agreed readily. Not once did suspicion enter his mind that the whole thing was a plant.

VIVIAN LEGRAND LAY back in the seat of Sammard's open car, a short cape of fur flung over her shoulders, talking lightly to the banker. They had covered half the distance back to Monte Carlo before she sprang her second trap.

"I wonder," she said hesitantly, in her low, throbbing voice, "if you are sufficiently familiar with Monte Carlo to recommend me to a banking house with international connections?"

"But naturally," Sammard answered with a smile. "I myself am of the firm of Courtois, Sammard et Cie. We are fully equipped to handle any kind of banking business that *mademoiselle* might care to entrust to us."

Vivian Legrand expressed her delight at finding a banker, and before she left him at her hotel had made an appointment to meet Sammard the following morning at his bank to deposit a large sum of money with his firm.

Despite Sammard's effort at polite unconcern as he made the appointment, she caught the tension in the banker's manner. It was eloquent of the fact that already he saw this American woman's funds in his hands. The fish had seen the bait, and Vivian Legrand felt sure that he would swallow the hook.

Soon after she left the banker, Wylie picked her up. They went to the cemetery, where they unearthed the money that Sammard had buried.

The next morning Vivian Legrand and Wylie appeared at the banking house of Courtois, Sammard et Cie. They were immediately ushered into the office of the junior partner. Vivian was polished, poised… emotionally untouched, hiding beneath her exotic polished beauty and suave manner the smoldering purpose that was fast sending her to the pinnacle of her particular field of crime.

Wylie, too, seemed the efficient, intelligent man of business as he sat there, leaning forward slightly, his hands crossed over the crook of his stick.

Within half an hour the two of them had left the bank again with a receipt signed by both Sammard and his white-haired partner for 300,000 pre-war francs— worth more than $60,000. Most of this was the result of their criminal operations in the Far East. But, unknown to Sammard, some 75,000 francs of this sum was his own stolen money, unearthed from his wife's grave.

That was Thursday morning. That afternoon Sammard instructed his secretary that he would be out of town for several days on business, and left a note for his father-in-law, Courtois, saying that he was leaving for Paris to be gone several days.

When he left the bank late that afternoon the 300,000 francs of Vivian Legrand left with him in the dispatch case. From that moment on he was never out of sight of a member of the Legrand gang. When he left Camilla's apartment, Vivian and Wylie again trailed him toward the cemetery.

She was taking no chances. There was the possibility of a breakdown; the possibility that they might not reach the spot in time, and she had no desire to see her 300,000 francs vanish into Italy with an absconding banker.

Earlier in the night she had planted a confederate in a car a little beyond the gates of the cemetery, with instructions to follow Sammard quietly when he arrived.

They were not far behind Sammard's car when he turned into the cemetery, as he had done the night before. Further on, beneath a tree, was the dark bulk of the car where the confederate was hidden.

The car seemed very silent as they approached it. And then Wylie says that he knew Vivian's intuition was working, that intuition that many times over was to warn her that danger was near long before the shadow of it had fallen across her path. For she broke into a little run.

There was nobody in the driver's seat of the car when they reached it. But the slant of the moon's dim rays through the opposite window showed them the interior of the car. Half on the floor and half on the seat lay the driver, blood slowly oozing from a wound on the back of his head. It was obvious that the man had been watching the approaching car through the rear window of his own, when he was struck down.

5

"**TROUBLE," VIVIAN LEGRAND** whispered to Wylie. "Someone ahead of us. Valente, probably. He may have been following Sammard on the chance that he could pick up something."

They shut the door of the car softly, started toward the gates of the cemetery. The road was dusty and soft. Their feet made no sound.

Crouching as they moved from one patch of darkness to another, they advanced close to the grave of Sammard's wife.

The snap of a twig not far ahead brought them to a sudden halt in the shadow. All at once there was a rush of feet. Sammard dashed past them, running at full speed, the bulging dispatch case in his arms. Close on his heels came a little knot of men.

Ahead of the running figure of Sammard a man leaped from the shadows into the road. A dagger of orange flame stabbed the darkness and a scream of pain came from Sammard. He took one or two stumbling steps, and crumpled up in the roadway, dropping the dispatch case. Instantly the man who had fired pounced on it. Another instant and the little knot of running men had joined him.

Almost immediately Vivian Legrand darted out,

followed by Wylie. In her hand she carried the gun that never left her. Wylie, too, had his automatic.

The men were too engrossed in the dispatch case to notice the movement in the darkness. At the last instant one of them gave a surprised grunt and half turned. Wylie shot. Without a groan the man slumped and fell sprawling almost across the body of the banker.

"Drop your guns!" Wylie ordered sharply. "You haven't a chance."

For an astonished moment the group of men stood frozen, crowded together. Seeing them clearly for the first time, Vivian Legrand knew that her first thought had been right. She was dealing with Valente and his gang.

One man at the edge of the group suddenly darted for the nearest clump of bushes. Before he had taken two steps she fired and dropped him on his face.

"There are plenty more where that came from," she told them crisply. "If you want bullets, I'll give them to you. I will, if you don't drop those guns."

There was only a moment's hesitation. Then four guns dropped to the roadway.

"That's better," snapped Wylie. "Now step forward into the moonlight. Line up and let's have a look at you. Do as you're told, you scum. There—hold it."

"Throw that dispatch case toward me," Vivian Legrand ordered the man who held it.

The man tossed it toward her formless shape in the shadows.

"Thank you," she said sweetly. "Now the guns. Toss them this way also." She waited until the man had gathered up the discarded guns and thrown them in her direction, then spoke again.

"Now listen! You, Raoul Valente—step out from the others."

One of the men stepped forward unwillingly.

"You have a reputation as a knife-thrower," Vivian Legrand told him smoothly. "Take that knife from beneath your armpit and throw it over your shoulders as far as you can into the bushes."

Valente reached inside his shirt, drew out the long knife, raised his hand to toss it over his shoulder—and suddenly hurled it at her shadowy figure.

It thudded into the trunk of a tree against which she had been standing a moment before. With the gliding ease of a cat she had moved at the first flexing of his arm to throw, and almost as the knife thudded into the tree she fired. A snarl of rage or pain came from Valente as the bullet smashed through his right wrist.

"You won't throw a knife for a long time, my friend," she mocked him.

She stooped, picked up the dispatch case and melted into the shadows with Wylie.

6

JUST A FEW moments after the doors of Courtois, Sammard et Cie. opened the next morning Vivian Legrand and Wylie presented themselves. M. Sammard, they were told, was out of town, and would not return; but Monsieur Courtois, the senior partner, would see them.

Vivian and Wylie exchanged glances in which there was something of relief. Sammard's body had not yet been discovered, so that factor would not complicate matters.

"I regret exceedingly," Vivian Legrand told Courtois, when he appeared, "that we must alter our plans. But I have just received a cablegram from New York and must sail at once."

The cablegram she extended was faked, of course, but so genuine did it appear that even an employee of the cable company would have been deceived. Then Vivian Legrand extended her receipt for 300,000 francs.

"In view of our sudden departure," she said smilingly, "I shall have to withdraw my funds."

They waited in tense anxiety as Courtois himself went to the vaults to obtain their money.

Within a few minutes Courtois returned, white-faced, grim.

"I regret," he said curtly, "that there will be a delay. There has been an accident—a robbery."

"Robbery!" Vivian Legrand said sharply. "But why should a robbery concern us? Am I to understand that Courtois, Sammard et Cie. is unable to pay its honest debts?"

"For the moment, *mademoiselle*, I fear that it is impossible," retorted the old Frenchman.

"I do not believe it," Vivian Legrand told him crisply. "My money was deposited here only yesterday. Today you tell me that you are unable to pay. You are attempting to trick me."

"Believe me, *mademoiselle*," the man said, "if you will but give me time—"

"I must leave Monte Carlo today," she put in sharply. "I cannot give you time. If you cannot produce my money, it can mean but one thing— that your banking house has failed."

"Today," said the old man curtly, "the robbers have left hardly sufficient cash in the vaults to transact the day's business. Tomorrow, when I call in my loans—"

"Then there is nothing to do," Vivian Legrand interrupted, "save consult my lawyer and see if he can save something from the ruins."

"If you make public the fact that the bank has been robbed, we will be ruined," the old banker said.

"But you are ruined."

"I can make good my losses if I am given time. I have a large private fortune. I can borrow. If you will only give me time, no one will lose a penny."

"I cannot wait," Vivian Legrand told him. "If you are in a position to pay me, I will keep silent about the robbery. Otherwise not."

For the first time Wylie spoke.

"I am not familiar with the laws of Monaco," he said smoothly, "but it seems to me that that is compounding a felony. In America or England it would be. And that places us, of course, in a rather dangerous position." Before the banker could speak he went on. "Naturally, if we are being placed in a dangerous position because we are willing to save a fine old banking house from ruin, that matter should be taken into consideration."

"Naturally," Vivian Legrand said. "I am sure that you appreciate that fact, do you not? We have on deposit here the sum of 300,000 francs. Now, your reputation in Monte Carlo banking circles is good. Your credit is excellent. We will wait here, while you approach your colleagues. If you are able to borrow 350,000 francs, we will keep silent about the condition of your bank. But if—"

"But you have on deposit here only 300,000 francs!" the banker snapped.

"I KNOW," VIVIAN LEGRAND told him, "but under the circumstances, the extra 50,000 francs can be considered as a bonus. Surely it is worth the extra 50,000 to you to stave off ruin. If not—"

The old man sat perfectly still. He looked for mercy in Vivian Legrand's eyes. There was none.

"Very well," he said, grimly. "To save the name of Courtois from disgrace, I will even pay a—er—bonus. Will you wait here until my return, please?"

He was gone for more than an hour. When he returned he placed in Vivian Legrand's hands 350,000 francs.

THE EPISODE OF THE
LEVANTINE MONSTER

*The Devilish Guile of Vivian Legrand Forces
the Monster of the Turkish Underworld to
Sell His Own Accomplice into the Harem*

1

VIVIAN LEGRAND WATCHED the disappearing lights of Monte Carlo with something akin to relief. Each turn of the ship's propeller was taking her further away from police officials who might, if the occasion arose, become exceedingly inquisitive about the large sum of money she had blackmailed out of Monte Carlo's leading banker. Then, too, there would undoubtedly be a disturbance over the death of Paul Sammard, the junior partner of the banking firm, and it was undoubtedly wiser to be on the way to Constantinople than in Monte Carlo when the storm broke.

Standing by the rail she gave the appearance of some great lady of the world. There was nothing about her to indicate that she was as deadly as a striking snake. And, as more than one of her victims could testify, she was as merciless, as utterly devoid of the usual human emotions as a statue. The weak rays from the deck light caught her red hair and caused it to take on something of the nature of a quivering flame above the exquisitely modeled, exotic face.

Suddenly, warned by some inner sense of the presence of another person, she turned with that catlike grace that always characterized her every movement and saw, directly behind her, the slim silhouette of a man—so close to her, in fact, that she instinctively threw out her elbow to avoid collision, while the other hand automatically dropped into the pocket of her light tweed coat to grasp the revolver she carried there.

The man halted abruptly.

"Pardon, *mademoiselle*," he said in French that was strongly accented, and moved the fraction of a step nearer. "In the dim light I mistook *mademoiselle* for a friend."

Then he stepped back as the deck steward came around the corner of the deckhouse and started folding up the deck chairs for the night. Without another word the stranger made a slight bow and moved on down the deck. But not before Vivian Legrand had noticed that one of his hands was deep in the pocket of the coat he wore, much in the manner of her own hand clutching the revolver in her pocket.

Nor had the man's accent escaped her. It was of the East. Perhaps Greek, perhaps Turkish.

Her eyes went back speculatively to the rail of the ship against which she had been standing. How easy it would have been to stun her with a blow from behind, and then consign her body to the waters over which she had been leaning.

But why? She could assign no reason. Certainly not the police. Agents of the French Sûreté certainly would not adopt such methods.

She moved on down the deck in a shimmer of light-struck silk, still turning the affair over in her mind, made her way down to her cabin and threw open the door—to stop in amazement upon the threshold.

THE CABIN HAD been searched, searched thoroughly and carefully. Her dressing case was empty and the bottom had

*A beam of light moved
slowly up to her face*

been slit with a sharp knife to make sure that it held no secret pocket. Dresses had been ripped from their hangers in the little clothes closet and tossed onto the floor until it looked as though a dozen birds of paradise had moulted there. The handle on her hand mirror had been snapped, perhaps on the assumption that it might be hollow. Not a thing in the room had been left untouched.

"So," she said softly, "that was *not* a mistake up there on the deck."

Sudden consternation flooded her. Swiftly she stepped inside the cabin, locked the door. Upon the wall hung a little drawing. Hurriedly taking it down she turned it over. The purser's receipt for the valuables she had deposited with him was still fastened to the back of the picture with the two pins she had used.

Satisfied on this point, she replaced the picture and set about righting the damage that had been done. And all the time her brain was working swiftly, with smooth precision. Now she knew the reason for the attempt on her life, there on the deck, and the reason for the search of her cabin.

Thoughtfully she poured out a glass of water from the carafe and put the glass to her lips. Then she put the glass down without drinking and rang for her room steward.

When he answered she handed him the glass of water.

"Drink this," she ordered curtly.

The steward, puzzled, took the glass and raised it to his lips. But before he could swallow Vivian Legrand struck the glass from his hand. It crashed on the carpet of her cabin and splashed his white coat with water.

The man recoiled and looked at her with amazement.

"When did you fill the water bottle?" she demanded.

"This afternoon, *madame,*" he replied. "You were here at the time, if you remember."

"I remember now. I'm sorry," she said slowly. "I had forgotten, and the water seemed stale."

"Shall I bring you fresh water, *madame?*" he asked.

"No," Vivian told him. "That is all."

But she had not forgotten and her eyes were deadly as the door closed behind the man. The water was poisoned. It had been poisoned during the time that she had been absent. The faintly bitter odor of almonds that rose from it was unmistakable. Whoever her enemy was, he meant to leave no stone unturned to kill her. It was evident that the steward was not concerned in the affair. He would have swallowed the water if she had not knocked the glass from his lips.

Quietly she went out into the corridor and, glancing about to make sure that no one was in sight, made her way to the cabin occupied by Adrian Wylie, her companion in crime.

The moment she entered the room he sensed that something was amiss and dropped the book he was reading. Swiftly she outlined to him the two attempts upon her life.

"Somebody," she finished succinctly, "knows that we have close to a million francs in bank notes and jewels—and that somebody means to have them."

"Valente," Wylie said thoughtfully.

2

VALENTE WAS A French criminal, a leader of the underworld in Monte Carlo, whom Vivian Legrand had outwitted and outshot in a struggle for the stolen funds of Paul Sammard, the banker. She had broken the man's wrist with a shot as a parting souvenir.

She shook her head emphatically at the mention of the name.

"Not enough brains. A shooting affair in a dark alley—a knife thrust into my back from the shadows—a body robbed and quietly disposed of—yes. That much he is capable of. But not this. This is big-time stuff."

"Who else knows that we have that much money?" Wylie said. "That is the crux. Whoever it is isn't taking a shot in the dark. *They know.*"

"Right," Vivian Legrand said thoughtfully. "Whoever it is knows."

She stopped and a slightly startled look flashed in her eyes.

"There is only one person who knows that we have that money. Camilla."

Wylie's eyes narrowed in thought for a moment, and he nodded slowly. "Camilla. Yes, it might be that Camilla is mixed up in this."

"That means," Vivian Legrand said, "that Camilla

bargained with someone for a share of the money we took from Sammard, in return for the tip on who had it. That someone is on board, of course; and Camilla, being no fool, is undoubtedly waiting at our first port of call for her cut. Tomorrow night we are in Naples. That was why he tried tonight, in the hope of being able to go ashore tomorrow with the money."

"Whoever it is may not be playing a lone hand," Wylie warned her. "There may be others here on board."

"One or a dozen," Vivian said recklessly. "If they want war, we'll fight."

"They have the advantage of us," Wylie pointed out. "We are fighting in the dark. They are not. We don't know who they are."

"We will tomorrow," she said grimly. With a curt "Good night!" she went out and made her way to her own cabin.

TWO HOURS LATER Vivian Legrand was lying in her berth, wakeful, the lights off, unable to sleep because of the heat, which pressed down upon the steamer like a giant hand. And suddenly she had become conscious of a round hole in the center of the copper screening that covered the porthole—a hole that had not been there a moment before, perhaps an inch across, which looked like it had been carefully cut with a sharp knife.

She lay very still, listening like a cat, her eyes glued upon the porthole. And, while she looked, the black silhouette of a man's head loomed against the light outside.

It moved as she stared at it. A deck hand, perhaps. Again, perhaps not. She glanced at the luminous dial of her wrist watch. Eight minutes after two.

The glow outside the porthole gave birth to a hand,

stamped momentarily in relief upon the lighted circle, and withdrew into the shadows that had yielded it. Vivian waited, motionless, barely breathing. Then she became cognizant of the fact that a face was peering in upon her. No light was cast upon it. The silhouette might have been cut out of black paper and suspended there. And she knew that invisible eyes in that black outline were staring into the cabin.

Never had she felt more keenly that death was stealing toward her soundlessly and unseen. Narrowing her eyes to mere slits, even though the room was in darkness, she watched breathlessly. The dull beat of the ship's engines, the slap of the waves, the whisper of wind, came clear and distinct.

Suddenly a beam of light flashed across the bed. Her eyes were closed. She seemed in deep repose. It darted across the tumbled cover, moved slowly up to her face and rested there for a short moment. For perhaps ten seconds it played upon her, as if that silent and sinister watcher outside the window were assuring himself that it was indeed Vivian Legrand lying there asleep in the bed.

Then the light flashed off.

She was out of bed and upon her feet, soundlessly, as soon as it vanished.

Slipping across the room to the doorway she threw on a dressing gown and picked up the revolver lying upon the table. Then she quietly unlocked the cabin door and crouched, eyes upon the porthole, and waited.

She had only a moment to wait. The black silhouette moved, and a slender rod of metal slid through the hole in the center of the screen. To it was attached a larger cylinder—a silencer.

The barrel of the gun with the silencer attached came slowly through the hole and pointed directly at the place where, but a moment before, she had been lying. Smiling grimly to herself Vivian Legrand picked up her

Vedova Bey

own gun and cautiously eased the cabin door open, her eyes fastened upon that black silhouette at the porthole.

Then six sharp daggers of orange flame stabbed the darkness, and the sharp, acrid smell of burned powder invaded the cabin. The reports made no more noise than the clapping of hands together. A score of feet away the sound would have been inaudible, mingled with the noises of the ship and the wash of waves against the hull.

Scarcely had the last of the daggers of flame pierced the darkness of the cabin when Vivian Legrand threw open the door, ran down the short corridor, and onto the deck. A tall, slender man was just turning the corner of the deckhouse aft, the pistol still in his hand. Throwing a glance to right and left, Vivian began to run, her bare feet padding on the damp planking. At the corner of the deckhouse she paused a moment. A few yards away a companionway light illuminated a door. Into this the man dived. When Vivian

Legrand reached the opening he was nowhere in sight. He had disappeared into one of the cabins that lined the corridor, or had vanished down one of the corridors that branched off. Useless to look further.

She felt convinced that it was the same man she had encountered on deck earlier in the evening, but to identify him would be impossible. There was nothing characteristic about his walk, and the description "tall and slim" might apply to any of a dozen men on board.

3

VIVIAN LEGRAND MADE an early appearance in the shabby little dining saloon of the steamer the next morning. The ship was ploughing through a calm sea and it was more than probable that all of the passengers aboard would put in an appearance.

Although supposedly strangers to each other, Adrian Wylie and Vivian occupied the same table through Wylie's maneuvers with the table steward. Tall, lean and impressive, Wylie gave far more the impression of a man of affairs, a banker, perhaps; than the whimsical, yet prudent and incalculably gifted criminal that he was.

The two sat there at their table, talking casually as steamer acquaintances will, but shrewdly sizing up every passenger who entered the saloon.

It was the two men and the woman at a table across the room who held Vivian's eyes longest. The girl was not particularly striking. She was probably French, and pretty in a superficial way. The younger of the two men Vivian Legrand had seen on deck several times since the ship sailed, and his appearance now struck a chord in her memory.

His name, she had learned, was Jacob Arbajian.

His companion was Vedova Bey, a Levantine turned Moslem to further his career. Vivian Legrand was not an impressionable woman. She had lived much and swiftly among many kinds of people, and it took something remarkable in the way of a man to surprise her. At first sight of Vedova Bey she had nicknamed him the Levantine Monster.

It was not the size of the man that had prompted the nickname, and neither was it the terrible physical power which surrounded him like an aura. It was the calm, ghastly brutality with which he fairly reeked, the complete brutality of an animal, dominated by a human intelligence far above the average. Levantine Monster fitted him well.

On first seeing him on board Wylie had made discreet inquiries and had learned a little of the history of Vedova Bey. With his notorious brother (who was later hanged by the Germans during the war as a spy) he did a brisk trade in girls in Turkey.

There, prior to the World War, it was not unusual for parents to sell their daughters into the harems of wealthy men. Not always were the girls sold by their parents, either. There was many a girl who vanished from villages in France or Italy who later showed up as a slave girl in a Turkish harem.

Of his companion she knew nothing, save that he was traveling in company with Vedova Bey. What she suspected, however, was that he was the bodyguard of the Levantine Monster.

She had almost finished her breakfast when Jacob Arbajian, the Monster's companion, caught sight of her for the first time. His face went white and he stared at her as though he were gazing at a ghost. He leaned across the table and spoke to Vedova Bey. An angry scowl crossed the latter's face as he shot a swift look at Vivian.

Satisfied, she finished her breakfast. Later she went on deck. These two, the foppish young man and the Levantine Monster, were the only ones who seemed plausible suspects, and the fright of the younger of the two on seeing her added confirmation to her belief. Already her agile mind was working out a plan whereby she might prove the correctness of her theories.

DUSK WAS FALLING over Naples when Vedova Bey and his companion disembarked from the tender at the wharf and hailed a taxi. Neither of them noted the two shadows that detached themselves from the shadow of a building and stealthily moved in their wake—two shadows that had been watching and waiting for their appearance for more than an hour.

And if they had noticed the shadows, neither of the two men would have recognized in them Vivian Legrand and Adrian Wylie. Vivian's flaming hair was hidden beneath a black wig, drawn back and curled over the ears. Her skirt had a pleated flare and her black silk stockings glistened. She gave the impression of a parlor maid who had just doffed her lace cap and lacy apron for a night out. A deft line or two of make-up about the eyes, a change in the curve of the eyebrows, had altogether altered the contour of her face.

Wylie was no longer the debonair, suave, well-dressed gentleman. His graying hair had been darkened with a temporary preparation. A cap was pulled down over one eye. A sweater and a pair of old trousers completed the transformation that was as complete as that of Vivian.

Keeping a cautious distance from the pair they trailed, the taxi occupied by Vivian and Wylie wandered half-way across Naples, it seemed, before turning into a black little street. Just ahead of them the other car was drawn up before a building where light gleamed through a door of painted green glass. As they watched, Vedova Bey and Joseph Arbajian passed through the door.

Waiting a few moments, Vivian and Wylie followed. The ceiling of the room they entered was low, the room narrow and not well lighted. The walls were askew, as if the house, growing old, had decided to fall down, but on second thought decided to wait awhile. One or two of the patrons looked up indifferently. There was no sign of the two men they had been following.

A man with a big mustache, dark eyes, pale face and short, stout body came on a trot to make them welcome.

Wylie asked for a private room.

The man's hands went up in a gesture of disappointment. There was only one private room and that had been engaged, not five minutes before. But he would give them a table in a corner where they would be secluded. He pointed to a table in a little alcove near the door.

Wylie shook his head and indicated a table at the far end of the long room—a table only a few feet from the door where the proprietor had emerged—most likely the private room that held the two men they sought.

For nearly fifteen minutes they sat, talking in low tones, giving a perfect impersonation of what they were supposed to be.

Vivian faced the doorway. At last she stiffened and broke

off in the midst of a sentence. Her glance, with startled intensity, struck on Wylie's face.

"Camilla," she breathed through half-closed lips. Her eyes were hard, as emeralds are hard, as she furtively watched the girl.

4

CAMILLA CAME INTO the room with an assurance that betokened familiarity with it, and the greeting of the proprietor gave evidence that she was known to him. A single word passed between them, and then Camilla made straight for the door beside Vivian and Wylie. Her glance swept them indifferently as she passed, but there was no recognition in it as she opened the door and went in.

Wylie looked up, a wordless question in his eyes. A furtive gesture of Vivian's hand bade him wait. For a moment or two they sat there until the stout proprietor passed out of the room into the kitchen in the rear. Then, with a swift movement, Vivian Legrand was on her feet. Noiselessly she opened the door and slipped through, followed by Wylie. So swift, so noiseless were their movements that none of the other patrons of the place had noted what they were doing.

They found themselves in a narrow corridor which ended in a curtain-masked doorway at the far end. Light filtered around its edges, and from behind came the voice of Camilla, mingled with that of Vedova Bey.

The two spies crept to the curtain on noiseless feet and peered through. The three were seated around a table, and with them was a fourth person, Raoul Valente, Monte Carlo underworld leader, his right hand still bandaged.

"You are late," Vedova Bey was saying to Camilla.

"I know," the woman answered. "Did you get the money?"

"Not yet," Vedova Bey told her. "We will get it between Naples and Constantinople, and you shall have your share in Constantinople."

Camilla's evilly passionate eyes were suspicious as she fixed them on the Levantine Monster.

"Have you tried?" she queried.

Vedova Bey nodded. "Tried—and failed. But there will be no failure next time."

"But I do not understand how you could fail," Raoul Valente put in.

"Jacob was a fool last night," snarled Vedova Bey, his yellowish, catlike eyes gleaming. "If he had been more careful the money would be in our hands now. Three attempts, and all three failures."

"It was not my fault," protested Jacob. "The first time was too public, too dangerous. You said yourself that it must be done without the knowledge of anyone. Then, I could not know that she would not drink the poisoned water. Not my fault. And the third time you could have done no more yourself. The woman was in her berth. I fired six shots at her. Is it my fault if she is a witch woman bullets cannot kill?"

"Witch?" snarled Vedova Bey. His voice spat venom as he turned to Camilla and her companion.

"The fool fired at a shadow, a fold of the bed clothes—anything except the woman. But tonight will be different. I will take charge myself, and she will be killed without a trace and her body tossed into the sea. Then we may walk ashore in Constantinople with the money in safety."

Vivian Legrand turned to Wylie and whispered hurried instructions in his ear. He nodded, but demurred at leaving her there alone. She overruled him and turned back to the curtain as Wylie, after peering through a crack in the door, slipped out without being seen.

"There is bound to be a stir when she is found missing," Camilla was saying doubtfully. "Even if your influence with the Turkish authorities is great enough to prevent anything more than a perfunctory inquiry, her consul will make trouble. There will be questions, a search."

The Levantine Monster chuckled. "Not for a suicide," he said. "The lady has been very disconsolate. So she leaps overboard."

"Disconsolate?" began Camilla.

"It will all be explained in the note she leaves behind," the Monster told her. "You are not aware that the little Suzette who travels with me has other uses besides that of being beautiful? There is no handwriting she cannot imitate. The French police know that even better than I do."

A DOOR THAT Vivian Legrand had not previously noticed on the other side of the room opened and the stout proprietor of the tavern entered. He was obviously agitated, and she watched in silence as he made his way to Vedova Bey and whispered. Somewhere inside her that little warning bell of intuition rang a sharp alarm.

Vedova Bey turned his head slightly and smiled.

"Won't you come out and join us, there behind the curtain?" he said smoothly. "You might as well, since the other end of the passage is guarded."

The man's words seemed to hang there in the air while the eyes of the four in the room converged on the curtains behind which Vivian Legrand lurked.

The shock of being discovered for a moment took her breath away. She wheeled to look behind her. The door which Wylie had closed when he left was slightly ajar, and silhouetted in the opening she could see the figure of a man with a gun.

She was in a trap, and a desperate one.

Hardly more than ten seconds had passed before she thrust the curtains aside and stepped into the room. With a cool smile on her lips she approached the table. Close to it she halted, her narrowed eyes flitting to each of them in turn.

Vedova Bey peered at her intently, with outthrust head. His yellow eyes were unwinking. Vivian Legrand met their stare steadily and calmly. Her brain was clicking with machinelike precision. Five of them to deal with, one in the passage behind her, and no telling how many cutthroats in the tavern outside. And there were six cartridges in the gun in the hand concealed by the folds of her wide skirt. In that she had the advantage. They did not know she was armed.

"And to what do I owe the pleasure of this—visit?" Vedova Bey inquired with sinister menace.

"You smiled at me out there," Vivian Legrand said. She nodded her head toward the other room. She was gay. Her eyes were sparkling, her mouth quirked in a mocking smile. "You did not come back—so I came in."

She took a step forward. Sharp apprehension flashed in the deep yellow eyes, but before Vedova Bey could divine her intent, she brought the butt of her gun down in a smashing blow upon his temple. It was a terrific blow, and he dropped almost as if he were dead.

A cry went up from Camilla—a cry like the merciless "Au-rr-ugh" of a wolf calling the pack to the kill.

Even as Vivian Legrand straightened up from the blow a thrown knife grazed her shoulder. She realized that Valente, now on his feet, could throw a knife with his left hand almost as well as with his right. A quick glance over her shoulder showed her the fifth man, his mouth open in astonishment, just pushing aside the curtains that masked the doorway through which she had come.

Valente was the only one who had made a move toward her. The others seemed, somehow, to think themselves unfairly tricked by seeing a gun in the hand of a woman they had thought unarmed.

Before they could recover from their astonishment, Vivian Legrand spun about and her gun spat flame at the man in the doorway. He dropped, and without pausing to see whether he actually was out of the fight or not, she wheeled around and put a bullet into Valente—who, too late, was attempting to rush her.

Long in the telling but short in the doing. Almost before Valente's body had crumpled to the floor and while Camilla's scream was still hanging in the air, Vivian Legrand was at the curtain-masked doorway through which she had entered, was down the passage and in the tavern itself. It was empty.

As she opened the door there was the noiseless tiptoe of a foot and the door to the kitchen opened. The stout proprietor peered into the long room.

He gave Vivian Legrand one long stare, caught sight of

the gun in her hand, turned with a yell of fright and bolted. A moment later there was the sound of a heavy object being pushed against the door. Silence followed, silence so complete and abrupt as to give the uneasy sensation that the sound had been only a fantastic trick of the mind.

5

VIVIAN LEGRAND DID not stop. At any moment Jacob or Camilla might burst out of the passage behind her with spitting gun. She wasted no thoughts upon the two men she had shot down. That was like her.

So now she fled down the long, empty room, jerked open the door and found herself in the dark street. At the corner a taxi waited, with the driver asleep on the seat. He woke to the prod of her gun and in another moment the car was bumping over the cobbled street.

A block from her destination she stopped the taxi and got out. It was a dark little side street, with an uneven narrow sidewalk and cobbled street. In the shadowy alcove of a huddle of buildings she found Wylie waiting as arranged.

Swiftly she gave him a resume of what had happened, and then asked a single question herself:

"Is it arranged?"

Wylie nodded. "No trouble at all. We deliver the goods and collect the cash."

There was little said after this. Vivian was keenly aware of the difficulty of the thing she had set out to do. Her brain was working coolly, methodically; and in her half-closed eyes was something more deadly and remorseless than is ordinarily found in the eyes of any woman.

Camilla Tomasino would fight her, would she? Fight Vivian Legrand? All right. But she would fight back. And Camilla, if she lived long enough to regret it, would rue to her last day the impulse that made her fight.

Cloaked in the shadows Vivian and Wylie waited until a car drove up and Camilla disembarked. Vivian did not move, but her hand tightened on Wylie's arm.

The car drove off and she whispered a single terse word to Wylie. With swift, noiseless tread he was at the side of the black-haired girl. Before Camilla could utter a word his arm had tightened about her neck and Vivian Legrand had pressed a handkerchief, soaked in chloroform, to her mouth and nostrils.

A few moments more and a man and a woman, supporting between them the limp form of a woman who had evidently had too much liquor, made their way down the street. Fifteen minutes more and the taxi they had picked up deposited Vivian, Wylie and their limp burden before a tumbledown shack at the corner of a smelly alley. An old woman opened the door at their knock, a woman whose gray, lank hair fell about her face.

The old woman looked at Camilla's still white face in the yellow rays of the lamp on the table and nodded her head.

"She will do," she croaked. "One thousand liras, you say?"

"Five thousand," Vivian snapped.

"I can never get that for her," whined the old woman. "Girls are cheap now."

"Not this kind," Vivian Legrand retorted calmly.

"Ai," whined the old woman, "but you are hard! However, there is a man in Salonica who wants just such a one as she—Gregor Vedova, with whom I have done business in the past. I will be hard with him as you are with me."

Irony lurked in the depths of Vivian Legrand's greenish eyes as the old woman pulled a roll of bills from beneath her filthy dress and began to count them out. It appealed to her sense of humor that Camilla should be sold to the brother of Vedova Bey, the Levantine Monster.

"There," the old woman said as she paid over the last bill. "You have your five thousand. And if you ever have another like her, Old Mother Salina will take her off your hands. But not at this price. Not at this price!"

She was still cackling and rubbing her hands when Vivian and Wylie closed the door and stepped into the street again.

"I think," Vivian Legrand said calmly, as they started for the ship, "that Camilla will regret for a very long time, that she did not remain in Monte Carlo and mind her own business."

THEY BOARDED THE ship separately, and her face was thoughtful as she hurriedly removed her disguise. The affair was not ended by any means.

Discreet inquiries of her room steward had elicited the information that Vedova Bey and Jacob had come aboard more than an hour before. Vedova Bey had been in an accident, the man informed her, and was wearing a bandage upon his head. Vivian Legrand smiled grimly at the information. The man was lucky that he was not lying in his coffin.

She was still thoughtful when she met Wylie a few minutes later. They were passing the purser's office when that worthy himself called to her:

"I am desolated, Madame Legrand, to have been absent this afternoon," he told her, "but my assistant conveyed your message to me. You may be quite sure that we shall say nothing of you having withdrawn your valuables. But are you sure, *madame,* that it is quite safe?"

Vivian stared at him incredulously for a moment. This was the one thing her agile brain had not expected, had not prepared for. And then into her mind flashed a sentence that the Levantine Monster had uttered an hour or so before:

"The little Suzette has other uses besides being beautiful. There is no handwriting she cannot imitate..."

A flash of inward lightning seemed to quiver across her face.

"You still have my receipt?" she asked abruptly, and at the purser's, "But, of course, *madame!*" he went on.

"Would you permit me to see it? I am not quite sure that I signed it as I did my deposit slip, and I should like the transaction to be quite in order, of course."

"It is the same, *madame,*" he assured her, as he opened a drawer in the safe and took out a printed form. "Had it not been the same you would not have obtained the envelope with your valuables, even though we knew you to be the owner."

Vivian Legrand glanced at the slip he laid before her. For a moment Wylie's eyes were caught by a glinting stare. Those green eyes seemed to flame with an emotion which did not appear on the carved ivory mask of the face. The signature was the same. It was one of the most beautiful forgeries she had ever seen.

Every nerve in her body was tense with the effort of

maintaining a careless smile as she handed the slip of paper back to the purser.

"It is the same," she said quietly.

So that was why her room had been searched. They were clever, this Levantine Monster and his gunman. They had found the purser's deposit slip in its hiding place, the girl had copied it, and then it had been cunningly replaced so that her suspicions might not be aroused.

Then the girl, disguising herself to look as much as possible like Vivian, had presented a forged deposit slip and received the envelope containing her jewels and nearly a million francs in currency.

That was why the girl had studied her so steadily that morning at breakfast… why, all through the day she had found the girl watching her furtively on deck…

They planned now to kill her and to walk off the ship in complete possession of the money and the situation. Vivian Legrand smiled grimly. That was their plan. But she had another.

6

WITH A FURTIVE look to make sure that she was not observed, Vivian Legrand closed the door of the Levantine Monster's cabin behind her and stepped into the corridor. Her search had been thorough. Secure in the knowledge that neither Vedova Bey or his pretty companion would leave the deck, where Wylie was entertaining them, she had ransacked every available hiding place. Her missing money was not in the cabin.

She had not expected the money to be so casually hidden that she would stumble over it immediately, but neither had she expected the man to take extraordinary precautions in hiding it. She knew that they were counting on her not learning that the money had been withdrawn on a forged receipt, and of there being no search made for it.

Noiselessly she slipped down the corridor to Cabin 51, occupied by Jacob. She knew that he had retired an hour or more before, and the fact that the room was in darkness would seem to indicate that he was asleep. She listened carefully at the door. The man was asleep. His deep, regular breathing was clearly audible.

Entering quietly with a skeleton key she found that sufficient light came through the porthole to make her electric torch unnecessary. Then she slid over to the berth and listened again. There was no doubt of it. The man was sound asleep.

Carefully she placed the peculiar weapon she carried on the edge of the wash basin—a weapon that seemed harmless enough and yet was, as she knew, much more effective than a gun in a situation where the sound of a gun would be fatal. It was something her fertile brain had devised, and was, in later years, to become part of the equipment of every member of the Legrand gang when on an errand like this.

Then she set to work. Every bit of baggage was gone through. Every space that could have possibly held the money and her jewels was ransacked, But without success.

And then her eyes lit on the one place that she had not searched. Noiselessly she crossed the cabin to it.

The steamer, like most of the prewar vessels in the Turkish trade, was not equipped with running water. Instead, each cabin had a small tank which was supposed to be kept filled by the steward.

Lifting the top of this white enameled tank, Vivian Legrand plunged her hand into it. A smile of triumph illuminated her face as she brought up a dripping package wrapped in oilskin.

And then tragedy swept upon her with sinister swiftness.

An intuition, a sudden leaping of her nerves from no visible warning, saved her. She leaped sidewise under this intuitive impulse as the extended hand of the man behind her aimed a blow at her head with a revolver held clubwise. And at almost the same instant she struck with the edge of her hand on the man's wrist, a short chopping blow that sent the gun spinning into the corner of the room.

Jacob Arbajian flashed on the light, and for a moment the two, the killer and the woman, stood there staring at one another.

Jacob was between Vivian and the door, and his eyes were fixed on her with a dancing alertness as he backed slowly, a step at a time, toward the corner where his gun had fallen.

For once, Vivian Legrand was not armed with a gun. True, she had that strange weapon, but it lay on the edge of the washbasin where she had left it to reach for the oilskin package. She could reach it in a single backward leap, but she dared not make that leap, because that single instant of time would give the man the opportunity to leap for his own gun.

Not a word was spoken by either. Slowly, so slowly as to be almost imperceptible, Vivian Legrand backed toward the washbasin where her own weapon lay, and slowly the man inched toward his own gun on the floor.

Then he flung himself forward, snatched it up. His finger was just curving on the trigger when some sixth sense caused him to glance at her right hand.

"Put your hand down!" he screamed. "I'll shoot. I'll—"

He broke off with a horrible, high-pitched, choking noise. He stumbled back and crashed to the floor, clawing frantically at his eyes.

"Oh, my God!" he moaned. "I'm blind! My eyes! You've put them out. I can't see!"

His lips slobbered. He kicked and writhed on the floor. Concentrated ammonia does that. It burns the eyes and scorches and strangles. Renders a man immediately helpless.

Vivian Legrand's weapon had been a small rubber syringe filled with the stuff, and she had squirted a fine spray full into the man's face. She dropped the syringe back into the washbasin and started toward the door.

Almost simultaneously there was the muffled sound of a shot from the porthole, barely distinguishable a dozen feet away because of the fact that the gun from which it came bore a silencer.

Jacob crumpled to the floor, a gaping hole in his forehead. Almost instantly Vivian Legrand threw herself to one side. Her hand found the light switch, plunged the room in darkness. Then, keeping out of the light that streamed through the porthole, she crept across the cabin and flung open the door.

Standing outside, blocking her passage, was Vedova Bey, the Levantine Monster.

WITH A QUICK gesture he thrust her back into the room, stepped inside and closed the door behind him. A quick turn of his wrist and the door was locked and the key in his pocket.

"I was a fool this afternoon," the man said. "I should have realized that a woman clever enough to have worked that trick in Monte Carlo would be clever enough to fit two and two together and get to the bottom of Jacob's rather clumsy attempts upon your life. But when you shot your way out of that trap this afternoon it did not occur to me that it might be you."

"Jacob," Vivian Legrand said with deadly calm, "seems to have paid for his carelessness."

"I do not regret having to shoot him," the Levantine

Monster said with an indifferent glance at the still form on the floor. "He deserved it."

"Now," went on Vedova Bey, his eyes again fixed upon her, "if you will be so kind as to give me the little package you have there you may go."

Fire flashed instantly into Vivian's greenish eyes. She struck out swiftly and boldly.

"Do you realize," she told him, with just the right amount of calm insolence in her voice, "that you have just murdered a man? Even though this be technically Turkish soil, there will be inquiries."

"I murder my friend—my very dear friend and companion?

"Do you think, my dear Madame Legrand, that I intend to take the blame for a murder that you committed? No. Most assuredly not. You had a rendezvous with my companion. You quarreled. You shot him. And now I, out of the goodness of my heart, am offering you an opportunity to escape before the crime is discovered. Will you give me the bag, now?" he added, apparently as an afterthought.

Instead he found himself staring into the muzzle of the revolver Jacob had dropped when he fell to the floor.

"If you will be so kind as to step aside," Vivian Legrand suggested, "you will live a great deal longer than if you compel me to shoot." Her voice came low, steady with threat. "The authorities might be interested in knowing that I was passing. I heard a shot. I flung open the door and found you standing over your victim, the smoking revolver in your hand."

The Levantine Monster shook his head. There was a

light in his eyes that warned her that he had not played his last card.

"That was clever," he said, and his slight smile deepened into a sneer. "It took an exceedingly agile brain to think of that on the spur of the moment. But, unfortunately, I had anticipated something of the sort. For that reason, I stationed my little Suzette in the hallway. We were together, Suzette and I, we heard the shot. I flung open the door and found *you* standing over your victim." He shot a glance at Vivian Legrand. "Ah, you do not believe." He raised his voice and called.

"I am here," came the voice of a woman from beyond the door panel.

"Now will you give me the bag?"

"I will not," Vivian Legrand said.

"IF YOU WILL hand the bag to me," said Wylie's voice at the porthole, "that will end the matter."

The slim and menacing muzzle of a revolver peered through the porthole, covering Vedova Bey.

"I witnessed the whole thing," came Wylie's calm voice. "It was most fortunate that I was on deck, just outside the cabin, and heard and witnessed the whole thing through the porthole. You, *madame,* if you will hand me the bag, I will deposit it with the purser for you."

Vedova Bey had stepped back involuntarily against the door jamb as Wylie first spoke. He leaned there, anger flaring in his eyes as Vivian Legrand swiftly crossed the cabin and handed the bag to Wylie through the porthole. He tried vainly to catch one glimpse of the face of the man to whom she handed it, but the darkness outside baffled him.

"You do not realize," he said slowly, "that I am powerful in Constantinople. That my power is great. You will surely be sent to prison unless you deal with me. You have committed a murder. I am a witness against you. No one will believe that I, Vedova Bey, would murder my companion."

"Beat it," Vivian told him, anger rising in her like a tide. Forgotten was the fact that her position in a court of law would be a dubious one. Forgotten was the fact that it would be futile to appeal to a consul for aid.

She walked determinedly toward the door.

But Vedova Bey did not move. He still stood there at the doorway, blocking her progress.

"I do not think it will be necessary for me to tell anything," he said softly. "While we have been talking, I have been leaning against the call bell, pressing it with my shoulder. Listen."

She did. There was the sound of voices in the corridor.

"The steward—the night watchman," explained the Levantine Monster. "The constant ringing of the bell has brought them."

A hammering sounded on the door, a shouted command to open.

"Turkish prisons are not pleasant places," said the Levantine Monster, as he took the key from his pocket and prepared to fit it into the door. "Perhaps after the experience of a few days in one of them you may decide to talk to me. I have great authority in Constantinople."

He turned the key in the lock.

"I may go to prison," Vivian Legrand told him grimly, "but I won't stay there. And I won't buy my way out by paying you, either."

Vedova Bey bowed with a smile, threw open the door.

"Summon the captain," he said curtly to the men on the threshold. "A murder has been committed."

THE EPISODE OF THE LEAGUE OF DEATH

*Vivian Legrand Uses Her Fiendish Genius
to Strangle a Turkish Warden and Escape
the Only Jail That Ever Caught Her*

1

THERE WAS MURDER in Vivian Legrand's eyes as she faced Vedova Bey across the table in the warden's room of the Constantinople prison; murder because the Bey was responsible for her being there; murder because for the first time in her life even her fertile brain could see no way out of the situation in which she found herself.

"Have you not learned your lesson?" demanded Vedova Bey, his yellowish, catlike eyes gleaming like twin flames. "Your life is like a speck of dust in my hands."

"Take care that the speck of dust does not blind you," Vivian Legrand flung back at him.

The brown mask of the man's face was turned toward her, a devilish and cruel cunning in every one of its creases.

"I warned you there on the steamer," he said, "that I had great influence in Constantinople—that it was a choice of revealing to me who has the money you stole from the banker, Paul Sammard—or of rotting in a Turkish jail. And it is in a Turkish jail that you find yourself now."

"But where I shall not stay," Vivian Legrand flung at him.

Her voice, ordinarily low and rich and marked by a musical huskiness, was hard now, hard as flint; and there was the glint of ice in the narrowed green eyes. Anger burned in her, burning darkly, like flames obscured by smoke, but she did not permit it to interfere with the chill precision with which her mind was working.

She ran no risk of falling into the error of misjudging her enemy. She was a keen judge of human nature, and she saw in the Bey a predatory monster. He was the sort of man who would stab even while he held out the hand of welcome. She had not been summoned from her cell for empty conversation, she knew.

The Bey laughed, a short ugly laugh. He shrugged.

"Did you ever hear of the bastinado, my dear lady?" His voice reeked with a calm, ghastly brutality, the complete brutality of an animal, dominated by a human intelligence, that had caused Vivian Legrand, on first meeting him, to nickname him the Levantine Monster.

"Ah, I see that you have. It is an old and very efficient method of extracting pearls of truth. You take a rod and strike the bare soles of the victim's feet. Not hard, my dear lady, not hard at all. Quite gently. But it is kept up. After a few hours… but I am sure you have sufficient imagination to understand what has happened by then, without being told. Of course—those little feet of yours are quite soft and tender—an hour or less might be quite sufficient for you."

Vivian Legrand made a quick gesture that brushed the words aside as being unimportant, but her eyes flashed ominously.

"I DO NOT frighten easily," she told him calmly. Her narrowed eyes, rather heavy lidded, were baffling as she watched him warily. Those eyes told an onlooker only what their owner wished them to, and just now there was nothing in them that he could read.

"Ah, no," the Turk protested. "I do not seek to frighten

"You'll live a lot longer if you drop that gun," Vivian murmured

you." A palpable emanation of evil struck from him, giving the lie to his words. "There is a great deal of noise, of course, after the first hour, but do not let that concern you. These old walls were built for just such situations. You might scream until your throat ruptured and no one would be the wiser."

"I don't doubt," Vivian told him contemptuously, "that you are perfectly capable of doing what you have described—but you won't have the opportunity."

"And why not, dear lady?"

"Because I have no intention of staying here."

"No?" He smiled a trifle grimly. "Possibly you look for aid from your accomplice outside... the man to whom you passed the package of money. Granted that I do not yet know who he is. But I will. He will make some move to communicate with you, and then I shall know."

Vivian Legrand's eyes were mere slits through which

green fire shone. She knew that Adrian Wylie would not be such a fool as to try to communicate with her here in prison, or even appear to be interested in her fate. Astute crook that he was, he would realize that such a move would stamp him instantly as the man who held possession of the money. And, equally well, she knew that he would make every possible undercover effort to rescue her from her perilous situation.

Vedova Bey spoke again.

"Are you willing to tell me where the money is?" he demanded. "Tell me, and you walk out of here a free woman, the charge of murder against you dismissed. Refuse and… well, some people are never able to walk again after a very short period of the bastinado."

For a second she felt a trickle of fear that was like an icy finger, a sensation that came to her with the thought of those slender feet of hers bruised and scarred. It was not cowardice. This extraordinary woman could not have done the things that she did and have the slightest streak of cowardice in her nature.

It was more a bleak realization of the fact that the perfection of her form and face was the basis of her success as the world's most dangerous and glamorous criminal. Fear of danger or death she had none. But fear that some part of her physical perfection might be marred was very real to her.

It was a fear that she guarded carefully, lest it became known and held over her like a club by some member of the gang. Even Adrian Wylie, her closest confidant, did not know of it until years later.

Her slim fingers went up slowly and gently touched

the red hair that covered her head. The simple gesture was innocuous enough—until it was quite completed. And the completion did not come until she had answered his veiled threat.

"I shall walk, Vedova Bey," she told him gently. She was smiling, but her eyes were deadly cold. "Walk sufficiently well to see you die by my own hands."

Then it came. When her hands dropped from arranging her hair she was all set for instantaneous action. That action was as swift and true as the snap of a steel trap.

Her hand dropped to the level of the table behind which she stood—and snatched up a heavy brass candlestick. She raised it in the air. Another instant it would have crashed across the Turk's skull, braining him.

But Vedova Bey seized her wrist, held it tightly. He called loudly. The door was flung open and two guards rushed in and dragged Vivian Legrand away. But not before she had managed to sink her teeth deeply into Vedova Bey's hand.

"You hell cat," snarled the Bey, as the two guards pulled her away from him. "You shall pay for that! I shall get a special order, signed by the Sultan's minister of police, to permit me to take you away, for the sake of your health."

Vivian Legrand read in his glittering yellow eyes just how much her health would be safeguarded once she were completely in his hands, and out of the prison, where foreign consuls might come prying around to see that the prisoner was not mistreated.

2

NEVER ONCE, DURING her career as blackmailer, had Vivian Legrand found herself trapped by the police, and it was the irony of fate that she should find herself immured in a Turkish prison for a crime that she did not commit.

With Adrian Wylie, her companion in crime and chief of staff of her criminal activities, she had been traveling from Monte Carlo to Turkey on a Turkish steamer. With them was traveling 350,000 francs, fruit of her blackmail of Sammard, the Monte Carlo banker.

Vedova Bey and a companion had embarked on the same steamer, intent on wresting the money from them, and had succeeded. In turn, Vivian Legrand had taken the money back again, and passed it through the porthole of the cabin to Wylie, on the deck outside—but not before Vedova Bey had shot and killed his accomplice, and fixed the blame on Vivian.

He gave her the alternative of revealing to him the identity of the person to whom she had passed the packet of money or of going to a Turkish jail on a murder charge on arrival in Constantinople.

Vivian Legrand chose jail, and immediately after the ship docked she was rushed to a filthy cell in the ancient prison. On one side a huge Negress, Galouba, was imprisoned, and on the other a Macedonian girl, Kara. Both of them were in prison on the charge of slaying a Turkish tax collector.

There was little privacy in these cells. They were merely stone boxes with grilled fronts of steel, and the three women had become acquainted because of their common suffering and their common misery.

As Vivian Legrand returned to her cell in the grip of the chief warder himself, Galouba, the Negress, flung an insulting phrase at the man. Once inside the cell Vivian turned.

"Would you like to make some money—a great deal of money?" she asked the chief warden.

"You have no money," the warden said shrewdly. He knew that she had not, because he had been present when she was searched.

"Not with me," Vivian Legrand admitted. What the warden did not know was the fact that in searching her a pair of jeweled garters, rolled in the top of her stockings, had been overlooked. "But I can get money—and you shall have it if you will smuggle a letter out of the prison for me."

"Be careful," urged the girl, Kara. "A writing is like a snake. It may turn and bite you."

"Silence!" snarled the warden with a threatening gesture.

"Bah! Fatted hog, the heel of my spine to your unclean father," retorted the girl with the ready abuse of the Orient.

With the complaisance of the East, which permits an insult to slide from consciousness like water from a duck's back, the warden ignored her.

"It is too dangerous," he said to Vivian. But there was a light of greed in his eyes.

"There will be no danger," she told him. "No one will ever know."

"How much?" he countered, the Oriental instinct of bargain alive in him.

"More than you have ever had before."

Without another word the warden turned on his heel and vanished down the long, gloomy corridor.

"He will betray you," the girl called Kara told her simply. "Dogs like him have no honor."

"I must take the chance," Vivian Legrand said. "If I can get word to a friend, he may be able to help me in some way."

"If I could get word to my father," Kara said wistfully, "he would come with his men and tear this prison apart, stone by stone."

The girl's father, Vivian Legrand learned, was Balthazar, a notorious bandit whose band roamed European Turkey, preying on wealthy Turks and robbing pretty much as they pleased. A bit of graft now and then to underpaid Turkish officials and he was left alone.

In a moment or two more the warden was back with writing material. Hastily Vivian Legrand scribbled a note to Wylie and addressed it in care of an Armenian dealer in rugs with whom she knew Wylie must sooner or later get in touch. The influence of Vedova Bey was great, but she knew that in Turkey judicious bribes were more potent, even, than influence. She handed the note to the warden.

"The money," demanded that individual.

SILENTLY VIVIAN LEGRAND extended to him through the bars the garter that she had taken from its hiding place beneath the rolled top of her stocking. It was one of a pair given her by the Rajah of Salingar, and was set with small rubies from the rajah's own mines in the East Indies.

The man's eyes gleamed as he saw the glittering jewels. Then his face fell.

"A woman's trinket," he said scornfully. "It is not real."

"Fool," snapped Vivian Legrand. "My other jewels, taken from me at the prison office, were they not real? You know that they were."

The man toyed with the garter thoughtfully, holding it up to the little light that filtered through the window of the corridor, so that the rubies seemed to glow like living, flowing blood.

"If you do not think they are real, then give it back to me," Vivian Legrand said impatiently, "and we will tear up the letter."

"By Allah!" the man swore, "but you are in a hurry! They may be real. I am no bazaar Jew to tell whether they are or not. But there are ways of finding out."

He pocketed the garter. Then, with a smirk, he took a poniard from his belt, slit open the envelope and opened the letter. His face fell. It was in English, and he could not read it.

"Vedova Bey will be interested in this," he said with a grin. "He is still with the governor in his apartment, and he will pay well for a sight of this letter."

"But I have paid you to deliver it to the address," Vivian Legrand reminded him.

Whatever she may have felt, her voice betrayed nothing. But her eyes had narrowed and the arches of her brows had drawn together. An idea had flashed into her mind, an idea in which there was a glimmering of hope. It was a terri-

bly faint glimmering; the
chances were a thousand
to one against it.

Almost a forlorn
hope, but it seemed the
one solution to her situ-
ation—the one road out
of her peril.

Vivian Legrand

"The jewels were
not pay," the warden
informed her compla-
cently. "They were forfeit.
I would have taken them from you, anyhow."

"But you are a fool," Vivian Legrand told him in a
wondering voice. It was with an effort that she kept her
face in an expressionless mould. "I have two legs, two
stockings, two jeweled garters."

She pretended to be stupid, as she stood there, every
nerve keyed and strained to concert pitch. The warden was
fool enough to believe that such a woman could really be
so stupid.

"The other one is yours also," she said sweetly, "if I give
it to you, you will deliver the letter?"

"By Allah, that I will!" the man swore, and Vivian
Legrand stripped the second glittering ornament from
her leg and dangled it before him. He reached for it. She
drew back.

"Can I trust you?" she demanded. "How do I know that
you will keep your word and deliver the letter? You might
take the two garters and tear up the letter."

She was playing the most dangerous game in the world,

and playing it not merely against a callous, greedy man, but against Vedova Bey, a monster who held human life even cheaper than she did. A man who held it as the cheapest thing at his command. Her life would go out like a snuffed candle if she failed and the warden reported what had occurred.

The two women on either side of Vivian Legrand's cell were listening intently to the conversation.

"Do not trust the son of a mangy dog," spat out Kara, her black eyes snapping. "He is a thief. He will keep the jewels, and not deliver the letter."

"I must trust him," Vivian Legrand argued, apparently on the verge of tears. "He can take it anyway."

She caught the eye of the Macedonian girl. The two women looked at one another. A quickly-veiled lightning flash of understanding passed between them as Kara studied Vivian Legrand's face. A light came into her own eyes, and she flung a swift, hurried phrase in a dialect that the warden did not understand to the giant Negress in the cell that adjoined Vivian Legrand's. A grunt told her that it had been understood.

Vivian leaned against the stone wall of the cell, on the other side of which was the huge Negress, Galouba, and held out the jewel again.

"Here," she said wearily, "take it."

One chance in a hundred that the scheme would work. Gambling odds. She had played longer odds during her career, and won through.

3

THE MAN DID not see danger in the cunning gesture. He leaned forward, his brown face etched in lines of greed, his fingers twisting as if he were already grasping the second jeweled ornament. He reached greedily for it—and, like a coiled snake, Vivian Legrand struck through the bars.

Her hand shot out and seized his right wrist—gave a swift jerk. Caught off balance, he reeled against the iron bars at the edge of the other cell. And instantly the great black gorilla-like paw of the Negress in the next cell shot out and seized him by the throat.

The man could not cry out, but he struggled fiercely. His freehand clawed at the dark fingers about his throat. Unable to release that strangling grip, his hand dropped toward his belt, where his poniard rested in its sheath. Vivian Legrand reached out and seized his wrist, grasping it tightly. If he got a grip on that poniard she knew they were lost.

There came a low mutter from the Negress, and although Vivian Legrand could not understand the language, she sensed what the woman meant. She was losing her grip on the warden.

Once his throat was free his call would bring aid.

All three struggled desperately. The fight became a silent, murderous stalemate. Reaching through the bars made it difficult for the Negress to get an effective grip on the warden's throat. She could not strangle him, and yet he could not tear himself free. For all three the poniard in his belt spelled victory. By holding his wrist, Vivian Legrand prevented him from reaching the knife, but if she released him to snatch for it herself her doom was sealed. The terrible irony of the predicament struck her like a splash of icy water, but her mind was working with the keen coldness that made her a criminal genius.

She must reach that knife herself, and she knew that her move would be effective only if carried out with instantaneous precision. She jerked the man's arm through the bar, savagely, exerting all her strength. She pushed it as far down as she could and pressed it against the bars. Her raised knee went against the arm, and then, with all the leverage she could muster, she snapped the arm back across the cell bar. The bone broke with a sickening snap. Even the grip of the giant Negress could not entirely stifle the howl of pain that rose in the throat of the maimed man.

With a swift movement Vivian Legrand dropped the helpless arm and snatched the knife. Neat and exact as a surgeon, she drove the knife home into his throat just below the dark fingers that were clenched about it.

"Don't let him drop," Vivian Legrand snapped savagely at the woman, and Kara, seething with excitement in the other cell, realizing that the Negress would not understand, translated the command.

The warden's one good arm thrashed for a moment, then he went limp. The jugular vein had been severed. Blood spurted all over the two women.

NOW THAT HE was dead their problem was even greater,

for his keys were attached to his belt by a chain. If the Negress let go her grip and he collapsed into the corridor they could only watch him sprawl there until a guard arrived to detect and punish their fruitless crime.

"Kara," Vivian Legrand gasped, "tell Galouba that we must pass the body along the front of my cell until it is close to the door. Then you can hold him upright while I unlock it."

From the Macedonian girl, dancing with excitement in her cell, came a string of swift, staccato syllables. The Negress grunted assent.

It was a desperate expedient. Even the giant strength of the Negress was beginning to give way under the strain of holding the limp body upright, and the strain would become even greater when the body was passed along the bars to a spot where Galouba's arms could no longer reach. Then Vivian Legrand would be compelled to depend on her strength alone.

Slowly the two women shifted the body of the dead warden along the front of the wall, an inch at a time. Vivian Legrand's arms ached, and she could hear the breath of the Negress coming in little hissing gasps as she strained to the utmost to reach an inch or two further. From between the bars of her cell Kara stretched out her arm.

Her fingers fell short by inches of reaching the body.

It was up to Vivian Legrand alone to move that limp, heavy bundle of dead flesh across those intervening inches, until Kara could aid her.

From some distance away came the clang of an iron door. The guard was in the next corridor. At any moment he might open the door of the corridor that ran along their own tier of cells, and, dim as the light was, he could not fail to note the situation in a single glance.

"Hurry!" gasped Kara.

The blood drummed in Vivian Legrand's ears as she tried to force the body further along the steel grating. Pressing herself closer to the bars, she exerted every ounce of her strength to move it. Using her knee as a brace, she shoved it between the bars as far as it would go, resting some of the terrible weight upon the iron. But even that was insufficient. The body began slowly to sag as she inched it along. The space between that body and the tips of Kara's outstretched fingers seemed vast, the time endless.

Footsteps were audible in the next corridor now. They were approaching the door of their own corridor. For what seemed interminable, slow-ticking minutes Vivian Legrand fought desperately. Slowly but inexorably the body began to slip from her fingers. She could hear the hissing, agonized breathing of the Negress as she watched the progress of the struggle and saw liberty slowly slipping through their fingers.

Then catastrophe. Vivian's grasp slipped. One hand lost its grip entirely, and the body slowly began to topple toward the floor. She strove desperately, but she could not halt it.

It was only the tiniest of incidents that saved them—the fact that the body of the warden toppled sidewise toward the floor instead of backward. That movement brought it within the range of Kara's fingers.

In an instant the Macedonian girl had a grip on the collar of the dead man's tunic.

Renewed hope ran through Vivian Legrand like the tingling of an electric shock. It gave her new strength, and she exerted all her power. Now that she had assistance the thing was easier. In a moment more the two women had the limp body at the stone wall that divided the two cells, holding it up on either side.

"Can you hold him up alone?" Vivian gasped in a whisper to Kara. "I'll need both hands to get his keys and unlock the door."

"For a little while, not for long," the girl said. "But hurry! The guard! We have only a moment!"

It was the feat of an acrobat for Vivian Legrand to seize the keys dangling from the dead man's belt and try them in the lock of the cell door, one by one, until she found the one that fitted. Only the fact that the whole front of the cell was an open grillwork of iron made it possible. In a modern jail it could not have been done.

There was a gasp of victory from Vivian Legrand, and the door of her cell swung open. And at the same moment she heard the rattle of keys as the approaching guard prepared to unlock the door opening into their corridor. Even as she stepped into the corridor she heard the key grating in the lock. The two women in the adjoining cells raised stark and hopeless faces toward the door.

4

SWIFTLY VIVIAN LEGRAND scooped up the poniard with
which she had killed the chief warden and rushed on noiseless feet down the stone-floored corridor, the bloodstained
blade in her hand. She had barely time to reach the end of
the corridor when the door opened. Fortunately it swung
inward, so that she was concealed as it opened.

The guard stepped inside and gave the door a careless
shove. The movement was his last. As the door slammed
the poniard was buried to the hilt between his shoulders.

For a split second the man stood as though carved from
stone. He might have cried out, but Vivian Legrand's palm
flashed across his face, sealing his lips. Then he gave a sharp
gasp and collapsed to the floor.

With a long-drawn sigh of relief she straightened up.
Within the space of fifteen minutes she had killed two
men, killed them as deliberately, as callously as a tigress.
Swiftly, with no more regret for what she had done than a
beast of prey, she went back down the corridor. Relief was
written on the faces of the two women who had aided her.
It was only the work of a moment for her to release them.

"Allah be praised!" Kara said. "Thou art a woman worthy
of the hills from which I come." She was tall and lithe, this
Kara, with black hair which fell in heavy braids over each

shoulder and bold black eyes set deep below boldly curved brows. She flung her arms about Vivian Legrand.

The Negress said nothing, but there was a look of deep gratitude on the blank face that had that faint purple bloom which is seen only on the skin of the pure-blooded African.

For a moment the three stood there in the corridor, bloodstained, looking like three strange furies. They were free of their cells. But how to escape from the prison?

"Are you familiar with the jail?" Vivian Legrand asked Kara.

The girl shook her head, and in answer to a rapid question from Kara the giant Negress shook her head also.

Motioning them to follow her, Vivian led the way down the corridor, stopping for a moment to rifle the body of the last man she had killed. In his pocket she found a gun, fully loaded, and she nodded her head in satisfaction. The Legrand brain was working full speed now. The plan that had been nebulous, indefinite, desperate in its first conception had taken form and substance. If luck was with her, their escape from prison was assured.

The door leading into the next corridor had not been locked when the guard closed it, but undoubtedly the one at the further end would be locked. Vivian Legrand took the dead man's keys, and the three bloodstained women made their way on down the corridor. The door was locked. Cautiously, Vivian tried the dead man's keys until she found one that fitted, and turned the lock gently. Opening the door the merest trifle she peered down the long, low-roofed passage, dimly lit by rays of light from narrow slits of barred windows near the ceiling.

Lounging at the far end of the corridor, the last of the

cell corridors, was a guard. Beyond him, she remembered, lay the office of the chief warden and the living quarters of the governor of the prison.

She knew that they could never reach that guard at the far end of the corridor without the alarm being given. Hastily she whispered instructions to Kara, who, in turn, translated them to the giant Negress. Then Vivian Legrand rapped sharply on the closed door.

The guard straightened up abruptly. He came slowly down the corridor. Vivian Legrand rapped again. There was nothing in the sound to rouse his suspicions. If he gave the matter any particular thought, the idea that it might be escaping prisoners rapping to attract his attention never entered his head. He reached the door—and Vivian Legrand flung it open, stepped swiftly across the threshold, and before the man could recover from his surprise had jabbed the gun against his stomach.

"One sound and I shoot," she said.

The man started to speak, but one look at her face, her bloodstained clothes, and the green light flaming in her eyes cut short whatever he had intended to say.

"Is his Excellency Vedova Bey still in the apartment of the governor?" Vivian Legrand demanded.

The man nodded dumbly.

"Take us there!" she ordered. "If you are questioned, you will say that you are ordered by the governor to bring us into his presence. And one false move, one false word, and I shoot."

Again the man nodded. Fear rode his face.

Silently the strange procession made its way down the corridor, up a flight of stairs. Both Kara and the Negress were armed now. Each had taken a poniard from one of the dead men, and had hidden them under their clothing.

Stopping before a door their guide indicated dumbly that it was the entrance to the governor's apartment.

Vivian Legrand rapped sharply, and as she did so Kara and the Negress ranged themselves on either side of the unfortunate man who had been their guide, their poniards held in readiness. The man's face was almost white beneath its brown as he glanced at the deadly weapons.

The door was flung open and an angry governor stood upon the threshold.

THE GOVERNOR WAS a Turk of pure Osmanli stock who, though belonging to a military family, had been sent by his father to England and the Continent for school and university education.

He took in, almost instantly, the import of the scene before him. With a quick motion an automatic appeared in his hand. He was quick, but Vivian Legrand was quicker. Her own hand flashed forward like lightning, and the governor felt the sharp jar of her gun muzzle as it came to rest against his body.

"You'll live a lot longer if you drop that gun," she murmured in French.

Her voice was biting. Her eyes were like twin green rapiers. The governor retired a pace, looking about him wildly, with unmistakable fear in his eyes. For a second he stared at the slim, red-haired girl, his fingers clenching and unclenching as though he would like to strangle her with his bare hands. Then the automatic dropped to the carpet.

Vivian advanced slowly into the room, the muzzle of her gun prodding the governor slowly backward with each step.

The two women, with their trembling prisoner between them, followed her into the room.

A man of more than usual acumen, the governor realized at once that his life was nothing to this red-head if it stood between her and her aim. Vivian Legrand flung a terse, whispered command over her shoulder. The door was closed and the key turned in the lock.

"Vedova Bey. Where is he?" she demanded tersely.

The governor answered instantly, instinctively lowering his tone to hers, as if realizing that it would not be safe to speak more loudly.

"In the next room."

"Go ahead," she told him, "but don't try anything. If you do the prison will need a new governor."

Vedova Bey was seated with his back to the door as she stepped into the room. From behind him there suddenly came Vivian Legrand's voice, full of mockery, yet deadly in its menace.

"An unexpected meeting, is it not, Vedova Bey?"

With a growl the man leaped to his feet and whipped out his gun. Death glittered in the black eyes, narrowed to slits, as he stared at the apparition of the woman he had thought safely caged in her cell below. But he was not a fool. His own gun was out, but her gun was held steady upon him, and he knew that she would not hesitate to shoot.

No one moved or spoke.

Then Vedova Bey shrugged and dropped the hand that held the gun.

"That's better," snapped Vivian Legrand. "It gives you a few minutes longer to live. Drop the gun."

He obeyed.

"Take that gun," Vivian ordered Kara, still keeping her own pistol trained upon the man whom she had nick-named the Levantine Monster.

"A foolish thing," he grated. "I do not know how you escaped from your cell—but you will never escape from the prison itself."

"Oh, yes we will," Vivian told him calmly. "Search him," she ordered Kara.

The Macedonian girl's hand ran over his clothing swiftly and she laid another pistol, found in a shoulder holster, on the table.

"Give it to Galouba," Vivian ordered. Then she turned to the governor. "Sit down," she commanded.

The man sank into a chair.

"Write us a safe conduct from the prison. Say that we are being taken to the minister of police by his Excellency Vedova Bey for questioning."

"It—it will do you no good," stammered the governor, his face pale.

"Galouba," ordered Vivian Legrand, "take your knife. I shall count. When I reach three, start sinking the knife you carry into his flesh, just a little deeper with each count, until he writes—or the knife can be driven no deeper."

Kara translated in swift, staccato syllables. The giant Negress moved up behind the governor, the point of her knife resting lightly on the flesh of his shoulder, just below the neck. She was a fearsome sight, her clothes blood-stained, her gigantic black paw grasping the handle of the knife, her thick lips curled back over ragged, yellow teeth.

"One," began Vivian Legrand. Kara translated the

numeral in the only dialect that the Negress knew. "Two. Three…"

"I'll write it," the governor screamed. He snatched up the pen and began to scrawl Arabic characters upon a sheet of official stationery.

5

"WE CAN READ Arabic," Vivian Legrand warned him grimly.

"Put in nothing that would not be an official order." Her sardonic gaze shifted upon the motionless Vedova Bey.

"It was more than kind of you," she told him smoothly, "to wait here until we had escaped from our cells. You see, you are going out with us. You will be our safe-conduct."

The Bey's muscles twitched like those of an animal about to spring, but otherwise he did not move.

"You need not hope to make a break—to escape," she told him. "There will be three pistols trained on you. If you make a single false move you'll drop with three bullets in you, and we'll shoot our way out."

He did not answer, and the girl, Kara, eyed him sardonically.

"It is a pity," she said, "that my father is not here. I would take delight in seeing him tie you to two wild horses, one leg to each. For that is what he would do to you."

Vedova Bey paled slightly. He knew of Kara's father, and there was no doubt in his mind that the stalwart chieftain of the Macedonian bandits would take delight in doing just that. He had done it before during the years that he had roamed the hills, working for the freedom of Macedonia from the Turks in much the same manner that the "invisible empire," years later under the leadership of his successor, the dreaded Ivan Mihailoff, was to work. It was this same organization, of which Kara's father was a high member, that assassinated Todor Alexandroff in Vienna in 1914 and King Alexander of Yugoslavia in Marseilles in 1934.

The governor laid down his pen. Vivian Legrand picked up the sheet of paper, extended it to Kara.

"Read it," she ordered curtly.

The girl read it swiftly.

"It is what you ordered, nothing else," she said.

Vivian nodded. "Tie up the governor and the guard," she ordered. "Tie them well, and gag them."

She watched as the two women tightened the bonds, using strips from the silken window drapes as ropes, and other pieces of the same material as gags. Then she handed the governor's order to Vedova Bey.

"I shall kill you," she said thoughtfully, "later. Your presence can be useful now. If we tried to escape without you some officer might get suspicious."

The words seemed to hang in the room. Coldly, implacably, without a shade of inflection in her level voice, Vivian Legrand read the death warrant of Vedova Bey. She was as merciless, as utterly devoid of the usual human emotions as a statue. Vedova Bey knew that, once outside those prison walls, his life would mean no more to her than a snap of her fingers; knew, also, that any suspicious move he might make now would serve only to hasten the end.

Slowly the three women, with Vedova Bey slightly in advance, made their way down the stairs to the great gate where a lounging guard came to his feet at sight of the approaching group and called an officer.

The rapid sequence of events had edged Vivian Legrand's nerves, and the delay was galling. Her face was set, tense, but her green eyes were cold and hard as ice and her brain was clicking like a machine. The final, culminating moment was at hand. Seconds were vital. Investigation meant defeat. At any moment the death of the two keepers, the two trussed-up men in the governor's apartment above might be discovered, the alarm given.

There was wonder in the officer's eyes as he surveyed the three bloodstained women, and then read the official order of release that the Bey handed him.

"It is unusual," he said thoughtfully.

"You have the governor's order," Vedova Bey said sharply, "and I brought the order for their release to his excellency from the minister of police myself."

He had not missed, from the corner of his eye, Vivian's little movement as she came a step nearer to him. He knew, almost as if she had spoken the words aloud, that if the officer refused them passage until he had consulted the governor that she would not hesitate to shoot them down and attempt to open the gate herself. And he knew that he would be the first to fall in the hail of bullets that would be turned loose. He threw every scrap of arrogance that he could muster into his tones.

"Are you daring to question me?" he roared at the officer in charge of the guard. "Do you dare to question the governor's authority, the authority of the minister of police? Why, you insolent dog, the Sultan himself shall hear of this!"

Had it been anyone except Vedova Bey the scheme would probably not have worked. But the officer knew the far-reaching influence of this Levantine who had turned Moslem to further his own interest—and knew that any complaint that the Bey might make could easily reach the Sultan himself. Your true Moslem hates the man who has embraced the faith of Islem for the sake of expediency, but nothing of this showed in the officer's face as he bowed low, with a murmured apology, and ordered the gate opened.

Vedova Bey, with the back of his hand, wiped cold drops of sweat from his forehead. The situation had been so tense that fear came after danger was past.

The slow swinging open of that massive gate was like a drink of strong wine to Vivian Legrand. Never again, in her hectic career, was she to feel the strong, lifting sense of freedom that came to her as the warm sun struck across her uplifted face. It would have been difficult to believe, seeing her then, that she was one of the most dangerous and glamorous criminals in the world. She had been allowed no change of clothes. Her dress was filthy with blood and dirt, and the red hair, above the exotic, exquisitely modeled face, was a tangled mass.

WITH VEDOVA BEY still slightly in advance, the four passed out into the narrow street. None of the three women, alert as they were, noticed the action of a chauffeur in the front seat of a big car parked near the prison gates. At first sight of Vedova Bey he had half risen from his seat, as if to get out of the car. A close observer might have noticed that the man sank back again almost concurrently with a singular gesture of Vedova Bey's hand.

The chauffeur was still watching the strange group as

they passed him and approached a carriage standing by the curb further down the street, and his gaze was more intent than the occasion seemed to warrant, almost as if he were waiting for instructions of some sort.

The byplay went unnoticed, however, and the four climbed into the rickety old vehicle with the three women entirely unconscious of the intent regard of the chauffeur.

A lemon-water seller, clashing together the two brass drinking cups, was calling out in strident voice:

"Cool water, Excellency, cool, sweet lemon-water."

He was an old man, but spare and straight; his steady black eyes as keen as those of a man half his age, yet his beardless face was crossed and crisscrossed by wrinkles so deep that in the strong light of day they looked like a mesh of black lines etched on a copper mask.

He swaggered up to them, his gaze arrogant, and extended one of his cups, the goatskin bag on his shoulder held in readiness to fill it.

"Will his Excellency drink?" he inquired.

It was Kara who leaned out of the carriage and answered him.

"Begone!" she said harshly. "His Excellency Vedova Bey is leaving the city and has no need to drink."

For a moment the old man stared straight at them. At mention of the Bey's name a flash came into his eyes and went like summer lightning. Then he stepped back with a little bow.

"Where are you taking me?" demanded the Bey as the vehicle started forward, rattling over the uneven cobble-stones.

"That need not worry you," Vivian Legrand said grimly. "You will not leave the place, wherever it is."

"I am worth a great deal more to you alive than dead," the Bey said shrewdly. "Soon your escape from the prison will be discovered and the alarm given. You will never be able to leave Constantinople. But I could get you out of the city."

"You *will* get us out of the city," Vivian Legrand told him curtly, "and there will be no bargain."

"You will be safe nowhere in Turkey without my aid," he insisted. "I can aid you to reach Salonika, where I have a brother. He will see that you cross the border without trouble."

Vivian Legrand's smile was sardonic. She knew of Gregor, the brother of Vedova Bey, knew that he did a brisk trade in girls destined for the harems of wealthy Turks. She could imagine the fate that would be in store for the three of them if she were fool enough to accept the Bey's offer.

"Will you bargain—my life against your safety?" he queried.

"No," Vivian said shortly.

The man's manner puzzled her. He seemed to be talking just for the sake of saying something. Stalling for time, as though he expected to keep her occupied for a few minutes to gain something.

The rickety carriage swung around a corner and suddenly Kara cried out a warning. But it was too late.

With a running leap a man stood on the little step on either side of the carriage. Steady guns covered the occupants. Another man had scrambled to the driver's seat, his gun held in readiness for trouble.

There was no time for defense. The grim realization of defeat when escape was in their grasp slowed the beat of Vivian Legrand's heart.

"Did you really think," the Bey asked, his voice full of venom, "that you had outwitted me? This carriage was followed from the moment it left the prison. I signaled my chauffeur, as we passed my car, that I was in trouble. And now, your gun, please!"

Silently Vivian handed it over. The pistols were taken from the hands of the two women with her.

But only Vivian Legrand saw the look that flashed deep in the black eyes of the Macedonian girl, the queer, cold expression that settled upon her face.

Vedova Bey gave a swift order. The driver cracked his whip, the mangy ponies plunged forward, and in a few moments the gates of a walled courtyard clanged shut behind them.

Torches set in holders, flaring red in the gathering dusk, lit up the flagged courtyard like a stage setting, outlining in the ruddy light the little knot of men who came forward to meet them.

From behind the house the mosque of the Five Holy Pilgrims reared its minaret of faience tiling. The muezzin's voice, chanting the *maghrib*, the last pray of the day, drifted out suddenly across the scene.

The carriage came to a halt and Vedova Bey alighted.

"I hope," he said, holding out his hand to aid Vivian Legrand to alight, "that you have not forgotten my suggestion of the bastinado. My little residence here is a superb place to put it into operation."

He added with a certain grimness:

"I realize that your weapons have been taken away, but I might remind you that my men are good shots—and will not hesitate to shoot."

6

IT WAS AT that moment that it came—the sound of a queer, wailing call came from outside the wall—the sound of a lemon-water seller crying his wares. And before they could stop her, Kara answered it.

Instantly a man appeared on top of the wall surrounding the courtyard, a ragged, lithe fellow holding a knife along which the light of the torches rippled like tongues of flame. He leaped lightly to the ground, and for the first time one of the men who had been Vedova Bey's guards saw him.

He gave a little cry of warning and sprang toward him. Without waiting for the attack, the newcomer leaped in. There was no foolish upward fling of the arm in his style of fighting. Like a streak of ruddy light the knife ripped in, straight for the heart. The Bey's man sobbed once, and sank to the ground.

"One move, one step, and your master dies," Kara cried in rippling Turkish. Then swiftly to Vivian, "My father and his men."

But the warning was hardly needed. By now there were other men on the wall, swarming over its top like cats. Caught between this new attack, and the thought that a single aggressive move on their part might cause the knife in the hand of the lemon-water seller to plunge into their master's body, they did not move.

In an instant the newcomers had swarmed over the walls. The quick hiss of breath as they closed in was like the sibilant fury of serpents. The little knot of Vedova Bey's followers were surrounded, disarmed, their hands bound behind their backs.

A frightened servant in the doorway of the house, who had witnessed the attack, turned with a squeal to flee. But he had waited too long. A knife caught him in the back even as he ran, and he plunged to the ground, his blood staining the marble doorstep on which he rested. Without waiting for orders a part of the group of men plunged into the house.

The lemon-water seller, who was Balthazar, Kara's father and chief of the Balkan robber band, thrust his face into Vedova Bey's and leered.

"Peace on Allah and his family!" he boomed. "Truly Allah is great. I followed you as soon as you drove away. We have been watching that accursed jail for days, waiting for a chance to get my daughter away."

A few swift phrases from Kara put him into possession of the facts, and he turned to Vivian Legrand and bowed low, his hand to his forehead.

"My house is thine, for what you have done for my daughter," he declared. "Shall I kill this dog for you?" He indicated Vedova Bey.

She shook her head.

"I have other plans for him. But first, there is still the danger of escaping from the city," she answered.

"By the horns of the Archangel Ishrafeel, you shall go with us, friend of my house," Balthazar declared, "into our mountains. It will be easy. The dress of a Moslem

woman—a veil which no man dare lift to see thy face—
and you can laugh as you pass the very soldiers who search
for you."

"Good," Vivian Legrand said. "Can you also take a
message to a friend who does not know that I have escaped
from prison?"

She had no means of reaching Adrian Wylie before they
left the city. The only thing that she could do was to send
him a note in care of the Armenian dealers in rugs, with
whom he would sooner or later get in touch. Once he knew
where she was, she knew he would manage to get in touch
with her. Wylie was much too valuable a companion in
crime to be deserted.

"The man who obtains the clothes can also deliver your
message," Balthazar told her.

She nodded and turned back to Vedova Bey, a smile
wreathing her lips.

"Take off his shoes and hold him," she ordered the giant
negress. Kara translated the order.

A cry broke from Vedova Bey as he realized the reason
for her order.

"No! No! No!—" he screamed. "I will pay—I am
wealthy—"

"We will discuss payment an hour from now," Vivian
Legrand told him.

"**DID YOU EVER** hear of the bastinado?" she went on. There
was an unholy light in her eyes. "Ah, I see that you have.
You take a rod like this"—she took the slender bamboo
cane that the grinning Balthazar handed her—"and strike
the soles of the victim's feet—like this." The Levantine
shuddered at the light tap upon the soles of his bare feet.

"After a few hours of this... but I am sure that you have sufficient imagination to understand what will happen by then."

Each sinister word filled with a terrible menace for Vivian Legrand's victim, was punctuated with a blow as the grinning outlaws gathered around to watch, offering advice as to the next spot for the cane to strike.

Balthazar swore deeply. "By the war cry of Mohammed, that is a woman!" he declared as he watched the blows fall on the bare soles of the writhing Vedova Bey. "I could love that woman!"

"We need not leave for another hour," Vivian Legrand reminded the Bey with sinister emphasis. "Many things can happen in an hour. People have been known to go insane—and I think my strength with hold out long enough to find out."

THE EPISODE OF THE ORIENT EXPRESS ROBBERY

*It Was One of the Siren Vivian Legrand's Most
Daring Crimes—! Here Is the Sensational Story
of How She Robbed the Rich Orient Express*

1

THE LADY FROM HELL was trapped.

She was a prisoner in the camp of Balthazar, the mountain bandit.

The thing had happened twice that day, and this time, as she halted before the extended rifle barrel of the ragged mountaineer in the shadow filled defile of the sun-baked hills, it was too obvious to be coincidence. The gesture was not threatening. The man was smiling, but he shook his head and held his rifle so as to bar her passage away from the camp.

There were only two exits from the hollow in the Macedonian mountains where Balthazar maintained his headquarters, two narrow winding passages whose sides a cat could not have scaled, between rocky, encroaching hills. An hour or so before at the passage at the northern end she had been halted with an almost identical gesture by a guard. And now this.

Her lovely oval face was thoughtful as she turned back toward camp where fires had already begun to spring up in the purple dusk. Trapped, separated from her companion in crime whom she had been compelled to leave in Constantinople when she fled, her situation was not a pleasant one.

Could this barring of her exit have any connection with the black animosity which had grown up in Kara, Balthazar's daughter, toward her? She could see no connection. By all standards, Kara should be eternally grateful to her. It had been Vivian who had made the escape of Kara and her companion, Galouba, the giant negress, possible from the Constantinople prison. She had been grateful… at first.

But within the last few days Kara had changed. Her friendship, eagerly given at first, had slipped into sullenness and now open animosity. Kara, savage and relentless, as cruel toward an enemy as the Lady from Hell herself, was not an enemy to be treated lightly.

Vivian stopped beside one of the fires, the light bringing out headlights of flame in her red hair. Kara, sitting near by, looked up, swept her with flashing black eyes, and then looked down again. Galouba, the giant negress, squatted on her haunches beside Kara, rocking from side to side like a chained jungle beast, to ease the strain on her ankles. She, also, did not meet Vivian's eyes.

And that was a bad sign. The sense of unseen danger was like a cold wind blowing on the back of the Lady from Hell.

"Tell me, Kara," Vivian said suddenly, "why have you come to hate me?"

She knew the dramatic value of sudden attack, and she counted on it in this instance to play in her favor. But it did not work.

"Ai, I hate you," Kara flashed back at her viciously, "and I shall feed you poison, as I did two others before you, if you try to carry out your purpose." She lapsed back into silence, but hate still lingered in her eyes, thrusting at the woman before her like a naked sword.

From the rocking negress came a rumbling assent, and

Wylie struck with his bound legs. The guard staggered

her hands slowly clenched and unclenched as if they ached to clasp themselves around the throat of Vivian. The Lady from Hell had seen them clasped about the neck of a jailer in the Constantinople prison, slowly squeezing life from him, and she had no desire to feel them about her own throat.

Without warning Balthazar suddenly stood beside them. He had donned a green turban, in token of his pilgrimage to the holy wonders of Mecca, and his beard had been freshly dyed scarlet with henna.

"Leave us alone," he said to his daughter without preamble.

Balthazar's orders were invariably obeyed, even by his fiery tempered daughter. Without a word she got to her feet and moved away, accompanied by Galouba.

"I wish to talk with you," Balthazar said in his vibrant bass.

"I am listening," Vivian told him.

"I am a clever man and a brave one," Balthazar told her with the simplicity and directness of the East. "And I would have a wife who is a fit mate for such as myself."

"There are many beautiful girls in your camp," Vivian told him. From the corner of her eye she could see Kara watching them from beside another fire, a dozen paces away, black anger distorting her face. An inkling of the situation began to dawn on her.

"Shall an eagle mate with a sparrow?" Balthazar flashed back at her. "Three wives have I had, but their beauty was like a candle's flame in the wind beside yours. No..." and he held up a hand as Vivian would have spoken. "There is no need to fear a rival in my heart. The three are dead. But if they were not, I would put them away for your sake."

HE SAID IT with simple, sincere ruthlessness. The green eyes of the Lady from Hell had narrowed until they were tiny thoughtful slits as he spoke. So this was the reason for the orders to prevent her leaving camp. She had no intention of becoming the wife of a bandit chief, yet, she knew that unless she could divert the attention of Balthazar from his wooing, he would be mortally affronted.

She leaned forward into the firelight.

"I will not marry a poor man," she told him, matching directness with directness. Yet, there was a light in her eyes that seemed to say that she would like to be persuaded.

"Am I a poor man?" he demanded. The colossal egoism of the man seemed to swell and expand before her hard green eyes. "Who else in these mountains can match their wealth against mine?"

"Horses... cattle... goats... sheep," she told him disdainfully. "Those are not riches to me. Gold… jewels… silks… those are riches for me."

He shrugged his shoulders and spread eloquent hands.

"I will buy them for you," he said.

"Why buy what you can take?" she demanded.

"By Allah, a woman after my own heart," he cried admiringly. "I will raid the palace of the Sultan himself and fill your lap with seventeen camel loads of red Persian gold and jewels." His was the extravagance of the Orient.

Her nostrils quivered. A light came into her green eyes. She knew that the wooing of Balthazar was but a cloak thrown about his real purpose. He would wait, with the patience of the Orient, for a time, then take her. That fact, in itself, did not disturb her so much as the thought that she might be held here in these mountains for months, possibly even years. Whatever she may have felt, her voice betrayed nothing of it as she spoke.

"Why stick your head into a noose, when the things I want lie at your hand, ripe for the plucking?"

"Where?" barked Balthazar.

"On the Orient Express," she told him.

For a moment the man stared at her in stupefied amazement. The Orient Express was, and is, Europe's most famous train, running from Constantinople through Central Europe. It symbolized luxury, wealth.

"By Allah, that is man's talk," he ejaculated.

"Can there be a richer prize?" she queried. It was a cunning thrust, but the man did not see the crafty purpose that lay behind her words.

"None richer," Balthazar said absently. "It has been talked of much, and more than one has tried to rob it, but all have failed. The train is not a beast to be stopped with a shot, and it is well guarded."

"You have men enough to overcome the guards," Vivian argued. She paused and then added insultingly. "But perhaps they are not good enough fighters to beard the soldiers on the train."

"By Allah, they are ten times better than those misbegotten sons of pigs," Balthazar swore.

For a moment the green eyes of the Lady from Hell seemed to flame with an emotion which did not appear on the carved ivory mask of her face. Then her eyelids dropped across them again.

"Then why not snatch the richest prize in the mountains?" she said. "There is often gold being shipped from Constantinople to banks in Vienna, Belgrade, Paris. There are wealthy passengers… women with jewels. They can be kidnaped… held for ransom."

SHE STOPPED SUDDENLY. An idea came like an electric shock. Like a flash across her mind had darted the value of such a passenger, and with it the chance to not only escape from Balthazar, but take with her the loot of the Orient Express as well.

"You have spies in Constantinople. Let them find out when there is to be an important passenger on the Orient Express at the same time as a shipment of gold… a very important passenger, an ambassador, a consul, a member of an embassy whose government will force the Sultan to pay well for his release. That part of it will not be difficult. There is a passenger list made out for each running of the train, and places are engaged far in advance. Send Kara to board the train in Constantinople, to make sure that the right man is kidnaped."

She paused a moment and looked at him with eyes that were as shallow and expressionless as Yunnan jade, then threw caution overboard.

"Two things you must do if you wish me to marry you... rescue Effendi Wylie who was left behind in Constantinople when I fled from prison... and rob the Orient Express."

"And suppose," queried Balthazar, his face creased in the travesty of a smile, "I do what a man should do and take you without talk of this or that to be done?"

He sprang to his feet and his hand shot out to drag her to him. He was quick, but the Lady from Hell was quicker.

He found himself staring into the muzzle of a blue-steel automatic.

"I should hate," she told him evenly, "to think of your men without a leader, your daughter without a father."

For a moment he stared at the lovely red-haired woman covering him so expertly with a revolver whose muzzle did not quiver by even a hair's breadth. Then he burst into a great shout of laughter.

"You are a woman who would get the best of Allah himself," he said. "If it were only the robbing of the train, you could prepare yourself for your bridal night. But this other... rescuing Effendi Wylie... that is another thing. Why should you want him here?"

"Because," the Lady from Hell told him slowly, "he has with him a million francs that belong to me. And I wish him brought here so that I may obtain them."

WHICH WAS TRUE enough, as far as it went. Wylie did have in his possession the funds they had taken from a

Monte Carlo banker, who had in turn been robbing his banking house. What she did not tell Balthazar was the fact that Adrian Wylie was chief of staff of her criminal operations, with a hand and a share in every operation she directed.

"Allah," swore the man piously. "A million francs!" His eyes lit with greed. Then his face fell, and he fingered his beard thoughtfully. "It cannot be done."

"Why not?" demanded Vivian.

"The man is no longer in Constantinople," confessed Balthazar unhappily.

Vivian sat up abruptly.

"How do you know?" she demanded.

"I know, because he is in the hands of Vedova Bey, from whom you escaped," the chief said. "There was a letter that you wrote in prison and left behind for him. Through the address on the letter, he was found and trapped. They left Constantinople two days ago for Vedova Bey's home in the hills, at Dedeagatch. Vedova Bey will torture him and get the million francs," Balthazar concluded regretfully. His tone conveyed clearly the idea that he envied Vedova Bey the opportunity.

"Then he must be rescued," Vivian told him calmly, "before it is too late."

Balthazar stared at her in astonishment.

"Rescue him?" he said. "This palace of the accursed Bey is a fortress of stone with high walls about it. Have I wings, that I could fly over those walls?"

"He can be rescued," Vivian said curtly. "I will tell you how. I will also tell you how the Orient Express can be robbed. Go now, and tell your men to prepare to start for this place where Effendi Wylie is held prisoner."

Shaking his head the man got to his feet and strode off into the darkness.

The Lady from Hell stared after him, her brows knitted, her lips tight. There was upon her lovely face a look of cold cunning.

"He is no easy one to trick," she murmured to herself. "But in spite of that, he himself will aid me in escaping from these mountains."

Despite her absorption in the plan already taking shape in her fertile brain, she did not fail to see the look on the face of Balthazar's daughter, Kara, who never ceased watching her.

2

THE OLD STONE structure, set in the center of its encircling walls, was in utter darkness as the Lady from Hell crept slowly across the stone-flagged courtyard toward it. It was shrouded in silence, the type of silence that precedes the advent of death. It inspired a tiny chill of dread in Vivian, not alone for herself, but also for the man whom she had come to rescue.

She made her way forward as silently as she could, taking every precaution against stumbling. Somewhere off to her left, she heard a tink-tinkle, the touch of a knife blade against stone, and knew that Balthazar and his men were waiting to swarm over the wall when she gave the signal.

Fifty feet and she was in the deep shadows beneath the walls of the building itself. She paused, a slender dark mark beneath the walls, and listened. No sound came. There was something too quiet, too lonely about the place. It seemed unnatural. Inside, she knew, was Adrian Wylie, facing death or torture, at the hands of his Turkish captors. And yet, no sound, no movement. Not even a guard seemed to be on watch.

Mentally she visualized the building as she had seen it from a nearby hilltop in the afternoon sunshine. It was a square, surrounded by walls topped with crumbling crenellations. Yawning gaps and breaches in the walls had been

filled with carefully fitted stones, and midway were ponder-
ous doors of iron-bound wood.

Slowly she crept along the base of the stone structure.
And then she stopped suddenly.

Her trailing finger tips had left the surface of the wall
and gone off into nothingness. There was an opening in
the blank face of the wall. It was a window, her exploring
fingers told her, an old casement window with a wooden
shutter that swung inward. It was swung open now. The
room inside was black and silent. It might be a trap but
unhesitatingly she swung herself up to the sill, felt with her
feet for the floor on the other side.

Once in the building, she stepped swiftly aside, out from
the square of the window. She stood still, listening for any
sound that might betray the enemy or give her a hint as to
their whereabouts. The blackness about her was unbroken
by one single ray or glimmer of light.

She shot her flashlight ray in a sweeping circle about the
room. It was small, and empty. On the further side was a
door, closed. Leaving the window open, an avenue of quick
escape should it be necessary, she picked her way across
the little room and opened the door cautiously. Blackness
again.

Once more she was conscious that this was an eerie,
ominous silence. The flesh at the back of her neck crawled,
not from fear, but from the intuition that told her of the
advent of danger. It was as if a score of unseen, hostile eyes
were watching her from the dark, watching and waiting
for her next step. More than once this intuition of the
Lady from Hell, this intuition that amounted almost to a
sixth sense had saved her from disaster. Now an alarm bell

was ringing inside of her. It was too perfect... that open window, the silence, the absence of life. She sensed a trap.

Carefully and silently, she slipped through the door into the hall, and crept down it with a feline assurance, passing her fingers delicately over objects that came into her path with a touch light enough to stroke a butterfly's wings.

THEN SUDDENLY THERE was a sound, faint but unmistakable, of a footfall. Ahead of her a door opened and she had a momentary glimpse of a larger room dimly lighted by a kerosene lamp on a stand. Outlined in the square of dim light this revealed a dark stocky figure carrying a lantern.

It was useless to hope that the man would not see her in the darkness, even without the lantern. The corridor was so narrow that he must strike against her in passing. She was quite calm, alive in every faculty. But, as she flattened herself against the wall, there was the faintest of clicks. The door against which she had been pressing her body had not been tightly closed and swung open under the pressure. Soundlessly she melted into the gloom.

The man scuffed along the hall until he was nearly opposite the door where Vivian lurked. As he approached she opened the door cautiously and brought down the heavy barrel of her automatic in a sweeping blow against the side of the man's head. Her free hand reached out and caught him as he toppled. A moment later, with the door closed on her victim, she tiptoed down the hall and with the lantern extinguished, peered through the doorway into the lighted room.

She realized then that her intuition had been right. The silence that hung over the place had been unusual, unnatural. It had been the silence of a baited trap, all set and ready to be sprung. But for that intuitive warning she would have walked into it.

Seated on a chair near the further wall was Vedova Bey, stark and sinister... Vedova Bey, her bitter enemy, the man who had taken advantage of one of the few slips that the Lady

Doc Wylie

from Hell had ever made, by taking Adrian Wylie, her companion in crime, a prisoner. Half hidden in the shadows of the vast room were half a dozen men, armed with revolvers and rifles. If she had blundered through that door, the trap would have been sprung with the Lady from Hell inside. With bated breath she watched Vedova Bey.

Even as she looked a tall Macedonian entered the room from a door on the further side.

"There are men outside the walls," he reported in excitement. "And there is a knitted rope hanging down on the inside of the wall."

"Good," chuckled the Bey. "We have made it as easy for the lady and her allies as possible. The guards are withdrawn from the walls... a window conveniently left open... and men waiting to pounce as soon as they enter. She is a very clever woman, but not clever enough to realize that a woman who hates will also betray."

Vivian caught her breath. The whole thing was clear to her now. Kara had betrayed her, Kara, who even then was in

Constantinople to board the Orient Express as a passenger and enact her rôle in the looting of the famous luxury train as soon as the propitious moment arrived.

"And the prisoner?" queried the Bey.

"Bound and gagged in an upper room where he will be safe," returned the man in the same Turkish patois in which the Bey had addressed him.

VIVIAN DID NOT wait to hear more. She had the information she sought. Soundlessly she moved away from the door and down the dark corridor.

Two weeks before Vivian had been in prison in Constantinople charged with a murder which Vedova Bey had committed. He had offered to use his influence with Turkish authorities to secure her release if she would reveal to him the whereabouts of a million francs that Vivian and her confederate, Adrian Wylie, had looted from a Monte Carlo banker.

She had refused, and with the aid of Kara, Balthazar's daughter, and the negress, Galouba, had killed two of the jailers, forced the governor of the prison to write them a safe conduct, and kidnaped Vedova Bey to use as their escort in leaving the prison.

But she had made one error, the error that was responsible for her present position.

Just before her escape from the prison she had written a note to Adrian Wylie, who was unknown to Vedova Bey, in care of an Armenian rug seller. In the confusion incident to the escape the note had been forgotten. It was found by one of the jailers, who turned it over to Vedova Bey. The Bey immediately had Wylie kidnaped, and started for the Macedonian hills where he knew Vivian had taken refuge.

He hoped to use Wylie as a basis for bargaining to obtain all or part of the million francs.

She reached the far end of the corridor and her foot touched an obstruction, a stone staircase. As she reached the top of the stairs she halted suddenly. Ahead of her was a thin pencil of light shining into a dark corridor from beneath a doorway. Vivian listened intently. There was no sound. Carefully she tiptoed to the door, a keen bladed knife in her hand. She was armed with a revolver, but the sound of a shot would bring the Bey and his men in an instant. Quietly she opened the door the merest trifle.

The room was shadowy, barely furnished. The smoky kerosene lamp shed a ghostly light which threw shadows from the furniture in giant, flickering shapes. In the far corner, on a ramshackle bed of rawhide strips lay a man, so completely bound in ropes, knotted and criss-crossed, that he was more like a mummy than a man. A cloth was tied about the chin and mouth. Only the glitter of the open eyes showed that the man was alive.

It was Adrian Wylie. And crouched on a stool at his side sat a guard, a rifle between his knees.

The guard drowsed as he sat there. He had not heard the stealthy opening of the door.

Slowly, inch by inch, so that each movement seemed an eternity, Vivian opened the door further. The remembrance of that sinister brown face with its cold eyes and cruel smile brought a new cunning, a new craft to her aid. The guard had not stirred. Slowly, noiselessly, she slipped through the opening and crept along the wall to get behind the guard.

The eyes of the bound man on the bed had seen her. They shone hopefully as she crept slowly along the wall. She reached a position behind the guard, and started to creep out across the floor toward him. Still the man drowsed on, unaware that the cold hand of Death was stretched toward him.

There were a dozen feet to be covered... the distance narrowed... two yards... then catastrophe.

THE GUARD TURNED his head drowsily and his gaze fell upon the slinking woman, almost upon him. A startled exclamation broke from his lips, he sprang to his feet and jerked the rifle to his shoulder.

But Wylie, as the man sprang to his feet, drew up his knees, and struck out with his bound legs. The blow caught the guard behind the knees, staggered him, almost knocked him down. From his lips came a startled gasp as he lost his balance and the rifle clattered to the floor. Like a swooping eagle, Vivian picked it up, and swung. The wooden stock clipped the man just behind the ear. He went down without a sound. All this passed in the flash of a second.

In another instant Vivian was slashing at the thongs that held Wylie, as she told him in whispered words of the situation.

"You have the money?" she queried when he was once more on his feet.

"It is in Paris," he said with a smile. "Deposited to our credit there by Thomas Cook and Son."

She nodded swift approval.

It was an easy matter, once the circulation had been restored to Wylie's limbs, to retrace her steps, and climb out the open window again. The knitted rope still swung from the outer wall, and in a few minutes they had climbed the wall and were on the other side. Halfway down the hill, Balthazar, the bandit chief, rose from behind a pile of rocks in their path.

His great voice was muffled. "I never thought to see you alive again," he said. Then he caught sight of Wylie at her side. "Is it the one we came to rescue?"

"It is the one," Vivian assented.

"Good," he told her, "now there is left only the robbery of the Orient express and you become my bride."

Wylie's startled eyes flew to those of the Lady from Hell.

"The robbery of the Orient Express… and then I become your bride," she told Balthazar. "But that is not yet accomplished."

"It will be," he told her exultantly. "A messenger reached me with a letter from Kara only a moment after you left. Here, read it," and he thrust it into her hands.

One of the men lit a candle and shielded its glow with his cloak. The eyes of the Lady from Hell glowed.

Kara wrote that on the Thursday of next week a shipment of gold was being forwarded to Vienna. That much she had learned from Balthazar's spies in Constantinople's underworld. And on the same train a member of the British Embassy, a Sir Robert Kerrington, had booked passage. She had seen his name herself on a list of the passengers.

She handed back the letter slowly. Sir Robert Kerrington. She knew of him. A minor member of the Constantinople Embassy, he would not be of sufficient importance to be well known, for people on the crowded train to be aware of his identity. He was little more than a glorified clerk, for all of his title, but he would be traveling on a diplomatic passport, and that was the thing that counted. That and the fact that he was not a person of importance. It was a perfect setup.

"Send the messenger back to Kara with word to take the train," she ordered. "This man is very important. He can be held for ransom... England will pay thousands of Turkish pounds for his release. We will rob the train and hold this man for ransom."

In the darkness Balthazar could not see the sardonic light in her green eyes as she gave the order.

3

FROM SOMEWHERE DOWN the hot, Macedonian moun-
tain defile a shot crashed, echoed and died back into silence.

For a lingering moment the immense stillness of the late
afternoon was shattered, while on the cliff on the defile, the
lounging group of men sprang alertly to their feet. They
had been hidden in a little hollow of rock. Behind them
was a gigantic pile of boulders and before them the expanse
of valley through which the shining tracks ran.

Vivian had been lying at full length on her stomach in
a cleft of the rocks when the shot rang out. She sprang
to her feet with the rest. It was the signal they had been
waiting for. The Orient Express was approaching. Within
ten minutes it would be thundering down the valley on its
way to Phillipolis.

Within ten minutes would be decided whether she
escaped Balthazar and fled to Europe with the loot of this
same express in her possession or remained here in these
mountains to face the poisonous hate of Balthazar's daughter. Had Kara betrayed her? Upon that hung the answer to
the problem. She had betrayed her once. If she betrayed
her now the guards on the train would be prepared, the
attempted holdup would be a failure.

Balthazar's piercing whistle rang out on the hot afternoon air. The floor of the valley, a moment before deserted,

now swarmed with gaily clad mountaineers, their rifle barrels and naked knives flashing in the sun. A babel of cries in soft, purring Persian, in limpid Turkish, in virile, guttural Arabic and high-pitched Macedonian dialect arose as swiftly they piled faggots of wood across the tracks, waist high.

Soon the train track was blocked. The scene was cunningly arranged. There would be no chance for the engineer to see the obstruction and slow down. The track here curved around a shoulder of the mountain that ran down into the valley, and the faggots had been piled just around the turn.

It was a daring and dangerous thing that Vivian Legrand was engineering. Never before had Europe's famous luxury train been held up and looted. As a matter of fact, it was not to be attempted again until 1922, when Tzataz the Great, king of all Macedonia banditti, derailed the engine and looted the train near the Jugoslav border.

Far down the valley was a plume of smoke. Balthazar's whistle rang out again and the toiling men disappeared. All save one man who crouched behind the faggots.

From her vantage point beside Balthazar, Vivian could see the approaching train, the rocky floor of the defile sloping toward the shining rails and the members of Balthazar's mountain outlaws crouching behind the rocks. A signal from Balthazar and the pile of pitch-soaked faggots burst into roaring fire that turned the bottom of the defile into a valley of flames.

The engineer saw his danger as the train rounded the curve and slammed on the brakes. The train jolted to a halt. The engine stopped not twenty feet from the roaring flames. Armed Turkish guards swarmed from the coaches as the train halted.

As they reached the ground a single shot rang out from Balthazar's aerie, followed by a volley from his men behind their barricades of rock. Two of the guards fell, and then came the answering fire of the train guards, for the most part rattling harmlessly on the boulders behind which the attackers lay.

There was a sudden yell and one of the men near Vivian threw up his arms and went toppling over the boulders to lie still on the stones below. He was followed by another, as the train guards spread out in skirmish order to repel the attack.

THEY WERE TRAINED men, these guards, the pick of the Turkish army, trained by German methods and commanded by an officer of the Turkish army. They were rising from the ground now, running in a crouching attitude for a few yards, firing, running again, firing. Some slithered into the dust as they came. But their return fire was deadly.

Balthazar, however, was not a novice at this kind of warfare. His own men, of the type later to become famous in the World War as the *Kamitadjis*, irregular scouts, were fighting sturdily. The chief's whistle rang out. From behind the train swarmed part of his men, hidden behind the piles of rock for just such an emergency. They came running, shooting as they ran.

The train guard was outnumbered, caught between two fires. The battle was over in a moment. Those who had not fallen beneath the bullets of the bandits were disarmed and bound, as others of the bandits herded the passengers from the train and lined them up in its shadow.

That was the cue of the Lady from Hell. Drawing her veil across her face, she ran down toward the train with Wylie by her side. From the straggling line of passengers, Kara stepped forward.

"This is the one," she said, pointing to an Englishman who stood near her. The man's gray eyes stared at Vivian standing before him, taking in the loose violet robe in which she was clothed. Of her face between the top seam of her veil and the triangular droop of her kerchief, hiding her betraying red hair, nothing was visible save a white forehead and two green eyes.

"You are Sir Robert Kerrington?" she said in French that was as flawless as that of a Parisienne.

The man nodded grudgingly. "What does this mean? I am…"

"You will come with me, please," the Lady from Hell cut him short.

"But why am I selected from among these others?" demanded the man, not moving.

Without a word Vivian whipped out a revolver. Its steady muzzle centered on the man's chest.

"You will never have the opportunity to find out, unless you obey my orders," she said. Her voice was silky, deadly, suave.

Without another word he stepped forward.

"Show me your compartment," she ordered, and the man preceded her into the train.

Vivian dropped back for a whispered word with Kara.

"Did you purchase the clothes for me as I requested?" she queried.

The girl nodded. Hate flickered in her eyes as she gazed at the other woman. "They are in my compartment. You will have to get them out yourself," she said insolently, then added, "but my father will not let you wear them."

Vivian did not answer her. They were at the open door of the Englishman's compartment and she nodded with satisfaction as she saw the amount of baggage he had.

"Search him," she ordered, and watched as Wylie produced a diplomatic passport, papers of identification, a well-filled pocketbook and a bunch of keys from the man's pockets.

"Have you friends aboard?" she asked abruptly.

The man shook his head.

"Good," Vivian said, and made a swift gesture with her hand, a signal that had been used more than once between Wylie and herself.

Before the man could realize what was happening and turn, Wylie struck at him with the edge of his palm across the nape of the neck... and struck again. They were deadly, paralyzing blows, product of the ju-jitsu art. Just the one blow, then the second. The man rocked for an instant, then crumpled to the floor.

Vivian watched as Wylie and Kara bound the hands of the limp man and stuffed his mouth with strips torn from the bedding.

THEN SHE TURNED toward Kara, and the Macedonian girl's black eyes leaped to Vivian's in startled astonishment at the sudden drama of treachery that unfolded before her gaze. Her hand stole toward the knife that she always carried, and stopped as Vivian's gun inched forward a trifle in a suggestive gesture.

"It's your turn now, Kara," the Lady from Hell told her in a gentle voice that did not match the hardness of the green eyes. "You betrayed me to Vedova Bey… warned him that I planned to rescue Effendi Wylie, so that he might set a trap to catch me. You should die for it… but I have not the time. So I am contenting myself with taking the loot of the Orient Express. It was very kind of your father to stop the train so that I might board it… and present me with the gold and jewels that he has so laboriously gathered from the passengers." She turned back to Wylie. "Bind her," she ordered.

"My father will kill you for this," the girl spat at Vivian, venomous hate in her glittering black eyes.

"Your father does not come to Paris," Vivian told her mockingly, "and that is where I am going."

Working in perfect harmony, Vivian and Wylie lifted Kara and the English diplomat through one of the windows, to the ground on the opposite side of the train from where the bandits stood. The train acted as a screen for their movements as the two were carried to a jungle of rocks that rose from the defile floor, their legs securely bound, their lips sealed with strips of cloth. Vivian did not know that her action in kidnaping a minor member of the British Embassy at Constantinople was later, during the World War, to be of importance to the Allies. During his imprisonment by Balthazar and his men, Sir Robert Kerrington made friends with them and later, through that friendship, was able to persuade them to enter into guerrilla warfare against the Turks when the English were marching on Jerusalem from Egypt.

On a cloth on the train step, just as Vivian had arranged it, lay a pile of jewels, watches, coins, bills of half a dozen different countries. Even as she and Wylie reached the train again, several of the bandits dropped onto the step beside the jewels six small canvas bags that clinked musically. The shipment of gold from the express car. A small fortune in itself, not to mention the jewels that glittered in the strong sunlight.

Swiftly Vivian dragged the cloth with its glittering burden into the car, placed it in Wylie's arms; on top of it dumped the bags of gold.

"Hurry," she told him, "empty the Englishman's baggage and put all of this in it. You have the keys. He travels on a diplomatic passport, and his baggage enjoys diplomatic immunity. His will be the only baggage on the train that will not be opened and searched by the customs as we pass the frontier."

Then she sprang down from the train and approached Balthazar. Minutes were precious now. Success was within her grasp. But the tiniest slip might undo her patient planning.

"Make all of the passengers climb into the first car and give them orders to stay there until the train departs," she told him curtly. "When they are aboard, have your man remove the barrier in front of the train. I go to search the compartments of the passengers. Some of the women may have hidden jewels there before they came out here. Kara and the Effendi Wylie have already carried the jewels, the money and the bags of gold to the top of the cliff," and she indicated the hollow in the rocks where the bandits had been hiding. "Do not let the train depart until you hear me fire a single shot. That shall be the signal. Then I shall join you."

Her quiet assurance dissipated any suspicion the men may have felt. She dominated the situation. Her vigorous personality made itself felt, even upon these men accustomed only to docile obedience from the Oriental women.

"By Allah," grumbled Balthazar. "Am I the leader, or you? Your plans are good, but you give too many orders for a woman."

BUT, DESPITE HIS growling, he turned away to give the orders to his men. Swiftly Vivian entered the train again and raced for a compartment. Hastily she stripped off the veil, the enveloping violet, silken *meleh'fah* that had made of her a woman of the Macedonian hills, and slipped on the clothes that Kara had purchased on her order. She was a woman of the Occident again.

Then picking up the revolver she fired a single shot through the window. Peering cautiously out she saw the bandits, laughing and exulting over the success of their raid, straggling back toward the hills. Any moment now the train would start and they would be on their way to Paris with the loot of the Orient Express added to the funds she had gathered in the Far East and the million francs she had looted from the Monte Carlo banker.

She smiled inwardly. Her green eyes glowed. There had not been a single hitch in her plan. She was gay, her eyes were sparkling, her mouth quirked in a mocking smile as she thought of that loot traveling across Europe protected by the might of the British Empire while the wires hummed with the story of the holdup.

As for herself, she would simply take Kara's place on the train. That had been one of her principal reasons for insisting that the Macedonian girl make the trip. The train would be booked full, she knew. It always was at this season. Wylie would occupy the stateroom of the kidnaped diplomat, she the stateroom of Kara, and continue the trip under their identities. There could be no possible suspicion attached to either Wylie or herself.

A preliminary snort from the engine ahead told her that the train was on the point of moving again. A hasty glance out of the window told her that the bandits still had some two hundred feet or more to go before they reached the hollow in the rocks and found that neither Kara nor the loot was awaiting them there. And before it could dawn upon them that they had been tricked the train would be off, and she with it.

Then she caught her breath sharply. The train was moving... and Balthazar was racing down the valley floor toward it. He had not had time to reach the meeting place. Evidently not seeing her disembark, he had become suspicious.

The train was moving faster now and it was nip and tuck as to whether Balthazar would reach it.

Vivian raced for the platform where the door still stood open. Even as she reached it, Balthazar reached the side of the train. A stalwart arm flashed up and he started to swing himself up through the open door.

Vivian's foot shot upward and the hard heel of her slipper landed full on the chin of the bandit leader. With a howl he dropped to the ground alongside the train. She glanced out. The train was moving too fast now for him to attempt to board it again.

With a contented smile on her face the Lady from Hell made her way back to the compartment where Wylie was stowing the loot of the Orient Express in the luggage of the kidnaped Englishman.

The sun, slanting through the window, gleamed on the little pile of jewels and glittered from the mound of gold coins that Wylie had poured from the canvas bags.

The Lady from Hell picked up a pair of emerald earrings that had been torn from the ears of a woman and held them up to her own ears. In the reflection from the little mirror they matched her eyes in hardness and color.

Contentedly she gazed at the reflection, a smile of triumph curling her red lips.

THE EPISODE OF THE
HOUSE OF SECRETS

*In the Street of Sinister Shadows the Villainess
Vivian Legrand Discovers the Way to Steal
a Fortune from an American Banker—the
Strange Episode of the House of Secrets*

1

THE RUE DE VERTUS was a street of sinister shadows. A street of stealth. Vivian Legrand, the Lady from Hell, crossed it lightly after leaving her taxi. Her green eyes darted from left to right, her ears tuned to the sound of any movement. For often shadows in this street of Virtue moved… and swiftly… and her jewels were sufficient temptation for any apache in Paris.

The Rat Mort, for which she was heading, was a café off the beaten track. It was not the sort of place recommended even to the most inquisitive visitor to Paris. Many of its habitués were apaches. And if anyone were rash enough to go there in search of local atmosphere, the later in the evening he went, the more trouble he was likely to find.

That was one of the reasons why the Lady from Hell had waited until nearly midnight before arriving. The man she was seeking was not likely to leave there much before that hour, she knew from the reports that had come to her in the past two days.

The painted sign of a rat lying on its back hung beneath the flicker of a lamp. She had almost reached the doorway when a figure moved from a shadow; a tall, lean man in evening clothes, a cape thrown over his shoulders. Her ears barely caught the whispered phrase from the man in the evening clothes as he stood in the fringe of a shadow.

The knife flew through the air as she swung to leap from the desk

"He's here," he whispered.

Vivian did not pause in her stride. But between them, in that instant, passed a look of understanding.

No one seemed to pay any attention to the lovely woman with the flaming red hair and the green eyes, who entered the door of the café with a rippling grace of motion, a light, lithe stride that told of perfect muscles and the agility of a cat. But Vivian was instantly aware of furtive eyes that took in her sleek, black gown, her glittering jewels. And she was aware of hands that went with those eyes.

That did not bother her. The deadly little automatic she carried hidden away was more than a match for the knives of these apaches. And the hint of latent cruelty that lay in the depths of her greenish eyes might have warned a close observer that the woman herself might be equally as dangerous as the weapon she carried. Not for nothing had she been nicknamed the Lady from Hell.

From the corner of her eyes she noticed the man she had passed on the pavement outside, entered the café and paused at the bar beside the entrance. Standing there he purchased a packet of cigarettes. He lit one, his eyes blank, incurious, roving. His eyes rested on the Lady from Hell for just the right space of time, flickered across her jewels and then passed on.

There was nothing in his manner, his glance to indicate that they had met before, that he was, in fact, Adrian Wylie, her companion in crime, her Chief of Staff, and partner in every criminal enterprise that she had engineered... crimes that had netted the two of them close to two million francs.

But there was one thing... one trifle that even the closest watcher might have missed. His eyes lingered for a trifle longer on one man as they swept around the room. And Vivian Legrand, watching those eyes, took her cue from them, even though she did not appear to glance at the man. **MOST OF THE** tables in the café were occupied, but at her entrance a man arose, a red-haired, red-sashed apache whose long, narrow feet were clad in espadrilles. The table he had been occupying was next to that of the man she had come to find. As she paused beside the slouching apache and sank into the chair he had vacated, neither of them betrayed by the flicker of an eyelash that he had been sent there to accomplish the very thing that he had done...

insure that the Lady from Hell obtain a table next to her quarry.

Seemingly indifferent to the furtive glances that were cast in her direction, Vivian opened her bag and began freshening her lips. Through the little mirror she was holding up, the two men at the next table were clearly revealed in miniature in its clear depths.

One of them… her quarry… was a tall, slender man, a lean saturnine figure in evening clothes. His face was unhealthily pale, the nose slightly crooked, the black eyes very sharp and alert, beneath the closely cropped and sleek black hair. Geoffrey Channing had the air of one to whom the world has been kind, and from it he had learned assurance and a kind of aggressive affability. Outwardly respectable Channing always moved in the best of Parisian society. But there were rumors that seeped through the underworld, of activities that were not respectable.

The man with him seemed familiar. It was a part of her business to remember faces, and she racked her brain to place that pronounced Roman nose, that short, clipped V-shaped beard, those heavy white eyelids that had a trick of drooping now and then as if they were tired.

It was those eyelids that finally made the identification click in her brain. He was Sanang Kostoff, a Bulgarian officer, the same man who later, during the world war, took pay from both sides and started importing anthrax into Roumania to infect Roumanian cavalry.

Her eyes were the hard glitter of emeralds as the identification flashed into her mind. Something was wrong here. In her profession nothing or no one was above suspicion, no incident, however trivial, below notice.

And she knew Kostoff's reputation. A dangerous man, with affiliations through the Near East, a man who would be in an excellent position to aid Channing in the thing the Lady from Hell suspected him of plotting.

During a lull in the music a few words drifted to Vivian's sharpened ears.

"He must go aboard at Marseilles..." then a lowered blur of their voices and suddenly the name leaped out in fragmentary relief... the name of the one man that Vivian wanted most to hear... Martin Wardell.

She had been sure of it, certain that this tall Englishman was linked with the fleeing bank head, Martin Wardell for whom an enormous reward had been offered. Now she knew.

The dancers were swaying once more in a tango, their expressions rapt, their feet never leaving the floor. The two men at the next table did not realize that the music had softened to a slow languorous murmur.

"It is a risky thing," the Bulgar said in German. "Once on board the boat at Marseilles, it will not be difficult, but getting him there..."

THE MUSIC CUT in again. Vivian looked away indifferently as the Bulgar glanced in her direction, the bright lights catching her hair and turning it into a halo of flame above her exquisitely lovely profile.

Not one of those men in the café dreamed that she was the Lady from Hell, whose fame had already filtered into the Paris underworld. It seemed incredible that this graceful, beautiful woman could have been implicated in the poisoning of her own father; could have just escaped from a Turkish prison with two deaths to her credit and fled to

Paris with the loot of the Orient Express whose holdup she had engineered... a deed whose repercussions were still filling the continental press, although her part in the affair was not even suspected.

She glanced down at the table. Every move that the two men made was clearly visible in the little vanity mirror that lay propped against her handbag. The Englishman was shaking his head decisively at some question from Kostoff. He did not even glance in Vivian's direction. Evidently he thought that the music and the fact that they were speaking German would cover up whatever they might say.

"Seinicht Narrisch," he said. "It must be tomorrow night. I will have him carried aboard the train in a wheel chair with Jeanette dressed as a nurse and with a doctor in attendance."

The music rose again, drowning the voices, and Vivian Legrand relaxed, a little smile of satisfaction playing around her lips. Those few words, those fragments of conversation, had given her more information than she had been able to gather in days of patient search and shadowing.

Through the mysterious underground channels of the underworld, word had come to her that Martin Wardell was in Paris... Martin Wardell for whose capture a huge sum had been offered. Martin Wardell, the banker, who had fled with the funds of his bank, leaving behind him a wrecked financial institution. That was all, just the fact that he was in Paris, but the Lady from Hell had reasoned, and rightly, that his presence in Paris was but the prelude for a flight to one of those countries that had no extradition treaties with the United States. She knew that the arrangements for such a flight would cost the absconding banker a huge sum, and she saw no reason why she should not have a share of that money.

It had proven impossible to locate Wardell's hideout, but she knew that there were only a few people in Paris who could arrange for the banker to flee from France under the very noses of the French police. She had finally narrowed her list down to Geoffrey Channing. And now, tonight, her suspicions had been verified. By all the laws of probability Channing would go from the café to Wardell's hideout.

She was on her second cup of coffee when the man she was watching got to his feet and threw a coin on the table for the waiter. With a swift gesture she summoned her own waiter. The man had scarcely crossed the sidewalk when she was at the door.

But she did not make the mistake of letting the man she was following see her emerge. She remained there inside the doorway for a moment, adjusting her wrap until the taxi into which he had stepped drove off.

"Follow that taxi," she said to the driver of a taxi standing beside the curb. "Ten francs above your fare if you do not lose him."

The driver grinned. He was hers. A Frenchman surrendered to beauty, intrigue… and ten francs.

"He shall not escape you, Madame," he said, and slammed the door behind Vivian.

2

THE STREETS GREW darker, narrower, twisting in and out as they followed the taxi. An occasional pair of slow-pacing gendarmes twirled their nightsticks. Men in caps and rope-soled shoes slouched by. Muffled sounds of accordions and violins quavered behind the checkered curtains of little cafés.

And then, as her taxi turned into the Quai du Tokyo, she leaned forward with a little exclamation.

The taxi she had been following was drawn up under the fringe of trees beside the Seine. A group of men swirled around a taller one... Geoffrey Channing... trying to drag him toward another car standing some distance away. Channing was battling furiously but the odds were against him.

Her eyes glowed in exultation. Here was a situation that could not have fitted her purpose more perfectly if she had planned it.

Her French came in a spitting stream. But the muzzle of the deadly little black automatic she shoved into the driver's ribs was much more convincing.

"Crash through," she ordered harshly, "and give that man a chance to jump in here. The tall one."

There was a surprising ease and richness about that

voice, despite its harshness. It rose resonant and bell-like, as if it came effortlessly.

With a startled glance at the woman behind him, the driver put on speed. In her excitement Vivian stood up, her slim body swaying with the gathering momentum of the car. For days she had been working on the slenderest of tips. For days she had followed one slender clue after another, only to encounter one baffling setback after another. And now, when she was actually on the verge of obtaining the information she sought, the information seemed to be on the verge of being snatched from her by other hands.

Her driver certainly knew his business. At full speed he made for trouble, urged on by the prodding muzzle of the gun pressed against his ribs. Bearing down on the struggling men like a war tank. So unexpected was the attack that the men barely had time to pull away from danger. But as their figures melted to one side of the Quai they took with them the tall man, still fighting.

For a second the taxi slowed.

"Jump," Vivian cried at the tall man, opening the door.

She had the impression of a flashing knife blade, of a choking cry as one of the apaches who held Channing staggered back, blood streaming from his shoulder. There was a sudden surge, and Channing emerged clear of the group, sprang for the running board and hurled himself through the open door.

Vivian had one glimpse of angry faces under caps. Hands reached out. Her heart skipped a beat as one of the lithe, deadly apaches leaped for the running board. There was the flash of an upraised knife. Then the tall man struck out through the window. The apache fell back with a yell.

The taxi plunged forward, leaving the group of shouting, cursing men.

THERE WAS A stillness in the poise of the man beside her,
a stillness in his opaque eyes. Vivian's nerves coiled like
springs. He must not guess that she had been following
him. She found it hard to keep her detached poise.

"Your arrival was most opportune," the man said.
"Another few minutes would have been too late." He peered
at her appraisingly, striving to pierce the veil of shadows
that filled the taxi. He seemed to guess her thoughts. "They
do not want to kill me," he said contemptuously. "They
were trying to kidnap me, the fools."

"But why?" she asked although she knew full well.

"Why is anyone kidnaped?" the other answered with a
shrug.

But Vivian knew without being told. With Channing
in their hands, his ransom would have been delivery to
his kidnapers of Martin Wardell, the fugitive banker.
Evidently she was not the only person who suspected that
Channing was hiding Wardell preparatory to slipping him
out of France.

"I have not yet thanked Madame for her rescue," Channing said.

"I was on my way home," Vivian said in her low, throaty
musical voice. "I chanced to see that you were in trouble
and ordered my taxi driver to give you the chance to leap
inside and escape."

"Madame was most kind… but is Madame in the habit
of going armed? Paris is not that dangerous for a pretty
woman."

Until that moment Vivian had forgotten that she still

held in her hand the automatic with which she had urged on the driver. With a laugh she opened her jewelled evening bag and dropped it inside.

"I learned a lesson once," she said it with something of defiance in her husky voice, her drooping lashes screening the cold calculation in her green eyes. "Once in Saigon I was held up and robbed. Since then I have never gone out alone at night without a guardian in my bag."

"A wise precaution," the man said drily. In the flickering street lights he could see that she was tall… almost as tall as himself… and with a nervous, panther-like grace of movement. "Allow me to present myself. I am Geoffrey Channing."

There was still suspicion in his voice, but he was aware of a leashed ardour in this woman like that of a caged tigress, of a promise that lingered in the husky tones of her voice and flickered in the depths of her green eyes. The ability to dispell suspicion in a man, by turning on the full force of her personality as one turns on water in a tap, was always one of the greatest assets of the Lady from Hell.

"I am Madame de Renard." Vivian told the lie without the quiver of an eyelash. "My husband is in the colonial service in Saigon. I am in Paris on a visit."

"Your husband's loss is my gain," he told her gallantly. He was subtly aware of a warm beauty that radiated from her. He took his eyes away slowly. It was a difficult thing to do.

Vivian was about to answer when she saw horror written on the face of her companion… or rather, that quick, complete concentration on the object which means horror.

And then, with a muffled curse, the man threw himself

against her. So quick, so unexpected was it, that she fell completely over, the man with her.

THE MOVEMENT SAVED both their lives.

She had not noticed a big black car which had crept up alongside them. Now a flash of orange flame came from the side windows of the black car. Steel ripped through the taxi, splintering wood and shattering the windows. One bullet tore through within an inch of Vivian's head. Another slashed the cloth of her wrap, barely touching the skin. Glass fell about them in a crystal rain. A moment longer on the seat of the taxi and both Vivian and the man would have been riddled.

No sooner had the firing stopped, than a man wrenched open the door of the car as it sped alongside the taxi and spanned the distance from running board to running board in a single leap. His automatic bore down on the two flat on the floor of the taxi. In that instant the Lady from Hell raised her little flat automatic and the slug ripped into the man on the running board. He toppled backwards and was dead before he struck the pavement. The taxi sped on.

Disregarding the dead man on the pavement the black car picked up speed also, and raced after the speeding taxi. Flat on the floor, Vivian and her companion escaped the second fusillade untouched. But a slug found its mark in the driver. With a coughing gasp he pitched forward onto the steering wheel. The taxi swung to the curb, climbed it and crashed against a tree.

With a squeal of brakes the black car came to a sudden halt several yards ahead of the wreck. Four men leaped through a hastily opened door. One held at bay the star-tled pedestrians. Another darted back to the wrecked taxi.

But when he wrenched open the door the taxi was empty. Vivian and the tall man had had time to leap from the cab and speed across the sidewalk to the safety of a recessed doorway.

Lights sprang up in the houses along the street, windows were flung up. Heads thrust out excitedly.

Shadows were flitting from shadow to shadow. Vivian knew that within a moment or two a bullet from the attackers would find them out.

Then, with astounding suddenness, a third car dashed up the street and stopped beside the black car. It was a large blue limousine. From its window came shot after shot. One of their attackers crumpled and dropped to the sidewalk. Heedless of the gun that held them at bay, the frightened pedestrians took to their heels like a flock of sheep that has seen the wolf approaching. As a second man dropped, the engine of the black car whirred into life; the remaining men dived for its open door and it sped down the street and around a corner.

A man stepped from the blue limousine, smoking revolver still in his hand. He came directly over to the wrecked taxi. Vivian and her companion stepped from their hiding place as he approached.

It was Adrian Wylie, Vivian Legrand's companion in crime.

"I am glad to have been of assistance," he said suavely. "These apaches become bolder every day."

Vivian's companion bowed. "We are very grateful," he said, "they had evidently mistaken us for someone else."

A police whistle shrilled down the street, another nearer.

"May I offer my car," Adrian Wylie said hurriedly. "I

assume that you would prefer not to visit the Prefecture, if it can be avoided."

He seemed to be everything that his appearance indicated. Tall, lean and impressive, he was a whimsical, yet prudent and incalculably gifted criminal now turning fifty, and the fact that he appeared to be a substantial man of the world was one of his greatest assets to the woman with whom he worked. They had first met in Manila where he was assistant to the ancient and incredibly evil Mandarin Hoang Fi Tu, and almost immediately their partnership had come into being. And he had brains enough to realize that he could not have continued to be a successful crook had it not been for his association with the Lady from Hell. Among other things he lacked the rare initiative and cold ruthlessness which distinguished her.

The three chattered together amiably until the car drew up before the house at 41 Montaigne Avenue, where Channing maintained his quarters.

And then came the opening for which the Lady from Hell had been waiting. An invitation from Channing to have tea with him the following afternoon. Her lips moved in a slow smile as she accepted, agreeing to meet Channing at the Café de la Paix, two miles away. She wanted him removed as far away from his home as possible.

When Wylie's limousine finally drove away any suspicion that Channing might have entertained of Vivian Legrand had been dissipated. He thought of her only as an exceedingly lovely woman whose husband was half way across the world. Channing's eyes were speculative as he walked away from the car. Madame looked as though she might not be at all averse to a little affair of the heart to wile away her stay in Paris, he thought. Which was precisely the impression that the gifted Vivian Legrand had intended giving.

3

THE AMERICAN AMBASSADOR twisted the card he held between his fingers, a perplexed look on his face. His desk was piled with papers that he had yet to go through. Then he glanced again at the card. "Mrs. James Stokes." The name meant nothing to him, and the cheap printing of the card and its texture indicated that the woman herself could have no very important business with the Embassy.

For a moment he thought of sending a secretary out with word that he could not see her. But the woman had been so insistent, so obviously unnerved and disturbed that he finally dropped the card with a sigh, ran his hands through his graying hair above the tangles of deeply chiseled lines about his mouth and said to the clerk who stood beside his desk:

"Show her in."

He rose courteously as the woman entered, and his heart sank. She had obviously been crying. That meant a story of trouble to which he would have to listen. She was neatly, if a trifle shabbily dressed in black, and, despite the lines on her face, and the threads of gray in the black hair beneath her cheap hat, traces of a former beauty still lingered on her countenance.

"I have come to you," she said a trifle tremulously, "because I did not know what else to do. Perhaps it would have been better had I gone to the police, but since he is an American citizen I thought you would be the proper person to see."

The Ambassador fingered the papers on his desk with a significant gesture.

"Perhaps," he said, "if you will tell me your story, I can advise you whether it would be best to go to the police."

"At home, of course," the woman said nervously, "I would have gone straight to the police, but seeing Martin Wardell over here…"

His Excellency sat up with a start.

"Martin Wardell," he ejaculated. "You have seen him?"

The woman nodded. "That is what I am trying to tell you. I saw him the other day, and have seen him twice since then. Every day he takes a walk for half an hour along the Rue De Seine. He walks along this street wearing a checked cap that hides his face, and a mackintosh of a peculiar yellowish shade. At the bridge a taxi awaits him. He gets into this and drives off. He has changed his appearance, of course, but I recognized him. You see, when my husband died, he left me comfortably fixed. Mr. Wardell persuaded me to deposit my money in his bank for investment. And when he disappeared I was ruined, of course. So I have good cause to remember him."

"Madame," the Ambassador said, "to come to me with this story was the wisest thing that you could have possibly done."

He picked up the telephone on his desk.

"Get me the Prefect of Police," he ordered.

The woman reached out a trembling hand. "But the reward… there is a reward of twenty thousand dollars for him, is there not? If he is arrested, the reward will belong to me, will it not? After all, he is the man who robbed me. It will repay me in a small measure for what he took."

"Madame," came the Ambassador's answer, "if Martin Wardell is arrested through the information you have given me today, I shall personally see that the reward is paid to you at once."

"In cash?" Mrs. Stokes asked in a low voice. "I have no banking connections now. A check might be difficult."

"In cash," agreed the Ambassador, and turned back to the telephone as the Prefect of Police came onto the wire at the other end.

He did not see the deep light that leaped into the greenish eyes of the woman beside his desk. Vivian Legrand, the Lady from Hell, might have difficulty in collecting the reward. But Mrs. James Stokes would have no trouble.

THE LADY FROM HELL walked leisurely up the steps of the house at 41 Avenue Montaigne. She had plenty of time. From the vantage point of a closed car parked half a block away she had watched Geoffrey Channing leave the house for his appointment with her.

To the butler who answered her ring she said:

"Mr. Channing is expecting me."

The man looked puzzled. His narrow eyes studied her closely. Vivian knew that those narrow hands would be much more at home wielding a knife in the dark than performing the duties of a butler.

"I am afraid not, Madame. He has just gone out."

"Oh, but I have an appointment to have tea with him this afternoon," she insisted firmly.

The butler's face lit up.

"Oh, you are Madame de Renard. There has been a misunderstanding. Mr. Channing is meeting you at the Café de la Paix."

"Mr. Channing is meeting me here," Vivian insisted firmly. "There has been no misunderstanding. If he is not at home for the moment, he will be shortly." She waited a moment, and then said curtly: "Well, do you intend to keep me standing on your doorstep until your master returns?"

"I beg your pardon, Madame," the man stammered. "But naturally not." He opened the door. "If you will come in, I will endeavor to reach Mr. Channing and tell him that you are waiting."

She followed the man into the spacious drawing room, and her eyes widened. If Channing was a crook, he was a cultivated one. On the wall directly opposite the door was a picture that she recognized instantly as a genuine Velasquez that had disappeared a month or more ago from a church in Naples. Flanking it were paintings by Correggio and Rubens, and she knew instinctively that they must also be real. Channing was not the sort of man who would flank a genuine picture with copies. Here in this room were hundreds of thousands of francs.

There was a telephone in the room, but it was probably an extension. Silently she stole to the door which the butler had closed. Opening it a trifle she could hear the man, at the rear of the hallway, calling a number. She knew that Channing would not yet have had time to reach the café where she had agreed to meet him, but it would be dangerous even to permit the man to leave a message for him. He was undoubtedly well known and would receive the message immediately on arrival.

The man's back was turned toward her and she stole down the corridor on noiseless feet. Some intangible sixth sense must have warned him of her presence, as she neared. He whirled and dropped the telephone instantly, the mask of butler falling from his face. He ripped out an oath and spun on his heel. One hand went beneath his coat, then fell away again as the gun of the Lady from Hell covered him. She was smiling, but her green eyes were deadly cold, and the man knew that he was looking into the eyes of death.

"Keep your hand down," Vivian told him harshly, "and give me your gun."

The man's eyes flitted from her set face to the wicked black automatic in her hand. Without a word he handed her a gun which he took from a shoulder holster.

She nodded down the hall.

"That way," she said, "And no funny business. If I shoot, I shoot to kill."

THE MAN BACKED slowly down the hall and stood against the wall beside the front door. Still keeping him covered with the revolver, she opened the door a trifle. Almost instantly a man who had been lounging near the steps entered.

It was Adrian Wylie.

"Where is Wardell?" Vivian demanded of the butler, once the door was closed and locked again.

"I don't know what you mean," the man protested, his eyes shifting from one to the other, glazed with the film that comes when the body is taut with fear.

"It is very easy to kill you and find him myself," the Lady from Hell told the man. "The only reason that I do not kill you, is that it is easier to have you show me. Where is he?"

"Upstairs," the man said reluctantly.

Vivian motioned him toward the stairs with her gun, and the two followed as he went slowly up the wide, carpeted steps. Wylie's gun was out now. They were on unknown territory. The butler might be the only person in the house. And again, the house might be filled with guards. Indeed, it was more likely that there were guards there. Martin Wardell was too rich a prize to leave unguarded.

But if there were guards, they were not in evidence. Their guide stopped before a door.

"In here," he said sullenly.

Vivian tried the door. It was unlocked. She nodded to Wylie. The man did not see the signal, but he did see Wylie's answering movement. It was the last thing he saw for several hours. The butt of Wylie's gun clipped him across the forehead, and with a faint groan he slipped to the floor. Callously the two dragged the unconscious form into an empty room across the hall and turned the key.

Vivian threw open the door of Wardell's room. It was then they discovered why the door had been left unlocked. The fugitive banker was bound. Seated upright in a big wooden chair his legs were lashed together, and his hands tied to the arms. Of his face, only his eyes were visible below his tangled white hair. A bandage across his mouth hid the rest of it.

Vivian stripped the muffling cloth from his mouth.

"You are Martin Wardell?" she demanded, her eyes coolly appraising.

The man nodded, miserably. His eyes held the look of a hunted animal which expects at any moment to hear the hounds on its trail.

"You have been promised escape from Paris tomorrow night," she said. "You are to be taken on board a train for Marseilles in the guise of an invalid with a doctor and a nurse in attendance."

A gleam came into the man's eyes.

"That is right," he said huskily. "Are you the two who are to accompany me?"

"It was never intended that you should escape," she told him mercilessly. "You have been betrayed. Tomorrow, instead of going aboard a train, it has been planned for you to walk straight into the arms of the Agents du Police. Then… America and prison."

A THIN SOUND… almost a wail… of protest rose from the stricken man's lips. "But I will pay… I have paid…" he pleaded. "Why should I be betrayed. Channing has received only half the price agreed upon. He is not to receive the other half until I am safely aboard the boat in Marseilles harbor."

"He has betrayed you for the reward," Vivian told him mercilessly. "We are the ones who are to deliver you to the police."

"But I will pay you," the man protested huskily. "I will pay you more than the reward to carry out the original plan. Listen, I will give you fifteen thousand dollars if you will deliver me safely aboard the boat."

"It is too dangerous," Vivian told him curtly. "Besides, how do we know that you will pay. You may have no money left, and we will have our trouble for nothing."

"I have money," the man whimpered. "Plenty of it. Thousands of dollars. I have it all in the Banque de Lyons. See, there," and he nodded his head toward a portfolio lying on the bed. "Open it and then press down on the clasp. You will see."

From the opening revealed in the stiff leather by the pressing down of the heavy metal clasp Vivian extracted a bank book and a sheaf of checks. Opening it she quickly scrutinized the contents. Deposited to the account of Harvey Chase, American, was more than two hundred thousand dollars. Then she threw it contemptuously on the bed.

"That means nothing to me," she said. "You give me a check... and how can I collect. The bank does not know me. I must prove my identity, and even then they may not pay me."

"Oh, they will pay," the man told her eagerly. "I have made arrangements that any check that carries a certain mark beneath my signature is to be honored without question. It is not like an ordinary check. The bank understands. I have told them that I have business deals that require secrecy and any check that carries that secret mark is to be cashed without question."

"Good enough," Vivian told him quietly. "We will help you to escape." From the table she picked up Wardell's own razor and slashed the cords that bound him. Then she smoothed out one of the checks on the table.

"The check first," she told him pleasantly. Her green eyes were veiled and guarded. She had read thoughts in eyes too many times herself, when the owner of those eyes were completely unaware of what they betrayed, to run the risk of having Wardell discern the plan that was rapidly taking form in her brain.

"But it was agreed… after you delivered me to the boat," he said hesitatingly.

"It is we who run the risk," the Lady from Hell said. "If you, by some unfortunate chance, should be captured by the police, we would be the losers. First the check… or the police."

Without another word the man picked up the pen, made out the check for the equivalent of fifteen thousand dollars in francs and added two cabalistic marks beneath his signature.

Vivian watched in silence, her green eyes glowing. It would be an easy matter for an expert forger to alter the figures on the check, raise it from the amount Wardell had written in to almost the full two hundred thousand dollars that he had on deposit. And there would be no danger; Wardell could not prosecute. It was easy.

She took the signed check that the banker extended to her and handed him in return a light mackintosh of a peculiar yellowish shade and a checked cap that Wylie had carried.

"Put these on," she ordered. "You will accompany this gentleman in a taxi as far as the corner of the Rue De Seine. There you will alight and walk up the Rue De Seine, keeping your cap pulled well down over your eyes, toward the bridge, where another taxicab will be waiting. That taxi will take you to a private hospital where we will join you and take you aboard the train tomorrow."

TOGETHER THE THREE descended the stairs. Vivian opened the door, then closed it again with a little exclamation.

"There is an agent du police outside," she said hurriedly. "We must wait."

She was genuinely disturbed. To wait meant to run the risk of having Channing return and discover them. And she dared not leave the house yet. She did not believe that the agent du police was there to watch the house, but with a fortune in her grasp it would not do to take any chance.

"Is there a back door?" she demanded of the shaking old man.

He shook his head.

"The house is built directly upon the property line, and backs up against a new apartment structure," he said sadly. Then his face brightened. "But there is another way out. It is in there," and he pointed to the room where Vivian had first been taken. "A secret passage somewhere that opens onto the side street. I do not know where the entrance is, but the butler knows. I was brought into the house, blindfolded, through the passage, and I heard Channing order the butler to close it after him."

"Get the butler," Vivian ordered Wylie.

Whatever Wylie did, it was efficacious. Within a few minutes the butler came down the stairs, his face drawn and pale, a swollen lump on his forehead indicating the spot where the butt of Wylie's gun had landed.

"I want you to open the door of your master's secret passage," Vivian told him. Then she held up a restraining hand as he started to protest. "Don't lie. Save your breath. I know that you know where it is and how to operate it. Open it or I'll shoot."

The man gave her a glance of deadly hatred, then slowly crossed the room and removed several books from one of the bookcases. Reaching in, he pulled a little lever that the absence of the books revealed. A whole section of the bookcase swung outward.

Vivian's glance flitted speculatively to the pictures on the wall.

"I'll follow you later," she told Wylie. She had no intention of leaving the house when there existed the possibility of taking with her paintings that could be disposed of for several hundred thousand dollars.

Together they bound the protesting butler and rolled him behind a settee in the corner of the room. Then, waiting until Wylie and the banker, who did not realize for a moment that he was walking straight into the arms of the police, had disappeared, she closed the entrance to the secret passage until it stood ajar only a fraction.

Then she tossed her handbag upon the table, dragged up a chair and took down one of the pictures. She was busily engaged in prying it loose from its frame when a voice came from the doorway.

"I see that Madame has made herself thoroughly at home."

She whirled. Framed in the doorway to the hall stood Geoffrey Channing.

A tremor ran over Channing's hawkish features, and he smiled.

"Madame would perhaps not attempt to reach the little gun she so thoughtfully informed me last night she always carries in her bag."

He indicated his own hand in which a gun gleamed and there was no human emotion in that cold face.

4

A CHILL CREPT along the spine of the Lady from Hell. And it was anger that crept over her like a sheet of black fire. Anger with herself for falling into the trap Channing had set. The Englishman evidently read the conflict of emotions that flashed across her face.

"You're trapped," he said with a ghost of a smile curling his thin lips. His deep-set, dark eyes held no recognition of the fact that she was a very beautiful woman. Vivian sensed, and rightly, that to him at this moment she was merely a woman who threatened to wreck his plans. "You evidently did not credit me with any great amount of intelligence." For a moment her eyes flickered to the table on which lay her handbag. In that bag was her revolver. Mentally she calculated her chances of reaching it before Channing could shoot. And dismissed the thought.

But, although she was trapped, the doors of the trap had not yet closed about her. Before Channing could interfere, even before he could pull the trigger, she had deftly opened the door of the room behind her, literally hurled herself through and slammed the door behind her.

Scarcely had she turned the key in the lock when the stout timbers quivered under the impact of a body hurled against it from the other side. And then she halted in dismay. There was no other exit. The one window in the room was barred. The door of the trap had closed.

There was a tremendous thud and the door creaked and yielded visibly as Channing crashed his weight against it.

But she had no weapon, but rapidly she mapped out a scheme. It was simplicity in itself. She would unlock the door and open it the merest trifle, so that when Channing hurled his weight against it, it would fly open and the sudden lack of resistance would send him hurtling halfway across the room before he could recover. And in that brief space of time she would slip through the door and lock it again from the other side.

It was an excellent scheme. There was no reason why it should not work. And it did work… up to a certain point. She waited with tensed nerves for the crash. It came. The door flew open, and just as she had expected, the man spun halfway across the floor before he could halt his progress.

The room from which he had come was brilliantly lighted. And in the doorway to the hall stood two men with ready revolvers, who stiffened to attention as they caught sight of the Lady from Hell.

DEFTLY, SO SWIFTLY that it all seemed part of one continuous movement, she was back in the inner room again, had slammed the door, turned the key and withdrawn it from the lock. Then she retreated warily toward the desk. If she must fight, she wanted the wall at her back.

The interior of the room was photographing itself on her brain with the rapidity of a motion picture camera. She could have shut her eyes after that one brief survey, and recited the name and position of every article in it.

She was looking for aid, for some solution to the problem of her peril.

Above the desk, fastened to the wall, were crossed rapiers, slender things of fine Toledo steel. As Channing advanced she leaped to the top of the desk and seized one of the rapiers. Then she stood tensely, the slender length of steel poised on guard, those strange, almost hypnotic green eyes watching the man before her warily.

Channing was almost as quick. His hand flickered up and Vivian sensed, rather than saw the play of light on the knife he held. His hand moved again and she leaped from the desk. The thrown knife flew through the air where she had a second before stood and clattered to the floor.

Vivian's leap had taken her from the desk. Channing followed his knife with a leap to the desk top, wrenched the second rapier off the wall, and was down on the floor again, facing her.

The green eyes of the Lady from Hell became more alert. Dimly she was aware of a pounding on the door, of voices pitched high in excited French; of smashing blows upon the barrier.

Channing came toward her slowly, his rapier held breast high, as though he meant to spit the woman before him like a trussed chicken. But he made the fatal mistake that almost any man might make when fencing with a woman. He underestimated his opponent. The Lady from Hell had a wrist like iron, and she had learned her fencing from a man, who, in his day, had been one of the world's masters. This Channing did not know.

She sidestepped swiftly, her rapier leaped out like a slender ribbon of blue flame and with an exclamation of

surprise Channing was forced to check his lunge midway
to guard against being spitted himself.

She laughed, a ripple that held the metallic tinkle of steel
on ice, and taunted him.

FROM THE FARTHER side of the door, above the sound of
the crashing blows rained upon it, came a shouted inquiry
as to Channing's safety. He shouted back.

Craftily Channing resumed his tactics of driving her
back across the floor, and little by little she gave way before
his fierce attack. As she circled, presently she saw the knife
that Channing had thrown, lying on the floor.

It was in her mind to kick it out of his reach, but before
she could do so, something whispered to her to halt the
movement. She continued to retreat, slowly fighting every
inch.

Now she had stepped beyond the knife.

Now it lay between her and Channing.

Now it lay between the man's feet and now, as Channing stooped to pick it up, Vivian, like a tigress, struck. It
was what she had foreseen, what had made her withhold
that movement.

The black anger in Channing's mind had made him
reach for the weapon. With a knife in one hand, a rapier
in the other, he would be more than a match for her. The
calmly reasoning brain in Vivian had foreseen that in his
movement lay her advantage. It was only for an instant
that he went down on one knee, his rapier still flickering
before her, a singing blue flame. But it was enough. It gave
the Lady from Hell the chance she sought.

Expertly, so swiftly that it all seemed one movement,
Vivian's rapier changed hands and her right hand snapped

out like the head of a striking cobra, snatched up the heavy brass candlestick that stood on the desk and flung it straight at Channing's head.

It went true and before Channing knew what had happened he had crumpled to the floor.

At almost the same instant came a thunderous crash, and the door fell inward. Framed in the doorway were a group of men, armed.

Vivian was standing over the prone man, the keen point of her rapier touching his throat.

"Halt," she cried in crackling French. "One step inside the doorway and I drive this through your master's throat."

Her desperate eyes; her chill, hard voice drove home her meaning. The men halted in confusion. She pressed her advantage.

"It will do you no good to shoot. Even though I am hit, I can still drive this through his throat before I die. Back out of that doorway, all of you." Her green eyes were hard.

The men retreated slowly until they stood outside the wrecked doorway.

"Into the hallway," she said, "and close the door."

She waited until the last of them had disappeared and she heard the click of the latch. Then, soundlessly, she sped through the door and across the room and closed the door. From the floor where she had dropped it she got the key and, inserting it in the lock, turned it.

Swiftly she bound Channing with strips torn from the window drapes, and then began again the work that his arrival had interrupted, the taking of the stolen pictures from their frames. Once off, she rolled the canvas as into a cylinder, and then picked up the telephone. She asked the operator to connect her with the prefecture of police.

When there came an answer she said rapidly:

"Monsieur, you do not know who I am, and it does not matter. If you will send *Agents du Police* to the home of Geoffrey Channing, 41 Avenue de Montaigne, you will find a thief for whom you have been looking for many months."

She hung up with a decisive click and opened the section of the bookcase that screened the secret passage. In a moment the room was empty, save for the bound figure of Channing on the floor, and the equally helpless figure of his butler behind the settee.

THE POUNCE OF DEATH

It Was One of the Ingenious and Cold-Blooded Vivian's Most Brazen Plots—the Plot to Sell an English Castle to the Heirs Who Already Owned It. Here Is the Story in the Episode of "The Pounce of Death"

1

THE CHILD DID not realize that it was in danger. There was nothing to indicate that the tremor of the nearby shrubbery was caused by anything more than the wind. She played peacefully with her toy on the edge of the grass in the soft English sunshine. The woman with her read contentedly on. The roar of London traffic, softened by distance, beat across the park in muffled waves.

Twenty feet or more away another woman sat on a bench and watched the child and its guardian. The sun picked out bright tongues of flame in the red hair beneath her smart hat and cast a sharply defined shadow across the greenish eyes that seemed to be watching nothing in particular but were, in reality, not missing a single move of the woman and the child.

The woman with the flaming hair was Vivian Legrand, the Lady from Hell. But no one would suspect that this lovely creature sitting in the park was really taking the first step in one of the most audacious schemes that she and her companion in crime, Adrian Wylie, had ever attempted.

She seemed the perfect woman of the world, but her eyes told a different story. At that moment they were old; filled with a cruel and ancient wisdom which belied the smooth untroubled contour of her face and the slim perfection of her figure.

It had taken her three weeks to establish the fact that the woman and her granddaughter came to this same spot in the park every fair day. This was the third day that Vivian Legrand had sat watching them, waiting for the right moment to strike. The bobby who patrolled that section of the park had passed ten minutes before. It would take another twenty before he returned.

Slowly the Lady from Hell opened her brightly-colored parasol. The bright spot of color was visible for a long way down the walk.

Almost immediately an altercation broke out between two men seated on a bench on the other side of the woman and the child. They sprang to their feet. A blow was passed. Another. They began to fight. The child's guardian dropped her book and looked up. People were running from all sides.

The Lady from Hell signaled again, this time by closing her parasol. From behind the shrubbery where he had been lurking a man darted. So intent were the spectators on the fight going on that his actions passed unnoticed as he snatched up the playing child, one hand over her mouth to stifle a scream, and vanished behind the shrubbery with his struggling burden. A moment later, from the nearby driveway, a motor roared into life.

Quietly the Lady from Hell got to her feet and strolled away, her green eyes glowing with pleasure.

TWO DAYS LATER the Lady from Hell sat in a luxurious car outside Winchester station. The man with her was, to the closest scrutiny, of the same fashionable type as the woman herself. His clothes had been cut in Saville Row, his manner was debonair and cosmopolitan, and there was

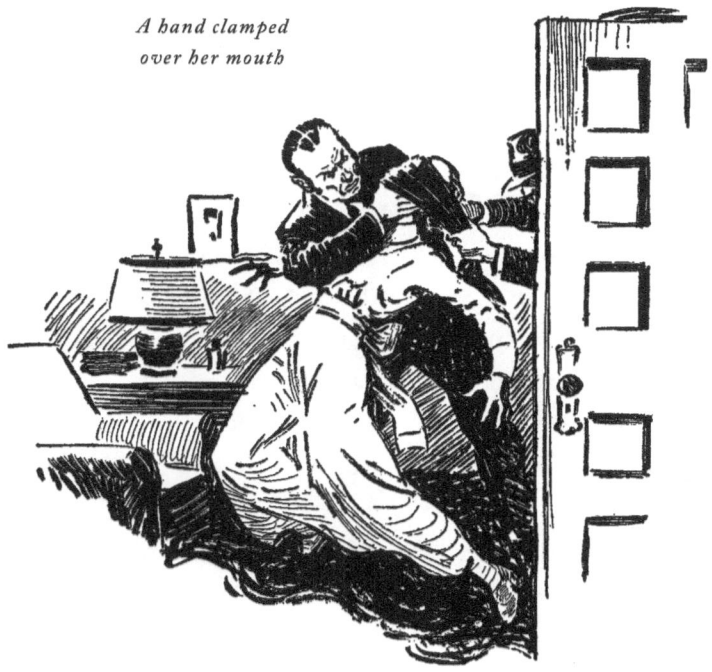

A hand clamped over her mouth

nothing about him to indicate that he was companion in crime to one of the most daring swindlers of the age.

Suddenly Vivian leaned forward and touched her companion's arm.

"There she is," she said, indicating an anxious-faced woman of about twenty-seven who was making her way through the crowd disembarking from the train. She was cheaply but neatly dressed in black.

"I knew our note would bring her," Wylie said with satisfaction.

Vivian leaned out of the car toward the woman, who had halted on the edge of the pavement and was looking about her with a bewildered and worried air.

"Are you looking for someone?" Vivian said sweetly.

The woman turned pale at the sound of the voice, and

her eyes rested incredulously on the expensively-clad form of the woman who addressed her.

"I—I was expecting to meet someone," she said anxiously.

"Perhaps we can drive you where you want to go," Vivian said quietly, "if you'll get in."

"Thank you, but I—I don't think I'd better," the woman said, her glance flitting about the platform.

"What's your name?" Vivian snapped.

"Lannin—Margaret Lannin. I was looking—"

"I know," Vivian told her sharply. "Get in." Her cold eyes slashed at the other woman's face.

The Lannin woman started at the harsh tones.

"Oh," she said, and her voice was high and shrill with excitement. "Are you the one who kidnaped my little girl—my Amy?"

Vivian's eyes passed swiftly over the crowded platform. Was the fool woman going to make a scene here, of all places?

"I don't know what you're talking about," she said quickly. "But if you've an appointment I'll drive you wherever you want to go—that is," she added with unmistakable emphasis, "if the person you have the appointment with is still alive."

In silent terror the woman climbed into the car. As it moved forward she leaned over and said huskily:

"What have you done with Amy? Don't you know I haven't any money? I can't pay any ransom. Oh, why did you do it? Please, for God's sake, don't let anything happen to her. I never did anything to you. Why did you do it?"

"The child is all right—so far," Vivian told the frantic

mother. "You must keep quiet now. You'll have plenty of time to talk later."

Her voice was calm, almost kind. Wylie knew, however, that the tone was deceptive. He had seen that cold glow at the back of the eyes of the Lady from Hell before, and he knew that it was like the warning rattle of a snake before it strikes. More than once the Lady from Hell had not even raised her voice before death spat from the muzzle of the revolver she always carried. Only that cold glow in the eyes told of the danger.

There was no further conversation. The woman huddled in the corner, sobbing quietly into a handkerchief. The car went noiselessly on, swept through the tall iron gates of a secluded house, and the three went indoors.

Once inside Vivian turned to the woman and said curtly: "Sit down."

Margaret Lannin sank down into a chair.

"You're a professional nurse, aren't you?" Vivian asked, running her hands through her red hair.

"Yes," the woman replied.

"At present you are on a case at Karnwood Hall, are you not?"

The woman nodded.

"You are nursing Simon Ashbrook?"

"Why yes," the woman answered in a puzzled voice, nervously twisting her handkerchief.

"Just how ill is Mr. Ashbrook?" Vivian demanded.

"HE'S MUCH SICKER than he thinks or knows," the trained nurse explained nervously. "It's a terrible responsibility for me. He can't live long, and he won't have a doctor."

Wylie leaned forward tensely.

"Won't have a doctor?" he asked sharply.

"No," the woman went on. "He's very old, but terribly stubborn. He says if he's going to die, he wants to die in his own good time, and not on a doctor's prescription."

"That's splendid," Wylie said with satisfaction. "Now, how about his heirs in America?"

"They've been notified of Mr. Ashbrook's condition," the woman said wonderingly. "They're on their way over now."

"What ship?"

"The Berengaria."

Vivian turned to Wylie.

"How much time does that allow us?"

"At most, four days," her chief of staff replied.

Vivian swung fiercely around. Her eyes were blazing now. Margaret Lannin shivered. Yet so great was the poise of the Lady from Hell that any chance visitor entering the room would have deemed them friends.

"If you obey my orders, everything will be all right and your child will be returned to you unharmed," she told the woman. "If you fail me... But then, you won't, will you?"

The woman hung her head miserably. "I'll do whatever you want," she said in a choked voice.

"Very well," the Lady from Hell said swiftly, stabbing each word at her as if it were a weapon. "You'll inform Simon Ashbrook that your daughter is very ill and needs you at once. Tell him that you must go away for several days, possibly a week."

"But I can't leave," interrupted the woman.

"Let me finish," Vivian snapped. "And don't make the mistake of thinking you can tell the police. We're holding your daughter as a hostage for your good behavior. She isn't here. I am the only one who knows where she is, and if anything should happen to me, if I should be arrested..."

She smiled thinly, and the air was suddenly filled with the portent of tragedy. The nurse caught the implication.

"But Mr. Ashbrook—he'll have to have a nurse."

"He will have. Your sister."

"My sister?"

"Naturally," Vivian Legrand said evenly, "you don't want to lose a good position as long as your patient lives. So you will send your sister, also a trained nurse, in your place, to take care of him in your absence."

"But I haven't got any sister," the woman protested.

Vivian laughed—that husky musical laugh that rippled low in her throat.

"Oh, yes, you have," she purred, and the heavy lids fell over the inscrutable green eyes. "You're sending me to Karnwood Hall in your place until your daughter recovers from her illness.

2

FOR THE NEXT twenty-four hours the secluded little house on the outskirts of Winchester was a hive of activity. In some respects it resembled a school, with one Nicholas Benton as the pupil and Adrian Wylie as teacher. It had taken Wylie three months to find Benton, and several weeks after that to persuade him that five hundred pounds easily earned in two weeks was much better than a few pounds earned over a period of months.

Benton had, at one time, been an excellent actor, but age and changing school of acting had gradually shoved him into the background. When Wylie found him he had not played a part for more than two years. His savings had vanished and he was desperate. He was seventy years old, but despite his age he was in robust health. It was Wylie's task, in a day or two, to make him speak, look and act exactly like Simon Ashbrook, the eccentric dying millionaire.

Just now Wylie was thoughtfully tapping a file of carefully accumulated data in regard to Ashbrook, as well as innumerable specimens of the old man's signature on checks and documents. Ashbrook was an American who had elected to live as an English country gentleman; a bachelor who avoided, although without dislike, his relatives and heirs; a very rich man who never trusted a secretary, but wore himself out attending to the most trivial details of the management of his fortune; who employed many gardeners but few household servants; who lived like a miser, yet catered to his own whims with the extravagance of an absolute monarch.

Wylie, among other things, knew that Ashbrook had a habit of rubbing his thin, tormented nose with the back of his claw-like hand. He knew also of Ashbrook's lifelong trait of shutting his right eye and squinting at the ceiling whenever matters of finance had to be discussed. And that Ashbrook frequently made a dry, clicking sound with his tongue.

He had Benton propped up in bed as Vivian Legrand entered the room. The shades were drawn, the lighting just right. She saw that the resemblance was astounding; the illusion of wizened feebleness nothing short of masterly.

On the bed lay a sheet of paper covered with a scrawling signature. Wylie picked it up and carefully compared it with the signature on several of the documents he took from the file.

"Good," he said. "Even better than good. You could have made your fortune as a forger, Benton. Ashbrook's signature as you write it now would fool almost anybody."

He held up a photograph, taken from the file, in front of the man lying there in the bed.

"Who is it?" he asked.

"Alice Merriweather, my sister."

"And this?"

"Marjorie Carr, my niece, daughter of Mrs. Robert Carr. Seventeen years old. Birthday... the twenty-first of next month," came the parched old voice.

One by one he identified the photographs Wylie held before him, until the photographs of all the Ashbrook heirs had passed in review.

"Good enough," Vivian said thoughtfully. "But how about the voice? I know. Get the Lannin woman in. If he passes muster with her, he'll do."

Margaret Lannin, quite unwarned, was ushered in from the adjoining room. She looked at Nicholas Benton lying in the bed, and her jaw sagged.

"Good heavens," she gasped, "Mr. Ashbrook! I thought you were safe at Karnwood Hall!"

"What are you doing here?" came in parched tones from the form on the bed.

Volubly the woman started to explain, but Wylie cut her short. After the astonished nurse left he turned to Benton.

"Good enough, she didn't suspect," Wylie said. "The others won't. This afternoon you're going to have your final rehearsal for the biggest part you've ever played. When I finish with you this afternoon you'll be Simon Ashbrook."

"Just give me a chance to hear him speak," Benton said confidently. "After that, even his own mother couldn't tell us apart."

IT WAS AN entirely different Vivian Legrand who arrived at Karnwood Hall late that afternoon. Her halo of flaming red hair was hidden under a smooth brown wig, and she wore the cap, the white clothes and the rubber-soled shoes of the professional nurse.

The man who answered her ring was tall and powerfully built, with broad shoulders and long arms. His face, a strange dead-white, was disfigured by a long scar running from eyebrow to chin that gave him a perpetual sullen expression. The Lady from Hell surmised at once that he was Martin, the butler. To him she presented the letter from Margaret Lannin, stating the reason for her absence, and saying that her sister, Miss Bailey, would take care of Mr. Ashbrook during her absence.

The butler fingered the letter thoughtfully, blocking entrance with his powerful body.

"I suppose it's all right," he said hesitantly.

A bright spark glowed in the narrowed eyes of the Lady from Hell for a moment. Why, she wondered, did this servant seem surprised—disappointed—that she was here?

"Why shouldn't it be all right?" she demanded curtly. "Now will you let me in, please, and place my baggage in my room. Mr. Ashbrook has been without a nurse long enough."

The butler's face darkened at her curt tone, and the sullen look on his face deepened, but he showed her upstairs respectfully enough.

A few minutes later she emerged from the sick room and rang for the butler.

"Where is the telephone?" she queried. "I want the village doctor, whatever his name is, here at once."

A look of alarm spread over the man's face. "Mr. Ashbrook is not sinking, is he?"

"I don't know," Vivian told him curtly. "But I don't want to take over the case without a doctor seeing him. Oh, I know," she said swiftly as the butler started to protest, "Mr. Ashbrook doesn't want a doctor. Has been refusing to see one. But I'll take the responsibility."

She met the doctor, a dapper little man, in the lower hall when he arrived half an hour later. It had not been a part of her original plan, but Ashbrook had seemed in much worse shape than she had expected to find him, and if he were to die before their plans were completed, this would be the man who would sign the death certificate. Then, too, there could be no suspicion on the part of the doctor, if he had already examined the man and found him seriously ill, if he were called in later to certify to the cause of his death.

The doctor confirmed her own suspicions.

"Mr. Ashbrook is very low," he said thoughtfully. "He is in a semicoma now. He may rally and his brain be quite clear again before the end. And again, he may never come out of it."

Vivian Legrand was thoughtful as she closed the door behind the little man. Ashbrook's death before their scheme was complete had not entered into her plans. And she knew that if he died, they could not postpone notifying the doctor more than a few hours. Any further delay might cause suspicion that would lead to an investigation.

That night silence lay over Karnwood Hall like a blanket. The only light was the little night light that glowed in the room of the dying millionaire. As midnight came Vivian stole silently to the door of Ashbrook's room, opened it, and listened.

Hearing nothing, she made her way carefully downstairs, opened the side door and stepped into the dim moonlight. Almost immediately there was a rustling in a clump of bushes near by and Benton and Wylie stole toward her.

"He's in a coma," Vivian whispered. "Has been all day."

"Low?" Wylie asked.

"Dying," the Lady from Hell told him curtly. "He may last a few hours or a few days. We've got to work fast."

A few minutes later, had anyone been awake in the house they would have witnessed the curious sight of two men carefully carrying the limp form of Simon Ashbrook up the stairs toward the rooms on the third floor that had been assigned to Vivian.

As a matter of fact, someone was awake, but the three conspirators did not notice that one of the doors that they passed stood slightly ajar, and if they had, would not have suspected that the sullen-faced butler was watching them through that crack. They deposited the limp form of Ashbrook carefully on Vivian's bed, locked both the door to the bedroom and the door that led from the little sitting room to the corridor, and hastened back downstairs. Then Wylie set to work. Under his skillful hands Simon Ashbrook appeared where Nicholas Benton had been.

3

BY MORNING THE conspirators were ready for the supreme test. Men employed on the estate, men who had not seen Ashbrook for several months, but who before the period of his recent infirmity had been accustomed to meeting him about the house or the grounds and talking with him almost daily, were cannily introduced into the room of the impostor on one pretext or another. If Benton passed their scrutiny, there would be no trouble, for none of the heirs hastening from America had laid eyes on Simon Ashbrook for many years.

The last of the employees was just bowing his way out of the room when the butler brought in a telegram. Vivian opened it, then caught her breath sharply.

The Berengaria, with the North Atlantic a mill pond, had made an excellent crossing, had docked ahead of time. The Ashbrook heirs were already in England, indeed, on their way to see their dying relative at Karnwood Hall.

At the entrance of the hall they were received by Vivian and Wylie.

"This," said Vivian, "is Sir Charlton Mayne, who is here because of the seriousness of Mr. Ashbrook's condition."

The Americans were impressed with Wylie. None of them had ever heard of Sir Charlton Mayne, who looked impressive enough to be the king's personal physician. He was courtly in manner, but appeared hardly to notice that the five individuals he was meeting were the only surviving relatives of a man worth several million dollars.

The most aggressive of the heirs was Mrs. Alice Merriweather. Wylie, bowing over her firm brown hand, recognized an adversary who would sooner or later put their plotting to the grim test of reality.

Then there were the Laurison brothers, Philip and Edgar—pleasant, immaculate young men who seemed to have anticipated their heritage by learning to be as idle and parasitic as was humanly possible.

Mrs. Robert Carr and her pretty daughter, Marjorie, were the fourth and fifth of the party. When millions were in her own name, attached to her, Wylie reflected, the charming, seventeen-year-old Marjorie was probably due to be sacrificed to some shopworn old-world title.

There was, in Atlanta, Georgia, a sixth Ashbrook heir. With him the plotters felt no concern. He was a criminal, and as such, would be in no position to contest the will.

"I am glad that you have come," said Wylie, addressing all of them. "Ashbrook is very low. As a matter of fact, his life hangs by a thread."

"Just how long do you think he will live?" Mrs. Merriweather bluntly demanded.

"Madame, a day, a week—at most a month," was the reply.

"May we see him?" pursued the old lady.

"That, I believe, was his purpose in summoning you here," Wylie told them. "Something has been troubling him, troubling him greatly, in connection with his will. And in this connection I cannot urge you too strongly not to allow your worry over his condition to show. He must not be permitted to know that his condition is as grave as it is. Even at that, I can permit this interview to endure only a very short time. We must do everything we can to insure his tranquility and ease of mind. I may rely on you all, may I not?"

Mrs. Merriweather nodded curtly. The others eagerly assured him that Simon Ashbrook's repose would be to them a sacred objective.

The Lady from Hell led them up the stairs to the suite that Nicholas Benton occupied. All the visitors had been tactful enough—with Ashbrook still presumably conscious—to leave their luggage behind in London.

When they entered the room of the impostor there was no show of affection, very little stir. Just a solemn scene of five uneasy people doing their painful duty, and wondering when the huge inheritance might safely be expected.

Nicholas Benton spoke a few words of husky greeting. Then he turned to Vivian.

"I want you to leave us," he said slowly.

THE LADY FROM HELL rose obediently from her seat beside the bed and Wylie stepped forward. "If this is to be a family conference, perhaps I had better leave also?" he suggested.

"No," came the studied reply. "You're a doctor. You might as well hear it."

Vivian made her way slowly up the stairs to her rooms on the third floor. The affair was in the hands of Wylie and the pseudo-millionaire. The scheme was hers, even down to the minutest detail, but for the moment there was nothing that she could do save to stand aside and let it be played to the end.

She unlocked the door of her little sitting room and started across it toward the bedroom, where the real Simon Ashbrook lay drugged on her bed.

And then catastrophe struck.

She was already through the door when she heard a quick, catlike tread behind her. She made an attempt to swing around too late. Someone leaped on her. A strong arm was locked around her throat. A hand clamped over her mouth. A knee dug into the small of her back. A black cloth was thrown over her head and drawn tightly.

She struggled to break the grip. She lurched toward the hallway. A leg tripped her. She pitched forward. Other hands seized and held her. A length of rope bit into her arms and legs. Helpless, she was carried to a chair and dropped into it while the deft hands bound a strip of cloth about her mouth. Not once was the dark cloth about her head removed, so that she might see who her captors were.

Then, for the first time, one of them spoke. There was something familiar in the man's voice. She racked her brain to place those tones, but could not.

"Get him downstairs and into the car," the man ordered, and the Lady from Hell knew that he must be speaking of the drugged form of the millionaire. "But handle him carefully. We don't want him dying on our hands."

Listening intently she could hear the sound of the limp form being lifted from the bed and the slow progress of footsteps as he was carried out of the bedroom and through the living room into the hallway.

"I hope," the man said again, and there was a mocking

note in his voice, "that you are gone by the time the police arrive. It would be difficult to explain, wouldn't it?"

Then a hard note crept into his voice. "So you thought you'd muscle into our racket, did you? You were big enough fools to think that with such a perfect set-up, nobody except yourselves would have any knowledge of it. Well, we've got the old man, and those heirs downstairs that you're fooling so nicely will pay through the nose to get him back before he dies, so he can sign a will."

Then the sound of a closing door. Silence, with the Lady from Hell bound and gagged in her room, while on the floor below the heirs gathered around the bed of the man they believed to be their dying relative.

The pseudo-millionaire shifted position slightly so that he might face the five people who had raced death across the ocean.

"You are my heirs," he told them bluntly, "and I am dying." Ashbrook himself might have envied his double's malicious tone. "Everyone dies once. How he dies doesn't matter much, I reckon. But I wanted to talk to all of you before the end came, to prevent a nasty scandal."

"Scandal?" Mrs. Merriweather asked. She glanced uneasily from one relative to another.

The man on the bed laughed, a mirthless and strangled sound. He tried to push himself up on an elbow, but it buckled beneath him and he fell back.

"Yes, scandal, my dear Alice," he croaked. "You noticed the nurse whom I sent out of the room? Well, she is my daughter—illegitimate, to be sure, but none the less my flesh and blood. She does not know it… I do not wish her to know it. That is why I sent her out of the room."

He paused a moment to let the astounding statement sink in, and then went on.

"I want to make my will, here, in your presence, so that there may be no lawsuit later. I want my child to get her share of the estate."

"You are going to leave that—that *servant* part of your money?" burst out Mrs. Merriweather.

4

"THAT IS JUST what I propose to do, my dear Alice." The laughter of the seemingly dying man lifted in the stuffy closeness of the room; it died away in a rattle of coughing. "She is my daughter. She has what I consider a valid claim upon my estate. In this my solicitors concur."

"She has no legal claim," Mrs. Merriweather said angrily. "No court would uphold her claim to any part of your estate."

The man on the bed stared at her for a long minute, while his slender fingers pulled at the coverings over his body. "I have no intention of permitting my bequest to her to be contested," he said in his husky voice. "I have no intention of dying and bequeathing you the savage enjoyment of fighting the child on the front page of every newspaper in America and England. Nor do I desire to mention her in my will as my daughter, because that would put a stain on the name that I have tried to keep clear."

"It's rather late in life, in view of the evidence you yourself have told us of, to be talking of besmirching your name," came from Mrs. Merriweather.

"We grow wiser as we face death," came the husky tones. "If I were to make any substantial gift now, it would appear under the English laws as an attempt to avoid inheritance taxes. So the solicitors I consulted—not my regular ones—have suggested another and a better way."

A spasm of coughing shook the pseudo-millionaire. It passed and he lay quietly. There even seemed to be beads of sweat jeweling his forehead.

"Not too strenuous, sir," Wylie said gravely.

He crossed the room, began ostentatiously taking the patient's pulse. He frowned, then poured out a glass of water and handed it to Benton, who reached feebly toward the table at his side and picked up a document.

"This is my will, prepared by my solicitor." His eyes had caught the agreed signal from Wylie and he knew that the time had come to rush the heirs. "In fact, here are two wills. One divides my entire estate equally between the five of you, except for a bequest of one thousand dollars to Arthur Ashbrook, Helen's son, who is now in prison in America. The other leaves one thousand dollars to each of you, and the balance to charity."

He paused as a gasp of consternation went up from the assembled heirs. In the silence there came the sharp sound of a crash from the floor above. Wylie's eyes flickered upward for a moment. The sound appeared to have come from the room occupied by the Lady from Hell.

The man in the bed appeared not to notice it, or if he did, ignored it.

"I intend to sign both of these wills," he went on relentlessly. "If you are prepared to do as I say, I will destroy the second will. If not, I destroy the first one, and my entire fortune goes to charity."

He lay back, squinting at the ceiling. He was clicking his tongue, burnishing his nose with the back of his left hand.

"What is it you want us to do?" asked Mrs. Robert Carr.

"I want each of you to make a present of fifty thousand dollars to my daughter. Make it here, before my death."

"Fifty thousand dollars!" gasped Mrs. Carr in consternation.

"I won't do any such absurd thing," barked Mrs. Merriweather. "It's the most preposterous thing I've ever heard of!"

"How do we know," spoke up Edgar, "that you've any money to leave? For all we know you may have lost your fortune."

"Oh, you know," the old man answered dryly. "You know down to a penny. I'll wager that Alice could tell you the exact amount of my holdings in every company."

Mrs. Merriweather winced. It was true. It had cost her a large sum, but the report that she had in her handbag at that very moment placed Simon Ashbrook's fortune at a little more than five million dollars.

"Give me a pen and something to write on," the feeble old man said imperiously to Wylie. Silently the five heirs watched as he scrawled his signature at the bottom of both documents. The signature, after hours of painful copying from the original, was sufficiently like that of the real millionaire to have fooled even the old man himself.

"How do we know," asked Mrs. Merriweather slowly, when the old man had finished, "that you will destroy the other will?"

"I thought you'd think of that," sneered the husky voice. "You're exceedingly practical, my dear Alice. If you'll just read the terms of this document which I also propose to sign—at the proper time—you will find that your "investment" is amply protected. It's an acknowledgment of indebtedness in the sum of $50,000 to each of you, collectible against my estate."

Mrs. Merriweather read it carefully, then passed it on to Edgar.

"It's an outrage," Mrs. Merriweather flared, "that we are expected to pay for the youthful indiscretions of a dying old fool."

The old man chuckled hoarsely.

"Just one of life's little ironies, my dear Alice. Take it or leave it."

Mrs. Merriweather bit her lip, then went on slowly:

"I suppose you've got us, Simon, right where you want us. You leave us no alternative. I'll pay the girl the fifty thousand dollars."

"That's very sensible of you—of all of you," he added as the others, having read the document, sullenly agreed to pay their share also.

"I don't expect you," the impostor went on, "to have the money with you, but checks will do. Bring them here this afternoon, and when my daughter tells me that they have been cashed, I'll destroy the will that leaves my fortune to charity."

MEANWHILE, ON THE floor above, the Lady from Hell had finally managed to get her head clear of the encumbering cloth. It had not been tied on, and by hooking it onto the back of the chair she had lifted it from her head.

Her eyes swept the room, hoping against hope that some avenue of escape, would present itself. And then a faint glimmer of hope came to her. It was a glimmer and noth-

ing more, but the more she thought of it, the more practicable it became.

On a pedestal beside the door into the corridor stood a
tall Chinese vase of porcelain with a glaze like the bloom
of grapes. It was upon this fragile thing, as fragile almost
as her hope, that her chances rested.

Slowly, ever so slowly, she inched herself out of the chair
and tumbled to the floor. Then, painfully, inch by tortured
inch, she worked her way across the floor until she could
raise her bound feet between the vase and the wall. One
sharp downward sweep of her legs, and the slender piece of
porcelain toppled over on the floor, breaking into dozens
of fragments.

Rolling over several times, she rested her back on the
jagged base. It took several minutes to adjust her position,
and then she began the nerve-racking torment of sawing
her bonds up and down the serrated edge.

Even when she had severed her bonds, she had to lie
motionless for several minutes before life came back to her
arms. After that it took but a minute or two to release her
ankles, then the gag. She raced down the stairs.

Wylie opened the door of the sick man's room at her
light tap. Only he caught her light, tense whisper:

"The old man has been kidnaped!"

Then she said in a louder voice, intended for the ears of
those within:

"Doctor, could I interrupt? One of the maids has been
injured, and I thought that perhaps you—"

"Certainly," Wylie said in his rôle of doctor. "I am sorry,"
he said, turning to the little group in the room, "but I must
ask all of you to come with me, please."

Once outside the room he faced the five heirs.

"I would suggest," he said gravely, "that you leave Mr. Ashbrook alone now. And also that you do not return to London at once, but remain at the inn in the village. His pulse is perceptibly weaker, and I am afraid…"

He broke off, but his implication was all too clear to the little group. In silence they made their way down the stairs.

Not a trace of their inward consternation showed in the faces of Wylie and the Lady from Hell as the five heirs drove off toward the village. But the moment their big car rolled through the iron gates of Karnwood Hall onto the road, a whirlwind broke loose.

And in ten minutes more Wylie and Vivian were facing the fact that except for Benton and themselves the house was deserted. Butler, housemaid and cook were gone, as was the big Rolls Royce in the garage. It dawned upon Vivian then where she had heard the voice of the man before.

"It was the butler," she said bitterly. "What fools we were. We've been so lucky that we've become careless. We simply stepped into the middle of a situation that somebody else was already working on, and they simply went ahead with their plans."

"The only thing we can do is take what we can get from the heirs and get out before it's too late," Wylie said uneasily.

Vivian shook her head vigorously.

"No. That would be fatal. We can't rush them. Then, we'd have to cash the checks, and if they hear from the kidnapers before we have the checks cashed… it would be prison for us. No, we've got to find the old man."

"Find him?" Wylie was one of the few who dared to use sarcasm to the Lady from Hell with impunity. "Yes! Why not call the police to aid us in finding him?"

"That," said the Lady from Hell, "is precisely the one thing the kidnapers won't expect—and therefore precisely the thing I intend to do."

5

IF VIVIAN HAD attempted to trace the abductors of Simon Ashbrook by any other means, she would have failed. And only the brilliant mind of the Lady from Hell could have conceived the idea of making the police her accomplices in a hazardous and illegal scheme.

A police constable, hurriedly summoned from the village of Karnwood, heard from the lips of the pseudo-Ashbrook that he suspected his butler was systematically robbing him; that only an hour before the butler had asked permission to use the Rolls Royce to visit an ailing sister. That he wanted the constable to trace the movements of the Rolls Royce and find where it went, without alarming either the butler or the occupants of the house. Then Scotland Yard would be communicated with, and a raid arranged.

A ten-pound note clinched the argument.

It proved absurdly simple, as all great schemes are. The Rolls Royce was well-known throughout the countryside and the kidnapers, never dreaming that the police would be called in, had made no attempt to cover their tracks. The constable ascertained by telephone that the car had passed through the little village of Leems, five miles away, and had not passed through Milwood, two miles further along on the same road.

Within an hour the car had been located in the stable of

an old farmhouse. An hour after that, Vivian, Wylie and Benton were watching the house from the woods near by.

There was no sign of life about the little thatched cottage. The doors and windows were closed. But Vivian knew that behind those closed windows were keen eyes, watching every avenue of approach. She knew, also, that to attempt to approach the cottage openly would be to invite death. The group that had been daring enough to kidnap the dying Simon Ashbrook would not hesitate to shoot them down if the need arose.

Her one hope was that the Ashbrook heirs had not yet been notified that the real Ashbrook had been kidnaped. If the abductors held off until dark, there might be a chance that the three conspirators could regain their pawn in the desperate game of double-cross and blackmail they were playing.

It was nearly five o'clock when the first sign of activity made itself manifest. The front door opened and a man ran out to the stable, where the stolen Rolls Royce was housed. It was Martin, the butler.

Instantly Vivian was on her feet. Her period of waiting had not been wasted. She had mentally provided for just such a contingency and now that it had arisen, she was prepared.

"Follow me," she said, and ran through the woods alongside the little lane. Wylie and Benton followed at her heels.

She stopped in a little patch of woods through which the lane ran, just before it debouched into the main road.

"The car will have to pass here," she said in swift sentences. "We've got to stop it. They may be sending a messenger to the Ashbrook heirs, or they may be taking

Ashbrook himself to some other hide-out. I'll try for the front tires. You," and she motioned to Wylie, "get the man at the wheel if I don't succeed in stopping them."

She took up her station hidden by a little clump of bushes, while Wylie and Benton ranged themselves further down the road. Hardly had the three taken cover when the car came into view, driving at the moderate pace with which the sick are conveyed.

Vivian waited until the car was nearly abreast. Her two shots sounded almost as one as she neatly punctured both front tires. Martin, at the wheel, stepped on the gas. One of the two women in the rear seat screamed. Despite the handicap of punctured tires, the car might have won through except for Vivian Legrand's generalship. As the car shot past her Wylie stepped into the lane from ahead. His shot shattered the windshield just to the left of the driver.

It was enough. The car came to a halt with a jerk, and the scarred face of the butler peered back at Vivian. In the waning light of the afternoon his face looked more sullen and cadaverous than ever.

"Get out," she told him curtly.

With a muttered curse Martin climbed out into the lane, followed by the two women, whose faces had faded to the shade of a dirty putty. With swift strides Vivian reached the side of the car and peered into the seat in the rear.

It was empty. Simon Ashbrook was not there.

She turned menacingly on Martin, and the muzzle of her revolver inched forward suggestively. The man feared that gun. He flinched and stepped backward.

"Ashbrook?" she demanded.

"Where is he?"

"Back at the house," the man said sullenly.

"You go up and see if he's telling the truth," Vivian said to Wylie and Benton. "If he is, put him in the back of our car and we'll take him to Karnwood Hall."

"Precious lot of good he'll do you now," Martin told her vindictively, "He's dead."

A little gusty sigh came from Wylie, as he saw his hopes of their big haul gone glimmering. With the real Ashbrook dead there would be no chance of using the double who had been so successful up to now. They could not risk police inquiries by producing the pseudo Ashbrook for the relatives, and then having a doctor make the discovery that Ashbrook had been dead during the hours that his relatives believed that they had been in personal conference with him.

"And that's the end of that," Wylie said sadly.

"Not the end," Vivian said swiftly. "I've still got a card up my sleeve. But we've got to rush the body back to Karnwood Hall."

MRS. MERRIWEATHER CLOSED the door of the room where Simon Ashbrook lay quietly in death, and confronted Vivian Legrand in the hallway outside.

The village doctor had come and gone. Again Vivian blessed the foresight that had caused her to call in the man earlier. He would swear to the death certificate without any suspicion.

"It was very kind of you to stay this long," Mrs. Merriweather said suavely to Vivian, "But now that Mr. Ashbrook is dead, there is really no need for you to be here any longer. I will order the car for you, if you wish."

There was contemptuous amusement in the eyes of Vivian Legrand, as green and as dangerous as the hundred-mile shoals off Formosa, as she faced Mrs. Merriweather. But her voice was quiet enough. The Lady from Hell was playing the most terrific gamble in her whole criminal career, banking, betting, coldly and unruffledly on an unpredictable factor—a woman's reaction to blackmail.

Had her opponent been a man, Vivian would have been sure of winning. But she knew, as every clever criminal knows, that a woman does not react to blackmail in the same manner as a man. And Mrs. Merriweather was no mean antagonist in any game. She was hard, she was stubborn, and she possessed a driving clarity of mind that was disconcerting. Her weakest point was her greed, and it was upon this that Vivian was playing.

"I shall be quite comfortable here until tomorrow," Vivian told her.

"Under the circumstances," Mrs. Merriweather told her briskly, "it will be better if you do not stay."

"Why?" the Lady from Hell asked.

Mrs. Merriweather gazed at her angrily. The effrontery of this green-eyed chit! She did not realize, any more than had many others who had been victims of the Lady from Hell, that she almost invariably and at once placed the other person on the defensive. It gave her an immediate advantage.

"I do not think that I need to go into explanations," Mrs. Merriweather told her curtly. "Your work here is finished. I will pay you whatever wages are due."

"Which come," the Lady from Hell told her calmly, "to

exactly one quarter of a million dollars—fifty thousand from each of you."

It was a blow below the belt. Vivian's face was impassive. Only her eyes seemed alive—cold, deadly bits of emerald. Mrs. Merriweather gasped. The fact that the woman before her was aware of the agreement made by the heirs with Simon Ashbrook took her breath away. Before she could speak Vivian went relentlessly on:

"Mr. Ashbrook died sooner than you expected. And I suppose under the circumstances you feel that you can escape paying me the money you had agreed to pay."

The older woman abandoned all pretense.

"You are quite right," she said curtly. "We have no intention of paying you any such sum. I don't know how you became aware of Mr. Ashbrook's ridiculous request, but since you are aware, you might as well understand that the thing is too absurd for words. Mr. Ashbrook was dying when he made the request. He was not responsible for what he was saying. The situation is, of course, regrettable, but it is not of our making.

"We might consider paying you, say, a thousand dollars, and you would be lucky to get that."

"AND YOU," VIVIAN LEGRAND told her softly, "would have been lucky to have paid me the quarter of a million. It would have been cheap at the price. Since you're prepared to welch on your agreement—I'm raising the ante. It will cost you three hundred thousand now."

Again that thin smile flitted across Mrs. Merriweather's face.

"I happen," she told the Lady from Hell, "to have a slight knowledge of both American and English laws. You haven't a leg to stand on in court. No judge would award you a penny." Her voice hardened. "Now, if you don't leave quietly, I'll ring for the servants and have you thrown out."

"In other words," Vivian told her mockingly, "the heirs are taking no chances of being disturbed while they hunt for Mr. Ashbrook's will."

Then, before Mrs. Merriweather could recover from her astonishment, the Lady from Hell calmly extended a document toward her.

"You may spare yourself the trouble. Here is the will."

Mrs. Merriweather seized the paper avidly, took one look at it, and gave a startled gasp.

"But this—this isn't Simon's will! Why, this is the one in which he leaves all his money to charity!"

"Exactly. There was another will, I believe, in which he left his money to you and the other four heirs. But I'm afraid that's lost."

"Lost?" gasped Mrs. Merriweather.

Vivian Legrand nodded. "Lost. He gave it to me to keep, after telling me to destroy this one." She nodded at the document in the woman's hand. "And I can't remember what I did with it."

"You must remember!" In her excitement the heiress gripped Vivian's arms tightly. "Try and remember!"

"I have such a poor memory," Vivian told her apologetically. "I'm always forgetting things and having to have my memory refreshed. I'm afraid it would take—at least three hundred thousand dollars to prod my memory into activity."

A grim look settled over the face of the militant old woman.

"Blackmail, eh?" she said.

For an instant there was a sardonic gleam at the back of the hooded eyes of the Lady from Hell; then it faded. It was more than blackmail. If the woman only knew, it was the most stupendous gamble of Vivian Legrand's career.

"Not at all," she said sweetly. "You see, I am a very busy woman, and my time is valuable. If I understand the trend of your conversation correctly, Mr. Ashbrook's will, in which he leaves some five million dollars to you and the other heirs, has become lost. You want to employ me to aid you in finding it. Very good. But, as I have intimated, I cannot undertake to enter your employ for a cent less than three hundred thousand dollars."

"It's an outrage," sputtered the woman. "Blackmail! I won't pay it!"

"You don't have to pay it," Vivian explained patiently. "It is unfortunate, of course, but then you're the judge of what the will would mean to you." She turned on her heel. "I shouldn't be surprised if it had been destroyed," she flung back over her shoulder.

Mrs. Merriweather ran down the hall after her.

"Wait!" she called. "I'll pay—we'll pay!"

"In cash?" Vivian queried gently.

"In cash," assented the panting woman.

"Then," Vivian told her, "I'm quite sure that I'll be able to help you find the will—when you've the cash ready."

Two days later Mrs. Merriweather handed Vivian Legrand thick sheafs of crisp English banknotes in exchange for the forged will. She did not know, and the Ashbrook heirs today do not know, that the will for which they paid three hundred thousand dollars was a piece of worthless paper. But, since there was no contest, the clever imitation of the millionaire's signature was never questioned, and never came under the scrutiny of handwriting experts.

www.ingramcontent.com/pod-product-compliance
Lightning Source LLC
Chambersburg PA
CBHW031150020726
47499CB00002B/315